I0773841

BIRTH OF A BABY DADDY

PIPER RAYNE

This book is a work of fiction. Names, characters, places and incidents either are products of the author's imagination or are used fictitiously. Any resemblance to actual events or locales or persons, living or dead, is entirely coincidental.

© 2019 by Piper Rayne

All rights reserved, including the right to reproduce this book or portions thereof in any form whatsoever.

Cover Design: By Hang Le

Line Editor: Joy Editing

Line Editor: My Brother's Editor

Proofreader: Shawna Gavas, Behind The Writer

About Birth of a Baby Daddy

If you're having fun living your bachelor life in your Alaskan hometown and out of nowhere a woman shows up holding a baby she insists is yours, you need a plan-a birth plan.

BP Step #1 - Lift your jaw off the floor.
BP Step #2 - Figure out the baby's age-do the math.
BP Step #3 - Try to remember the woman and with any luck, her name.
BP Step #4 - Double check that she's not confusing you with your twin brother.
BP Step #5 - Ignore your five sister's scowls as your entire family watches the drama unfold.

There's only one thing you shouldn't do.

BP Step #6 - Don't assume she's there because she wants your daughter to call you Daddy. You'll only end up disappointed.

Time to figure out a new plan-one that changes her mind.

Birth
of a
Baby Daddy

The Baileys

Austin Bailey - 32 years old
(*Biology Teacher/Baseball Coach*)
Savannah Bailey - 30 years old
(*Runs Bailey Timber Corp*)
Brooklyn Bailey - 27 years old
(*Runs Essential Oil Company*)
Rome Bailey - 25 years old
(*Chef*)
Denver Bailey - 25 years old
(*Bush Pilot*)
Juno Bailey - 24 years old
(*Matchmaker*)
Kingston Bailey - 21 years old
(*Smokejumper*)
Phoenix Bailey - 20 years old
(*Student*)
Sedona Bailey - 20 years old
(*Student*)

ONE

Harley

I hoist Calista higher on my hip as I drag our suitcase along the half-melted ice up the quaint path that leads to the front door of Cozy Cottage Bed and Breakfast.

This is the cheapest place to stay in Lake Starlight, and it doesn't look as rundown as I expected. It actually looks well cared for, but a little... peculiar. I'm not a judgmental person—not with my past being what it is—but most people wouldn't match pink siding with yellow trim. The plethora of garden gnomes and metal sculptures poking out from the clumps of snow around the yard ramp up the weird factor. I don't remember them from the pictures when I booked online, but it wouldn't have made a difference.

I'm here for one reason and one reason only—to track down my baby daddy.

God, that sounds so cliché, but it's true.

Denver Bailey. My one-night stand turned baby daddy.

It wasn't until his picture was plastered all over the news—a plane went missing in Alaska, carrying a famous Hollywood music producer—that I knew where I could find him. Denver was the pilot. That was when I learned his last name.

I'd had no intention of seeking him out. But now six months later, here I am in his hometown. Because I need something from him.

Calista's fussing draws me from my thoughts, and I stop to readjust her. I don't have a chance to knock before the door whips open, revealing a woman. She's middle-aged, maybe mid-fifties, wearing a colorful dashiki with black leggings. Her shoulder-length black-and-gray hair sticks out from under the scarf wrapped around her head. She frantically waves with dried-paint-covered hands. The neon pink of the paint is set off by her dark skin.

"Heeelllooo," she draws out the word with a huge smile. "You must be Harley!"

She steps onto the porch and wraps my daughter and me in an embrace. My back stiffens and I let out a breath of relief when she pulls away, directing her attention to Calista.

"Hello, you sweet thing." She scoops up Calista and my arms instinctively reach to grab her back, but the woman pulls her securely into her chest. I open my mouth to say something, but she beats me to the punch again. "Bring your suitcase in. You'll catch your death out here. It's not too spring-like yet." She turns and heads into the house with my daughter. "Is this your first time in Alaska? How was your flight? What brings you here? I'm Selene, by the way, like the Greek goddess of the moon."

My brain stutters to keep up with her rambling. I have no idea which question to respond to, so instead, I drag my suitcase through the door and close it. Selene takes off Calista's heavy coat.

I peek around what will be our home for the next few days. The inside is just as colorful as the outside. Bright, abstract oil paintings cover the walls, and trinkets decorate every available surface. That will be a nightmare now that Calista puts everything into her mouth.

"Did you paint all these?" I ask Selene, who's busy tickling Calista under her chin, but Calista isn't giggling. She's staring at her as if Selene just stepped off a UFO.

"I did. I'm not only a patron of the arts, but I'm an artist myself. Made all the lawn decorations you saw outside too."

I smile. "Cool."

An awkward silence hangs over the room.

I use the moment to get another word in before Selene starts up again. "It was a long day of travel, so I think we're going to go lie down for a bit before we head out to get a couple things done."

Selene frowns. "I can keep her with me if you want to rest."

She seems genuine, not like a crazy murderer who will hurt my daughter, but I'm not about to leave my infant with someone I don't know.

"That's okay, she's due for a nap too." I take her from Selene. "I think we'll just go lie down and I'll unpack if that's okay?"

"Of course. No problem at all. Dinner is at five. Is that too early for you? I'm an early riser which means early to bed, but I know some people prefer to eat late."

Calista whines because at this point, we're way past nap time, so I bounce her on my hip, hoping to speed this conversation along. I worried about staying at a bed-and-breakfast instead of a hotel—because of the nosiness from owners and other guests—but I don't have money to blow on the Glacier Point Resort.

"Five is great."

Selene claps, startling Calista. "Perfect. We're having zucchini noodles with avocado pesto. It tastes better than it sounds, I promise."

I smile and head toward the stairway. *Guess I'll grab something to eat while we're out.*

"You're in the light blue room."

"Thanks."

"By the way, what's your daughter's name?"

I stop to face her. "Calista."

"Calista." She smiles. "Most beautiful. Did you know that's the meaning? In Greek mythology, Calista was a mythological Arcadian who transformed into a she-bear, then into the Great Bear constellation." She ends the conversation in baby talk as though she's telling Calista instead of me.

"That's good to know."

My chest weighs heavy as I walk up the stairs. I hope my daughter is a she-bear, because she'll need to be fierce for what lies ahead.

Selene was right. Dinner did taste better than it sounded.

After dinner, I grab our coats and button Calista up to venture out to find out more about Denver. Lake Starlight appears to be a small town where everyone knows one another, and hopefully I'll run into someone who might be able to tell me where he lives or hangs out.

As luck would have it, I get an Uber with a car seat and

it drops us off downtown in front of the local hardware store, Hammer Time. Well, he was good with his hands. The memory of his skilled callused fingers over my nipples surfaces, but I shake my head to push away those thoughts.

The bell on the door rings when we enter. Once I'm inside, I inhale a deep breath, loving the smell of cut wood and building materials.

A man stands behind the counter, bearing a genuine smile. "Can I help you find something?"

I return the smile and walk over, taking a quick glance at his name tag. "Hi, Jack. This is going to sound strange, but I'm wondering if you can tell me where I might find Denver Bailey?"

"Well, I talked to Austin earlier and he had some big plans tonight, but then they were all going to meet at Rome's new restaurant. It looks over the town courtyard. It's not open yet, but I'm sure if you knock, they'll hear you. It's just down the street to your right a couple of blocks. Called Terra and Mare."

"Great, thanks so much for the information." I turn and head for the door.

"Hey, what's your name?" Jack calls.

"It's not important," I say, the door chime ringing as I leave. I poke Calista in the belly. "Your mommy made a smart decision by going into that store. Jack is like an encyclopedia."

She giggles and I kiss her forehead.

As I walk the streets of Lake Starlight in the direction Jack sent me, my stomach turns over and bile creeps up my throat. Calista stares at the sky, and every once in a while, she juts out her mittened hand to catch snowflakes.

Only minutes later, the sign with Terra and Mare in gold script on a maroon background comes into view. It's definitely a classy place. When I peer inside, the restaurant is empty except for a long table in the center that's surrounded by a bunch of people.

I don't see Denver, but a few guys' backs are to me, so he could be one of them. It's been more than two years since I've seen him, so I'm going on fuzzy memories at best. More than what he looks like, what I remember most about our night together is how he made me *feel*.

I inhale a deep breath, reminding myself of why I'm here. The wind picks up when I push the door open, and a cold draft travels into the warm restaurant. All heads turn simultaneously in my direction. I take in each of them as I step toward the table. I scour them for familiarity, but when my eyes land on Denver, my heart beats triple-time.

All the memories of that night and what drew me to him rush to my mind. His good looks and hazel eyes. The way his arms and chest fill out his shirt. How the stubble on his face scraped against my inner thighs.

But he's clearly not on the trip down memory lane with me because there's zero recognition on his face, which stokes my anger.

"I'm sorry, this is a private party. Family only," a pretty blonde says, sliding out of her chair.

"Well, then I guess we're in the right place," I snipe.

Everyone at the table exchanges looks of confusion.

A man in a chef's uniform emerges from the kitchen and walks across the dining room, carrying a platter of beef.

Wait... what the hell is going on?

I glance from the chef to Denver.

Somehow, the chef doesn't notice me, placing the tray in the center of the table. "Why is everyone so quiet?"

He follows the others' gazes over to Calista and me.

My mouth drops open and I prop Calista higher on my hip. "There's two of you?"

Denver tilts his head and the chef rounds the end of the table, growing closer.

"I'm sorry, how can I help you?" the chef asks.

The fact that there's zero recognition in the chef's eyes either fuels my anger like gasoline thrown on a fire.

My eyes narrow. "You can tell me which one of you is the father of my little girl."

Everyone's head swings from one man to the other. I glance from the chef to Denver, both wearing an identical expression of panic.

What have I gotten myself into?

TWO

Rome

"Which one of you is Denver?" The woman looks between my brother and me.

I'm not ashamed to admit that relief envelops me like that heavy blanket Savannah bought for herself last month. The relief is bone-deep, because I have no idea who this woman is, and based on my guess about her daughter's age, I was in Europe when she was conceived.

Win for me.

Not so much for my brother.

My brother glances back at me, slowly standing from the chair. He steps in her direction as if he's about to be sent to jail with no chance of parole. "I'm Denver. You are...?"

She cocks her hip farther out, raising an eyebrow. The baby tugs at her hair, but she absentmindedly lowers the baby's hand without a complaint. "Really? I know we'd both had a few that night, but I thought you might remember my name. It's Harley."

Harley? The name rolls around in my head. Nope. Not the baby daddy.

It's clear from the way Denver keeps turning in my direction with his pleading stare of "it's yours, right?" he has no idea what the hell is going on either.

If neither of us recognizes her, then maybe we're both in the clear. Maybe we're being set up. This is totally something Liam would do.

My eyes shift to Liam. He's leaning back with both arms resting along the backs of the neighboring chairs. The life-is-great grin splashed across his face says he's enjoying this, but there's a note of surprise in his features, which tells me this isn't an early April Fool's prank on his part.

After I scan the room to make sure no other assholes in my family thought it'd be funny to play such a prank, I examine G'Ma D twice because this would be up her alley. Asking a woman to come in and pretend, then lecture us about safe sex and how if we don't start settling down, this day will likely come.

"Rome?" Denver's soft plea brings my attention back to him.

Shit, he wants help. What am I supposed to do? He knocked her up.

"Listen," I say, stepping forward, "I think maybe you have the wrong person."

Harley's eyes narrow and her head whips in my direction. "And you are?"

"Rome Bailey. His twin brother."

"I'm not blind," she murmurs.

I refrain from reminding her that she's the one who asked. This is a stressful situation all around, so I keep my sarcasm to myself. "If he thought he was this cutie pie's father, he'd say so."

The baby interrupts all the dramatic tension by patting the woman's face over and over, saying, "Mama. Mama."

Brooklyn rounds the end of the table with her arms out. "Would you like me to take her so you can—"

Harley swivels so the baby is as far from her grasp as possible.

"Or not." Brooklyn puts her hands up in the air and sits in an empty chair. She's closer now, and I watch her scour the little girl's face for any resemblance to the Bailey features.

The little girl is adorable, and I'm totally on board to play favorite uncle. Her hair isn't blond like her mother's, it's a light brown, but her eyes are the same green as her mom's. Her chubby cheeks are pink from being outside. She throws one of her mittens across the room, hitting Savannah in the face. My family laughs and Savannah picks it up, slowly approaching Harley as if she's a hungry tiger wanting to feast on us all.

"Thanks," Harley says, taking the mitten.

The little girl takes off the other one and throws it. It lands in the cream sauce I put out earlier.

My soon-to-be sister-in-law, Holly, picks it up and heads to the kitchen. "I'll go clean this up."

"It's no—" Harley's words die on her lips because Holly's going to do it no matter what.

"Where were we?" Harley grabs hold of the baby's hand from her face, kisses her palm, and places it by her side, then lasers those green eyes my way. "Since your brother Denver is playing dumb, let me fill everyone in. We met in Seattle a little over two years ago. He had a layover and came into the bar I worked at. He stuck around after closing time. One thing led to another and this is the result of our one-night stand." She nods at the baby who's now looking at me with rapt attention.

Denver raises his hands as if we're in the principal's office in high school again. "I wasn't in Seattle two years ago." He looks around for a witness or someone to agree with him. What, are we on Maury Povich here?

"You sure you'd remember?" Austin asks.

Denver turns to our eldest brother with a scowl like Austin's losing his man card once we figure out this situation. "Because I think I would remember if I took a trip to..."

Denver continues, stating how he couldn't have been in the lower forty-eight when the baby was conceived. We all know he rarely leaves Alaska, since his schedule can be grueling. The man makes his living as a bush pilot, and ninety percent of his business is in Alaska. As my family argues and the woman grows quiet, the hairs on the back of my neck stand up.

Seattle? Layover? Two years ago?

Fuck.

Denver might not have been in Seattle, but I was. I had a layover right before flying to New York and then on to Florence. There was a snowstorm out east. I remember being pissed about it because I had to call my new mentor in Italy and tell him I'd be a day late.

I examine the woman again. Her green doll-like eyes had to be what captured me first. I'd remember those, wouldn't I? The thought triggers something in my mind, and déjà vu hits me like a brick to the head. I've said that to someone before—doll eyes.

My mind was all over the place that night. The fear that my mentor would say the hell with you. The fear of leaving my family for so long. The fear of my dream being only a few flights away but delayed once again.

"Holy shit."

Denver's head whips around, and he blanches when he sees my expression. "You?"

The sound of a chair scraping across the floor breaks my trance. Austin stands, walking over to us. "I'm sure we can figure out what's going on here."

I'm surprised Savannah hasn't demanded a paternity test and kicked Harley out. And I haven't heard this much silence from G'Ma D since our parents' funeral.

I ask Harley, "Can I talk to you in the back?"

"It's admirable that you want to help your brother out here, but Denver is the father." Her eyes narrow on Denver, and he coughs as if he might vomit all over my new floor.

"About that..."

She tilts her head, waiting for me to fill in the blanks. "I saw him on the news, and unlike him, I remember his face and his name."

"Well..." I run a hand across the back of my neck, gripping tight enough to spur me to speak the truth.

Denver stares at me, his eyes conveying that he's not taking one for the team this round.

"I gave you his name in Seattle." I blow out a breath again. "It's this thing we used to do when we were younger. He'd tell girls he was me, and I'd do the same. It's stupid, I know."

The entire room groans before everyone questions when I'll grow up.

She blinks a few times, staring between the two of us. For a new mother, she's sure got the disappointed look down. "Unbelievable."

"I didn't think we'd see each other again."

"So why give me your twin brother's name?" She swings the baby around to rest on her other hip like a pro. Of course she's a pro. She's been doing this for a while now.

It's then the realization that I'm a dad and my daughter is right in front of me hits me. A heavy feeling invades my chest, and before this moment, if you'd asked me, I'd have told you it's because I don't want to be a father. But instead it's the fact that I've missed out on a helluva lot in my daughter's life.

A million questions rattle my brain. Why is Harley here now? Why not before? Is she here for money? Has she been looking for me for two years? Does she want a relationship? Like an instant family? I'm not one to settle down. Regardless, we need to clear some things up now, and the last thing I want is my family more involved than they already are.

I step forward toward Harley and the baby. "Can we talk?"

Holly rushes over with the cleaned mitten, and Harley thanks her with a tentative half smile.

"There's no need for that. All I need from you is a swab of your DNA." She shifts the baby again and digs into her purse before handing a business card to me. "Go there. They have the instructions."

"Wait!" I call.

She stops but doesn't turn around.

"What's her name?"

The room silences and she pauses as though she's not going to tell me.

"Calista," she finally says, and leaves as if she didn't just up-end my life.

THREE

Harley

I wait until I'm around the corner of Main Street, outside a diner, before I lean my back against the wall and finally breathe.

"Sweetie, that might've been hardest thing Mommy's ever had to do. Well, other than all the hours of labor, but I got you, so that was a win."

Calista giggles and pats my cheeks like she was doing in the restaurant. I love that she unknowingly kept me from going ballistic after discovering a new fact about her father—he's a liar.

"Oh, I've seen that look before." A blond woman surprises me to my right. She's in a turquoise diner uniform with pink polka dot fringe around the collar and sleeves. "Come on in. Pie's on me."

Her smile is welcoming, and after a bunch of strangers' judgmental eyes were trained on me, I could use someone who might be Team Harley. At the very least, she has pie. I glance at her black name tag and find "Karen" printed there in white.

"Thank you. Pie sounds great, but I'll buy it myself." I follow her through the open door.

"Can you believe we have snow this late in the winter? I guess that's what we get for living in Alaska. Are you new in town?" Karen grabs a menu and a high chair before leading us to a table in the back of the diner. She sets down what she's holding and holds her hands out for Calista. "May I?"

My baby is only growing heavier and this lady seems like she gets my struggle, though I know nothing about her. I hand Calista over and shrug off my now-wet coat. "Thank you."

"Oh, she's adorable. I keep nagging my daughter to give me a grandbaby."

"Nagging is putting it lightly. She just got engaged. Give her a minute." A man behind the counter circles around with a warm, welcoming smile, obviously teasing Karen.

She shoos him away and rolls her eyes. He nods like "listen to me." They're cute.

"Anyway." Karen secures the belt around Calista and ruffles her hair. "What kind of pie would you like?"

I glance over the menu. The meal Selena made was better than I thought, but I'm kind of hungry. Or my emotions are starving. Isn't that always the case?

"I'll have an order of fries, and how about the blueberry pie?" I ask Calista, whose eyes are busy staring at the man at the counter.

I turn to find him covering his face with his hands and sticking his tongue out when he removes them. Calista lets out a laugh that rings through the entire diner.

"And I'm the one who wants a grandbaby so bad." Karen laughs, shaking her head at the man. "I'll be right back. Drink? Coffee?"

"Please. Decaf though." Long gone are the days I could drink caffeine after dinner. When your schedule revolves around an eighteen-month-old, it's early to bed, early to rise.

She nods and disappears.

I hear the man behind me talking to Karen about how cute Calista is. I dig in my bag to pull out her soft cloth book and set it in front of her. She touches the cow embroidered there and says 'moo.'

"Oh, she knows her animals already?" Karen flips the cup on the table and fills it with coffee. "I remember being so worried about my daughter hitting all those milestones."

"Yeah. I never thought I'd be reciting the alphabet this early and hoping it clicks. I mean, she doesn't even use a toilet yet."

Karen laughs. "The pressure on mothers is intense." She eyes my hand as I reach for the sugar. "Single mothers especially?"

I retract my hand for a moment. This woman is observant. I remind myself that I can't trust anyone in this small town. What was I thinking? "Actually, can we get our order to go?"

She frowns and glances at the man who I'm assuming is also staring at us. This isn't Seattle. This is some small-ass town in Alaska. They probably already know how I barged into a restaurant to find the father of my baby. I'm sure word travels quickly around here.

"I'm sorry. I didn't mean to pry." Karen brings her hand to her heart. "I was a single mother and I just wanted to help you out. That's all. I'm sorry if I overstepped. But please, stay in the warmth, eat your fries, and let Brian keep

Calista occupied with peek-a-boo so you can have a moment to yourself."

Her kind smile confirms my gut reaction outside—she's a nice woman. I always go with my gut. Half the reason I went home with Denver, err... no, Rome. Man, that's going to take some time to get used to. How many letters did I start over the past couple of years by writing the name Denver at the top?

"Thank you," I say to Karen, mostly so she'll stop staring at me with pity.

I'd usually scoff at someone looking at me as though I'm some kind of project for them, but if she's telling the truth and she was a single mother, then she understands that over the past eighteen months, the only peace and quiet I've had is when I'm at school or work. Not that I'd change a thing.

Calista's head falls back, laughing at who I guess is Brian. I smile, wondering what this town, these people look like through her eyes. Everything we've known is different, yet it's still just us.

My phone dings inside my diaper bag, so I grab it.

Miranda: *Did you do the deed?*
Me: *You say that like it's a pleasurable experience.*
Miranda: *You available to talk?*
Me: *No. Too many ears where I'm at. Later tonight?*
Miranda: *But you saw him?*
Me: *By him if you mean Rome not Denver, yeah.*
Miranda: *You lost me?*
Me: *Denver IS Rome. They're twins who like to play games with the women they sleep with.*
Miranda: *Like they switched spots on you midway thru the night?*

Sometimes I wonder about Miranda.

Me: *I'd know if someone switched spots.*
Miranda: *But if they're identical, think about it. You're passed out on the bed from one guy and then he slides out of the room and his IDENTICAL brother comes in. I mean you said you guys did it how many times that night? I always thought you were exaggerating. I mean a man...*
Me: *Thanks for taking me on a trip through your warped brain.*
Miranda: *Anytime. You know my delusion is your delusion.*
Me: *I think he has a big family.*
Miranda: *Do identical twins have the same DNA? How would you really know for sure whether it was Denver or Rome?*

I roll my eyes. My best friend has a hard time staying on topic.

Me: *I have no idea but since I only slept with ONE of them I'm not worried about it.*
Miranda: *How's Calista doing? I miss my chubby-cheeked girl.*

I glance over to find her playing peek-a-boo. She's a kidnapper's dream. All it takes is a game of hide-and-seek and she's in love with you. Brian is now back behind the counter, pretending he's riding an escalator or walking down a set of stairs. He's bringing out the big guns.

Me: *She's good. Already has admirers.*

Miranda: *Of course, she does. I'm telling you, she'll break hearts.*

I nod and type my response.

Me: I just need to get out of this town...

Screw it. I press her number and she picks up.

"I can't keep texting you. I'm exhausted and my fingers hurt," I whine.

Karen slides the fries in front of me and silently points at the ketchup on the table. Then she sits down and grabs a clean fork, puts a little pie on it, and holds it out to Calista. Calista's eyes widen immediately. Seriously, I warn her all the time about strangers and how to be wary of anyone we don't know.

"You sound tired," Miranda says.

"I am, but I'll be home soon."

"When?" Miranda asks.

I can tell I'm on speakerphone now. In the background, I hear some soft music and a few grunts and moans.

"Are we alone?" I ask.

"No worries, my client has headphones in."

I chuckle.

She's back in Seattle, another step closer to becoming a registered massage therapist, and I'm here in Alaska, trying to get a guy who gave me the wrong name to give me his DNA.

"I don't even want to know how you managed to text me. I'll let you go. We can chat tomorrow." The fries are calling my name and serving as a welcome distraction from the curveball life has thrown me.

"Yeah, I probably should go. I don't think this guy understands this isn't a happy-ending parlor."

I hear the man's voice, which makes me wonder whether he really had headphones in or not. They begin to argue, and I hang up to enjoy my greasy fried potatoes in silence. Well, not silence, because Brian has brought over a chair and he and Karen are enjoying entertaining Calista. They do the train and the plane with Calista opening up as though she's the easiest baby ever.

Try feeding her squash or green beans and see how accommodating she is.

"That a friend?" Karen asks, her gaze falling to the phone.

"Yeah." I dip my fry in ketchup. I look around the diner, figuring this woman must have other patrons, but all the booths are empty, so I guess she's got all the time in the world.

"She from here?"

"No." I shake my head.

"Man-da?" Calista points and screams when my phone lights up with my friend's picture.

I click the ignore button before they can follow her line of vision.

"Are you new to Lake Starlight?" Karen asks, but there's hesitancy in her tone. She's worried she's going to scare me off.

"I'm just here for a couple of days."

"I thought so. I'd remember this little one." Karen inches closer to Calista and scrunches her nose.

I smile. Brian looks oddly familiar. Do I know him? Of course I don't.

The three of us sit there while I eat my French fries and let Calista be our entertainment. Sometimes it's easier with her around. She takes the pressure off making awkward conversation with people.

"Are you staying at Glacier Point?" Brian asks. "We know the—"

"Cozy Cottage B&B," I say before realizing I gave these people information they could use to track us down. *Okay, Benson, cool it. This isn't an episode of* Law & Order: SVU.

"Oh, Selene's the best." Karen points at Brian.

"She's always been eccentric, but she's kind. I'm sure you'll enjoy your stay," he says. "Plus, she's on the outskirts of town, so you won't be bothered by all the tourists."

"Tourists? Is Lake Starlight a big enough town for that? It seems small." I bite a fry, unsure of why I'm asking questions that don't matter to me.

Karen glances at Brian.

"People like small towns. But with snow still coming, my guess is Glacier is filled. Wyatt was telling me the other day about record bookings this winter," he says.

Karen nods. It's clear they must know the owner of Glacier Point.

"And with all the shops downtown, I'm sure my nephew's new restaurant will grab some attention, what with him studying culinary arts in Europe before he moved back home."

I choke on my fry, coughing to get the potato back up. "Nephew?"

Brian gives me a second to gather myself. "Yeah, it hasn't opened yet. He's actually having the entire family over there tonight, but Karen was called in at the last minute and we're a duo now so..."

"I told you to stay there," she says, shaking her head in a way that shows she tried more than a few times.

"Not without you. We'll experience it together." He pats her knee and she looks at him as though he's her savior.

What must that feeling be like? I wouldn't know. I've only ever had myself to depend on.

"What's the name of the restaurant?" I ask.

Surely there are two restaurants about to open that had a large table full of people tonight, right?

"Terra and Mare."

"Denver, err... Rome is your nephew?" I ask, grabbing Calista's book and tossing it in my diaper bag.

"Both of them, yeah." He smiles like a proud father. His gaze falls to Calista. "Do you know them?"

I grab our jackets, swing my diaper bag over my shoulder, and pluck her up, but her belt keeps her restrained. She chants "Mama" over and over and starts crying.

"Here." Karen unbuckles the strap. "Are we missing something?"

I glance back, getting Calista free, my heart racing as I swing her into my arms.

"Thank you for everything," I say, digging cash out of my bag and tossing it on the booth.

"Wait," Karen calls, but I push open the door and walk as far away as fast as I can.

Once we're around the corner, I stop to place Calista on the ground then hunch down to put her coat on. "If you weren't the most important person in the world to me, we'd never have come here."

Calista steps into me, her head falling to my shoulder. I pick up her and order an Uber, wishing it could drive me all the way back to Seattle tonight. Adulting sucks!

FOUR

Rome

I stand slack-jawed, watching the little girl stare over her mom's shoulder, her green eyes wide with curiosity as they leave my restaurant. The edges of the small card poke my palm as I crush it in my fist.

"What the hell is that?" Denver's gaze falls to the card that's now a ball of paper. I open my palm, and he takes it. "It's for some diagnostic place in Anchorage."

Austin takes it from him, but Savannah quickly snatches it from Austin. "I'm calling Uncle Brian."

"No." I put up my hand. "This is my business and I'd like it to stay that way."

"Rome, sweetheart, you need your family at a time like this." G'Ma D's kind and nurturing side is showing itself, which speaks to the severity of this situation. If memory serves, we usually only ever see it for a few moments on

Founder's Day every year, when remembering what we've all lost is front and center.

"I just need time to think."

"It might not even be yours," Savannah says. "Maybe that's why she's sending you to do a paternity test. You could be one of five."

"Savannah," Brooklyn scoffs. "This isn't an episode of Maury Povich."

"Sav's right. I mean, seriously, Rome doesn't even recognize her," Phoenix jumps to my defense.

I think I remember her. Kind of. Sort of. Those eyes. I know those eyes. I run my fingers through my hair, expelling a long, deep breath.

Denver kicks out a chair and shoves my shoulders down. "Sit."

I do.

"Rome was in Seattle. He admitted it," Juno says.

If my sisters don't stop arguing right now, my head is literally going to explode.

"It's mine." I hold out my hand for the card and Savannah passes it over. Twirling it, I try to figure out a plan.

I'm a plan guy. Not like life plan, but when I'm thrown an off-speed pitch, I know how to react. Excuse the baseball analogy, but when you grow up playing the sport, you relate everything to that play when you have half a second to decide if you're swinging or not.

I wasn't as good as my brother Austin, but I had an eye for the ball. Off-speed, lay off until it crosses the plate. Curveball, look to take it on the inside. This is like a wild fucking pitch I didn't see coming that hits me right in the helmet. Now I'm lying in the dirt, trying to figure out if I'm still that guy who can take a pitch.

"You okay, man?" Denver grabs a chair.

Denver's voice draws my attention from looking at the floor between my legs.

I glance at my brother. "It's gotta be a joke, right?" I stare at the card. Diagnostic testing.

Denver presses his lips together but doesn't say anything. He doesn't need to. Not only are we brothers, but we're twins. Not creepy telepathic twins, but we tend to know what the other is thinking.

"I don't understand. Why did she track you down if she's going to run off?" Liam asks.

"Because she wants money," Savannah says.

Liam rolls his eyes at her. "You're way too cynical."

"I'm a realist. She got wind that Denver was some hero, and since doofus here used Denver's name, she probably thought Griffin Thorne gave Denver loads of money for saving his life. Or she found out about Bailey Timber and is under the impression that we've got millions."

"What must it be like to be in your head." Liam shakes his head and tucks in his chair. "I think it's time for guy time."

Thank God for Liam.

"You want me to clear everyone out?" Denver whispers.

I say nothing but express my feelings with my face.

With a few hugs and pats on the back, my sisters and Holly leave. A cold rush of air floats through the restaurant as Brooklyn holds the door open and waits for G'Ma D—because right now, G'Ma D's standing in front of me. waiting to say her piece. I heave a sigh and tilt my head up to look at her.

"I can't say I didn't warn you." She looks down at me.

I nod.

"Baileys take care of what's theirs, Rome. I hope I don't

have to remind you of that if that little girl is a Bailey. You need to figure out your priorities and do it fast."

I nod again.

She pats my cheek. "First great-grandbaby. Ethel's going to be so jealous." A spring grows in her step as she heads out the door.

At least one of us is happy, even if it's only out of spite.

Thankfully, it's only the guys left—my brothers Austin, Denver, and Kingston, along with Brooklyn's boyfriend, Wyatt, and my buddy Liam sit around the table. I don't bother saying anything to them, but I head straight behind the bar, grab a shot glass and a bottle of Jack, and fill the small glass with amber liquid before tossing it down my throat.

"Isn't that what got you into this mess?" Austin says from across the room.

I stop what I'm doing and give him the best "fuck you" look I can muster. "How about being a brother instead of a father tonight?"

Denver pats Austin on the shoulder and sits on the barstool in front of me. I put out a shot glass for him and he watches as I pour.

"If there was ever a night to tie one on, it's now," Denver says before downing the whiskey.

"Pour me one too," Kingston says.

"Don't leave me out," Liam says.

One by one, they each take a spot on the barstools in front of me.

I line up the glasses in a row and pour us all a shot then slide one in front of each of them. Wordlessly, we raise the glasses and down our shots.

Kingston grimaces. He still prefers the taste of beer over hard liquor. Thankfully, he didn't ask for a chaser. If he had,

I might've had to take his Bailey man card. It's not summer yet, so he can live a little before his obsessive physical conditioning to fight bush fires takes over.

"So you think you're the dad?" Kingston asks.

"Could be." I sigh. "Probably. I didn't recognize her at first because she had her hair back the night we met and more makeup on, but I did sleep with someone in Seattle around when she probably would've gotten pregnant."

Each one nods slowly with their lips pressed together.

I get their sympathetic half glances. None of them want to make direct eye contact with me. From the time you start having sex, this is pretty much your number one fear as a guy—some girl showing up, telling you you're her baby daddy.

Everyone but Austin and Wyatt, because they'd probably welcome a kid in their lives at this point. They're established.

I still sleep on a mattress on the floor. No frame. Just there, tucked into the corner with the cord for my phone in the nearest outlet. The makeshift apartment above the restaurant is less than stellar. Making it a decent apartment is part of my plan. Nice enough to have girls come back to. All that seems stupid and childish now. A father should have his shit together. A damn bed frame at the very least.

"Savannah's on it. She'll call the diagnostic place first thing in the morning and figure out how we can get the DNA results back ASAP," Austin says.

"No surprise there," I mumble.

"What do you think she wants?" Kingston asks.

He seems the most thrown. At almost twenty-one, he's just starting his bachelor life. I'm sure he gets plenty of offers when he's out fighting fires. Then again, Kingston isn't Denver or me. He's always been more like Austin.

"I have no idea." I reach for the whiskey bottle again and pour myself another shot.

Denver slides his glass over. Never one to let me go through shit alone. I'm close to all my brothers, but we're twins. Our connection is on a whole other level. We clink our glasses and toss them back, the liquid no longer burning as it runs down my throat.

"I always told you two that little game you played, pretending to be the other, would come back and bite you in the ass," Austin says.

"C'mon, man, you can't be a twin and not do it." Wyatt chuckles.

I stretch my hand across the bar, and he fist-bumps me.

"It didn't do anything to me except make me almost piss my pants for five minutes." Denver leans back and catches my eye, guilt coating his features. "Sorry, man."

"Maybe so, but you're twenty-five. Time to grow up," Austin says in the dad voice he's perfected in the decade since our parents passed.

"I was twenty-three when I did it," I argue the moot point. "Doesn't matter. What's done is done."

My jaw twitches under the strain of clamping it shut so I don't say something I'll regret. I know my big brother can't help himself. He was forced into the dad role, but right now, I don't need the lecture. I need someone to tell me that it'll be okay, that I can handle this, that if this is my child, I won't be a shitty father.

I release my aching fingers gripping the neck of the whiskey bottle.

"What are you gonna do?" Liam asks.

"What can I do? I'm gonna figure out if I'm her father, and if I am... I don't know. I guess I'll figure it out from there."

I've always been the guy who's comfortable winging it through life, but there's no flying blind in this situation. If I screw up a little girl's life, there's no sorry big enough to make up for it.

G'Ma D is right. I need to get my priorities straight.

FIVE

Harley

This morning, I'm thankful we're off Calista's normal schedule, because I get to enjoy a warm cup of coffee on the back patio of Selene's house with the mountains as my view. My mind is a jumbled mess from last night. My biggest regret is running out of Terra and Mare like a coward. I should've held my head high and told him everything.

Then again, he didn't chase us down. Not like I expected the guy who left me with only a lame note on the pillow to jump up and down with glee that he has a daughter with a virtual stranger. I actually hope he's the guy I thought he was when I found the note, because we're here for only one reason and it's not to woo Calista's dad into becoming a permanent fixture in our lives.

"Oh dear, let me put on the gas fireplace." Selene comes out, her dark hair streaked with gray pulled back, and wearing a pair of colorful printed pajama pants cinched on her small waist and a T-shirt with a cardigan sweater over the top. She clicks on the gas fireplace, and the warmth from the flames feels nice.

"Thank you."

"You got in late last night. The little one still sleeping?" She sits in the chair next to me, sliding her legs so they're tucked under her. The dried paint on her hands confirms my thoughts that she was working this morning.

My eyes fall to the baby monitor next to me. "Yeah. You painting? I heard Neil Young playing." I sip my coffee.

I wish I could be like Selene at times. I wonder what her upbringing was like to allow her the freedom of self that seems to come naturally to her. She beats to her own drum and doesn't seem to give a shit what others think. We're similar in a way, I suppose. I do what I want without asking permission or caring what others think, but I'm always on edge, anxious... never mellow like Selene.

"My aunt got me hooked when I was young. Neil always gets my creative juices flowing." She looks into her tea. "I'm a transplant, if you haven't figured that out."

"Transplant?"

"I wasn't raised here. Although I feel like it sometimes."

I stare at a statue with a turquoise ball on the top that's out in the yard. "You like it here?"

"Love it. I'm sure you will too."

I sip my coffee. "I'm only here another day." Mostly because I'd never travel longer than two days in a row with Calista unless I wanted to torture myself.

"I do hope you take today to enjoy yourself then." She looks sheepishly. "I don't like to pry, but may I ask if you're here for business or pleasure?"

I raise an eyebrow. She may seem a little flighty, but I

don't get the feeling she's an easy woman to pull one over on. Selene knows as well as I do that a woman doesn't show up dressed in jeans and a sweater with a hole in the armpit and a baby on her hip for business.

"Neither really."

We sit in silence. Still not even one peep from the monitor.

"Okay..." she says it rushed as if we've been playing a game of chicken and she's the one to lose.

"Selene?" There's something she's not saying.

"Lake Starlight is a small town, and well, people find out pretty quick when there's someone new in town. Someone saw you and snapped a picture and... well, there's this online blog thing. I don't really follow it, but I was bored this morning, waiting for a portion of my art to dry before I could start on another layer and... well..."

"And well what?"

"People are speculating about why you're in town."

I stand, my coffee spilling as I place it on the table. "I thought this town was a little bigger than someone recognizing someone new from the moment they set foot on the sidewalk?"

"You'd think." She rushes to her feet but is able to keep her teacup in the palm of her hand. "I'm thankful it wasn't around when I showed up. Anyway, this isn't about me. Jack said you asked about Denver Bailey and the Baileys are kind of a big deal around here."

I snap my line of vision away from the turquoise ball to her. "What does that mean?"

She sighs. "They own Bailey Timber, which funds a lot of the town. You add on their parents' accident, and well, I think the town almost feels like they're our responsibility. I guess it's a small-town thing. My daughter is good friends with Kingston Bailey. He's so sweet and kind." She waves her hand like "silly me." "I have no idea why I'm telling you any of this, other than my own curiosity as to why you showed up in Lake Starlight for a two-night stay and your first line of business was to track down Denver Bailey?"

My heart sinks. This woman standing in front of me knows more about Calista's father than I do. What does that say about me as a mother?

It says that I don't know what kind of genes he might pass on to my daughter. How could I let her travel through life never knowing her genetic makeup or family medical history? She'd ask me how she got brown hair and what was my plan? To tell her I dyed mine? That's the whole reason I'm here—to get answers, not a daddy for my baby.

Selene patiently waits. I'm not sure if she really expects me to answer. She's a B&B owner, not my therapist.

I owe her nothing is the first thought to go through my head. Then I realize how alone I feel. Sure, I have Miranda and Shane back in Seattle, but she's moving on with her life and about to get her massage therapist license, whereas I had to take time off because I have daycare to pay for. Miranda wasn't stupid enough to get knocked up by a stranger.

I hate when I think that way, because it makes me feel as though I didn't want Calista. I didn't know I wanted her until I confirmed that she was growing inside me. Since that moment, I knew I'd do anything for my child. I'd sacrifice being a massage therapist for her. Hell, if we didn't need money to survive, I'd sacrifice everything, but life doesn't work like that.

"More coffee?" Selene disturbs me from the rambling in my head.

Selene would be cheaper than a shrink, and she doesn't seem to be a judgmental person.

I shake my head. "I thought I was here for Denver, but turns out I'm here for Rome."

She makes this low *uh-huh* thing like she understands completely, which makes me assume he has a reputation in this town.

I scan the monitor. Still silent. I guess I can't dodge this conversation by using Calista as an excuse.

"Rome is Calista's father." Saying it out loud feels weird.

"Oh," Selene says it as though she's trying to act nonchalant, but I can tell that she's excited to be one of the first to know.

"He didn't know about her until last night, and I'm only here for his DNA." I sip my coffee, the turquoise ball calling my name once again. Why is it so alluring?

"Why his DNA if you know he's the father?"

I shrug, not really wanting to get into my whole life story and Calista's. No need for our story to end up in whatever this gossip thing is that takes people's pictures without permission. I should ask Shane to look into the legal ramifications of that.

"Oh, you don't have to tell me."

I nod as a thank you, although I feel like I could trust her.

Another long stretch of silence ensues. I hate silence. It either means someone doesn't want to tell you something or you feel uncomfortable in their presence. I remember my foster mom's silence when I was a week away from eighteen. Not that I thought she'd like me to stick around after the checks stopped, but she could have brought it up before she was packing my bags.

"I feel like I need to prepare you for what coming here might bring." Selene sits in the chair next to me, and I follow suit. "You said you only want his DNA, but I can tell you that's not all you're going to get."

I sit up straighter. There's no denying this lady has intel I need. "What do you mean?"

"I told you the Baileys own Bailey Timber. There are nine siblings in all. Two sets of twins. Rome and Denver being one, then the youngest are a set of twins—Sedona and Phoenix."

I nod, remembering the two girls who looked alike at the restaurant even though the whole showdown is a blur.

"Then there's Grandma Dori. How do I politely say this... she's a meddler. If she finds out about you... well, the fact that she has a great-granddaughter isn't going to be ignored." She places her hand on my knee.

My heart wrenches because the grandma was there last night. They all were. The entire family.

"Do you think they'll try to take her from me?" Bile rises up my throat. How did I not consider that before coming here?

Because you thought you were approaching a guy who didn't care to say goodbye after you'd slept together. Not exactly a ringing endorsement for a guy looking for a commitment.

"No. They wouldn't do that, but..."

"What?" I sit up straighter, my chest constricting making my breaths grow shallow.

"They'll want to be a part of her life." She says it like she just told me I have cancer.

To me, it sort of feels that way. You don't come out of the foster care system soft with dulled edges. You leave with scars and edges sharper than a shard of glass. You cut first and ask questions later. Selene seems to understand me more than anyone I've ever met.

"What about Rome? He's the father. Last night it looked like he and Denver were willing to duke it out over who was going to have to accept responsibility for getting me pregnant. He didn't even remember me, which means I'm only one in a long line."

Selene giggles. "If you stick around, Calista will have a loving uncle Denver because Rome and Denver are one and the same. And yeah, both of them have reputations in this town. Neither of them are the settling-down type. So it could very well be that Rome wants no part of being Calista's father. But I'd be surprised."

Speak of the devil, my baby girl murmurs through the monitor, stirring before she fully awakes.

How could he not want his little girl?

Don't think that. If we're lucky, he doesn't want his little girl.

But then she could grow up with daddy issues and...

I stop the war in my head. "I'm going to get her. Thanks for the information."

She smiles and follows me back into the house, walking toward her big picture window in the front of her house.

"Um... Harley?" she says, looking out the window.

"Yeah?" I say, one foot on the stairs.

"Rome's here."

My throat closes up, and I'm torn between wanting to run and grab Calista and crawl out the window upstairs or shove Calista into his arms, telling him what a fool he'd be to not love her. Damn, I need to compartmentalize these feelings. Selene's opinions have me wavering about what I really came here for.

"Can you stall him?" I ask.

"Oh, honey, you know I can." She winks, taking the two sides of her cardigan and wrapping it around her middle.

By the time I'm at the top of the stairs, it's settled. I'm going to get Rome Bailey's DNA and get the hell out of Dodge, leaving no trace for him to follow.

SIX

Rome

Thanks to the good folks of Lake Starlight, it didn't take me too long to find Harley. I'm grateful that Holly's mom, Karen, sticks her nose in business that isn't hers and that my uncle Brian likes to brag about his nieces and nephews to anyone who will listen. It made finding Harley and Calista pretty damn easy.

I paced my floor with a dull headache most of the morning because I had no idea when a good time to stop by would be. When does a baby wake up? Fuck if I know.

I walk past the Cozy Cottage B&B's lawn, which is littered with what Selene calls art, when my phone vibrates inside my pocket. I pull it out of my jacket and see Savannah's name on the screen—again—and send her to voicemail —again. She's in fix-it mode, but there's nothing to fix until I know exactly what's going on.

Shoving my phone back into my jacket, I raise a hand,

but before I can knock, the door swings open and Selene stands there wearing bright pants and a cardigan. There's a splatter of paint in her hair and small dots on her sweater. Always making something with her hands.

"Rome, what a surprise! What are you doing here?" she asks.

I doubt I'm much of a surprise. She had the door open before I announced myself and, hello, this is Lake Starlight, the land of Buzz Wheel. Rumors are already spreading, but no names have been given. Thank God.

"Hey, Selene. How are you?" My hand falls to the back of my neck, my headache now radiating down my spine. Damn whiskey. Nothing good ever comes from it.

"I'm good. Just getting some pieces ready for the farmer's market this summer." She leans against the frame. "You interested in seeing any for the restaurant?"

She's blocking me, which means she knows. Either Harley told her, or she's a detective—like every other Lake Starlight resident—and has pinned me as the father.

"Not today. Is Harley around?" I stuff my hands into the pockets of my jeans, rocking back on my Converse.

"Oh." Her hand comes to her chest and a smile tilts up the corners of her mouth. "I didn't realize you knew my guest?"

Selene's not one for lying, so my assumption is she knows everything right down to the fact I gave Harley the wrong name.

"We can keep pretending you don't know why I'm here or you can let me in to talk to Harley and we'll figure this out."

The smallest of smiles tips the corners of Selene's lips and she steps back from the door, allowing me in. "I always liked you, Rome. How is Grandma Dori?"

I forgot how filled with knick-knacks her place is. It's like a horror movie. I can't help but feel as though all the creepy figurines are staring me down, seconds away from coming to life and attacking me. "She's good. I wouldn't be surprised if she's next to show up on your doorstep."

Selene laughs. "Well, she's always welcome."

"How's Stella? I heard she's back on the east coast, getting her degree?" I hate this small talk. Not that I don't care about how Stella or Selene are doing, but I really want to speak with Harley. But Stella is a friend of Kingston's, and she used to hang out at the house all the time when Kingston and his buddy Owen thought they could be rock stars.

"I miss her so much, but she's where she needs to be."

I nod. Everyone in Lake Starlight knows Stella should be as far away from Kingston and Owen as she can. The three of them together never worked.

A child's scream floats down the stairs before Harley appears around the corner with Calista on her hip. The baby is blubbering, her bottom lip quivering while tears run down her cheeks. My chest squeezes and I'm overcome with the need to try to soothe her, do whatever it takes to make her happy.

"Hey," Harley says, not at all surprised to see me. She stops at the bottom of the stairs and looks from Selene to me and back.

"Someone's not happy, is she?" Selene says and wipes a tear off Calista's cheek.

Harley tenses and holds Calista a little tighter to her hip. "She's hungry. She's off her schedule which means..." Harley stops talking, adjusting Calista on her hip.

Of course I've shown up at the worst possible time. I should've consulted a mom, but I don't know any moms, and since mine is resting at Union Cemetery, I don't have anyone to go to for advice.

"Sorry, I should've called," I say, feeling like an idiot. Except Harley never gave me her number anyway.

"Why don't I feed Calista and you two can go out back for some privacy? The path is clear of snow since it's melting and it's a pretty nice day out."

Selene is right. Spring isn't here yet, but it feels downright balmy after the long winter we've endured.

"I don't know..." Harley appears hesitant to give her daughter—our daughter?—to Selene, but I know her. She's good people.

"Selene can handle it," I say, not sure if Harley will kick me in the nuts for speaking my mind. I don't quite remember the edge she holds from that night. Usually my type are easier-going and pleasant.

Harley's lips press together for a second before she passes Calista to Selene. Calista finds the dried paint in Selene's hair and fixates on it.

"Is grilled cheese and some applesauce okay for her?" Selene asks.

"Yeah, she'll like that."

"Okay then, you two catch up. We'll be in the kitchen." She walks away, but Harley stops her.

"Just make sure to open up the grilled cheese so the inside isn't too hot for her."

I'm not sure Selene needs the guidance, but she's gracious enough to nod before disappearing to the back of the house.

"She has a grown daughter," I say with the hopes it puts Harley at ease, but her head snaps in my direction and the look on her face has me wanting to cover my junk and cross my legs just to make sure. There's a beat of awkward silence before I speak again. "Do you have a coat?"

"Oh, right." She walks over to the front hall closet and pulls out a black coat. She struggles to get the hood of her sweater out from under the coat, so I step up behind her to help her.

She smells like a fruit platter—berries with a twist of citrus. And the skin on the back of her neck is so soft as I brush her hair aside and pull her hood out from under her jacket. Bad move on my part, because now my dick has perked up and is in full chub mode.

This is exactly what got me into this situation in the first place.

I clear my throat and step back.

"Thanks," she says in a rough voice.

Does she know? Did she feel it against her leg? I really need to get it together here.

"No problem." I motion for her to go ahead of me out the front door. "We can take the path around the side of the house into the backyard."

Once we're out back and looking over Selene's yard that's dotted with gardens, paths, and fountains that aren't working yet, Harley stops. "This is quite the setup."

"Wait for the warmer months. Lots of people come here to have their wedding photos done."

Not only is Selene into art, but she has a master green thumb. I remember the flower arrangements that were laid over my parents' caskets, courtesy of her.

"I can see why," she says.

We walk down the path for a few seconds, neither of us saying a word, until I can't take the silence any longer.

"I might as well start with the obvious question... how did you find me?" As soon as the words leave my lips, I realize how they must sound. God, I'm messing this up big time. "I don't mean it in a bad way, I swear."

She ignores my backpedaling. "Well, when I thought your name was *Denver*—"

"Before you go on, I have to apologize to you for that... again. I don't know why I gave you his name. I wasn't myself that night. I was pissed about my flight delay and was moving away from home and well... it just slipped out. At the time, I didn't know we'd end up going home together."

"It's fine. Truth is if you hadn't, I probably wouldn't have found you. Like I said, I saw him on the news when his plane went down with that music producer." She stuffs her hands in her pockets.

I nod. That was national news for a hot minute because of who Denver's passenger was.

"Wait. That was more than six months ago." My forehead creases.

She glances away from me.

I stop walking when realization dawns on me. "You had no intention of letting me know I had a daughter, did you?"

A black hole opens in the pit of my stomach. Maybe I'm not the only one who needs to feel guilty here.

She faces me, blowing out a breath. "Look, I'm not here to up-end your life. I get that I showed up out of the blue and you were in no way expecting for this to happen."

I'm so confused. I push a hand through my hair and try to sort this out in my head. I know I'm hungover, but I can't make sense of what she's saying. She travels all the way here from Seattle to confront me with the fact that I have a daughter, yet she doesn't want me to be a part of my daughter's life?

"I don't get it. What are you here for? Money?"

"Money?" She rears back as if I'd offered her a twenty to suck me off.

My own anger feels like poison on the end of my tongue, so I better tread carefully here. This isn't how I want to start my co-parenting relationship with a woman I barely know.

She steps forward. "I found you because I need something from you."

"You didn't try to find me to tell me about the baby. Then when you do find me by some miracle, you wait six months before coming here. I just asked about money and from your reaction, it's clear that's not why you're here. I don't understand what's going on here."

Her back stiffens. "Even if I had tried to find you, *Rome*, I wouldn't have been able to because you gave me a fake name. And hello, I didn't have a last name. Your cute little note on the pillow in the morning conveniently left off a phone number." She circles around, her hand on her hip. In my experience with my sisters, nothing good ever comes from the hand on hip, hip jutted out pose. "I needed six months because I didn't know what to do. And I don't want your pity money. We're doing fine." She spins back around and stomps off farther up the path.

I catch up to her. "What is it you need from me then?"

"Same thing I said last night. Your DNA. Your medical history. Your family's medical history."

I scrunch my forehead. "Okay, but you thought I'd give it to you without wanting a relationship with my daughter?"

She glances at me. "I figured you'd be thankful not to be burdened. You didn't exactly seem like a 'settle down with a family' type of man."

The look of disgust on her face has me wanting to cast stones. She was a willing participant that night. I may not have remembered her immediately, but the more I scour my brain, the more it's coming back to me, and I distinctly remember her hand down my pants before we even walked into my hotel room. She knew the score before she walked in there.

But reminding her of that won't get us anywhere right now.

"Maybe you figured wrong. So you want this medical history for what?"

I have a feeling it's not just so Calista will have the information when she grows up. I mean, a woman who chose to hide the fact I had a kid for six months after finding me isn't coming here and risking the chance that I could argue my parental rights just so our daughter knows where she got her brown hair from.

"My..." Harley glances at the ground before she raises her head and meets my gaze. "I mean *our* daughter... is sick."

SEVEN

Harley

The color drains from Rome's face as though I punched him in the stomach, or lower.

"Calista is sick?" He says it softly, as if he's doing his best to wrap his mind around this new information.

His reaction takes me by surprise. Maybe I shouldn't have just blurted it out. Of course, I didn't expect him to show up here, so I'm not exactly prepared. This was supposed to be a quick in and out, "no worries, I want nothing else from you, see you later" kind of thing. It was supposed to be easy-peasy, because the man I met two years ago would've thanked me on his knees for not uprooting his life with a child. But the despair on Rome's face tells a different story. His shocked eyes and ghost-like appearance say that just like everything else in my life, this isn't going to go as planned either.

"Want to sit?" I ask, finding a bench that overlooks where I'm guessing the majority of wedding pictures are taken. There're no flowers or greenery at the moment, but there's a beautiful arbor I imagine looks gorgeous in the summertime, with ivy tracing up the spindles.

He hesitates but does end up sitting next to me, his elbows resting on his knees, his eyes on the hard ground.

"She was only diagnosed recently. Calista has Von Willebrand disease. It's not super serious, but... we're fortunate it was caught early. Once she started walking and moving, bruises started to appear on her arms and legs. I freaked out, but my doctor told me I was overreacting. My gut kept me going back. Finally, when she had a nose bleed I couldn't get to stop, I went to another doctor who took my concerns a step further and tested her."

"I don't get it. What exactly is it?"

"It's a clotting disorder. She's making the proteins we all do, but hers don't work right. There are different levels you can be at—she's a level two."

He pushes a hand through his thick hair. "Is there a cure?"

I shake my head. "No, she'll live with it her whole life. As she grows older, I'll have to make sure to tell surgeons, if she ever has to have surgery, and her period could become too heavy, which I'll have to address once she hits puberty. She can live a normal life, there are just precautions that need to be taken."

"Is there a medicine she can take? Anything to make it go away?" he asks, a crease between his eyes.

I'm speechless and taken aback. He's actually... concerned? I thought for sure he'd shrug it off and think I was using Calista's illness as a way to get his DNA and force him into paying child support. But I don't think he's putting on an act. I think he's honestly worried for my—err, our daughter.

"No, but honestly, she's good. I mean if she does bleed, I have to be cautious. Some people go their entire lives with it and never even know. You could have it."

He narrows his eyes at me. "I would know."

"Not necessarily. The doctor said most likely it came from one of us and I was tested. I don't have it."

He paces in front of me, eyeing me every once and a while. "So you're here to blame me for my genetics because I gave her this disease she'll have to live with the rest of her life?"

And there goes calm Rome.

"I'm not blaming you. I'm here so I know what she has to face going forward. So I won't be surprised again. So she has somewhere to look for answers if need be in the future." The edge in my tone reappears.

I have to remember I've had two months to process this. He's just learned he has a daughter and now one with a medical condition.

He sits back down. Thankfully. I hate when people pace in front of me. I once had a foster father who did that across the length of the couch as he dictated what I'd be responsible to do in the house the next day.

I wrap my arms around myself, hating that I have to bear my soul to a stranger, but if I want him to cooperate, he needs to understand. "I grew up bouncing around from foster home to foster home."

His shoulders slump and I see pity flaring on his perfect features before I can tell him not to feel sorry for me. I'm fine. In one piece and happy.

"I don't know much about my own family history, and when I first realized that something was wrong with Calista, there were a lot of doctors' appointments. Each one wanted a full rundown on Calista's maternal and paternal family history, and I had nothing to offer. Nothing. I felt powerless to help my daughter, and I promised myself I'd never be in that situation again. So I'm asking you to please get the DNA test. I swear I don't want anything from you. Calista and I are leaving tomorrow, and you can open your restaurant and go on with your life."

He stares at me, his eyes narrowed with an angry glint. "You think I'm the kind of guy who'd find out he has a daughter and not take care of her?"

I stand, stuffing my hands into the pockets of my coat. "I don't want your money."

"Too bad," he says, his voice rising.

I'm suddenly glad we took this conversation outside so that Calista and Selene don't have to listen to us argue. "I don't want to up-end your life. That wasn't the point of my coming."

"So you've said. Many times. Just a swab of my saliva and you'll be on your way, right?"

"Right." I nod.

He stands so fast I rear back in fear of what he's going to do. His hands fall to his sides when he looks into my eyes. There's that look of pity again. *Ugh!*

He stuffs his hands into the pockets of his jeans. "I'm not that guy. I can't go on with my life, knowing I have a daughter out there and not be a part of her life."

I knew this could be an issue as soon as I walked into that restaurant and found all those family members there to celebrate his restaurant opening. This is his hometown, not just a place he's been holed up during our years apart. How stupid am I for not doing more research? When your child is sick, you don't really think rationally. You just do what you need to to make sure she has everything she needs. And she needs her father's DNA.

"I'm sorry, but we live in Seattle. I don't really see how that will happen."

He gives me a blank stare as though he doesn't understand the words coming out of my mouth. From what I remember when we met, he was a guy who was never at a loss for words.

"I think we need to make it happen. If the DNA test says I'm Calista's dad, I have rights."

"If? You think I sleep around and don't know who the father of my baby is?" I raise both eyebrows, waiting for his answer. "Probably because now that you found out I'm a foster kid, you assume I have all these issues and I sleep with men because I'm looking for someone to love me since I didn't grow up with anyone who loved me unconditionally. Is that it?"

"No!" He steps closer.

I step back.

He blows out a long, tortured breath. "I don't think that at all."

"Oh, that's right, you don't remember me."

"I do."

I quirk an eyebrow.

"I mean I'm starting to. Your eyes. I remember them, and God, I know what a fuckup I sound like that I wouldn't remember your name. But I was a mess at that point in my life. I was a different person then. But the more I think about it, the more that night is coming back to me."

Figures. A night that I remember practically every

second of with complete clarity is blurry at best for him. By the time we were in my car leaving the bar, the sexual tension was at a ten and I wanted him like my next breath. I guess I forgot how much alcohol might have clouded his judgment that night.

"Good for you, but it's no sweat off my back if you remember or not."

"You seem hell-bent on throwing the name thing in my face as often as you can. It seems you are upset I don't remember you." The corners of his lips tilt slightly.

I get the impression, both then and now, that Rome's not normally a serious guy. Seems he doesn't want to feel the emotions running through his system.

Look at that, we have two things in common now.

"Just take the test so I can get out of this town."

"The test is important to you, huh?" His smirk says his mind is working something over.

"Not at all. I love traveling over two thousand miles with my eighteen-month-old daughter, finding her father in a room full of strangers, and finding out some random blog is talking about me. I'm weird like that."

He smiles. An amused, cocky, arrogant smile. The same smile that drew me in the night we met. My stomach flips.

"Well, it's important to me that I get to know my daughter."

I glare at him.

He laughs. "Yeah, looks like we find ourselves at a crossroads."

"Are you saying you're not going to take the test?"

He sits on the bench, his demeanor much different than minutes ago. He leans all the way back with one arm stretched across the back of the bench and his ankle on his one knee. The cocky smirk has yet to fade from his face. "Not at all. I'll take the test. I'm not a monster."

"I hear a 'but' coming." I raise an eyebrow.

He winks. "Yeah, you do."

I grunt and he chuckles. I hate it when I give people exactly what they expect. Like I'm playing in their hands instead of them playing into mine. "What do you want?"

"Give me a week. I get to spend time with Calista, and at week's end, you get your DNA test."

"And then what? You'll just be done with her?"

He laughs. "Sorry. You're stuck with me for life. Who would've thought you'd be the lucky girl?" He pats my knee.

"Lucky? Lucky as getting audited by the IRS." There was nothing sexual about his touch, but it still causes me to stifle a shiver.

"Lots of women would think they were winning the lottery." He winks.

I roll my eyes. "Don't we think highly of ourselves."

He stands and puts his hand out between us for me to shake. "The ball's in your court."

"And if I don't?"

"No test and I sue you for parental rights." He drops his hand when I don't move to shake his. "I'm not trying to torment you, but I want to be involved in my daughter's life."

Men like Rome Bailey have been my kryptonite my entire life. The cocky swagger makes me bite every time. I should say no. But it's too late. Rome will be a part of our lives forever. Might as well give him this week to find out how hard raising a toddler is. With any luck, he'll prove me right. Men like Rome Bailey don't stick around when things get tough.

"Deal." I put out my hand.

He cocks his head back in surprise and wraps his large hand around my small one. A flutter of goose bumps scatter up my arm.

"Let's get started." He winks, turns and heads for Selene's back door.

EIGHT

Rome

Leaving Harley, I walk to Selene's back door. I'm not sure I had a clue what I was going to do when I rang the doorbell after I first got here. The hesitancy I felt when I walked in is gone now though. There's a little girl I believe is my daughter who is sick and that changes everything. I'm not wasting any more time.

"Rome." Harley steps in front of me before I can open the back door.

"Yeah?"

"What are you planning to do? We need to talk about this. You can't just barrel in there and pick her up and take her somewhere."

I shake my head. "I'm not going to do that, but I'm not a sit-on-the-sidelines kind of guy either."

"Can we at least establish what your intentions are this week?"

I slide my arm under hers to the doorknob, but she slides her body in front of it. "My intentions are to get to know my daughter."

"And then what?"

I blow out a breath. "I thought we'd been over this. I'll get the blood test and we figure out how to make sure we're both a part of her life."

"We live two thousand miles away from one another," she yells then lowers her voice. "We can't exactly do joint custody."

"We don't need a plan right now. I'm just going in there to play with my daughter and tell her I'm her daddy." I get my hand in the small opening she's leaving next to her ribcage and turn the knob.

"Rome," she says through gritted teeth.

Frustration looks cute on her.

"I remember now the way my brother's name sounded from your mouth. It was more pleading in a 'don't stop' kind of way. Makes me wish I hadn't lied about my name."

My remark sets her back. Her grip on the doorframe falters and I step into the house.

"I'm not sure we'll both survive this week," she says, following me.

Selene looks at us when we enter the room, seeming surprised that we're together.

Calista smiles at me for a split second but looks past me almost as fast. "Mama!"

Her smile grows and jealousy takes over any rational thoughts I had. I want that smile directed at me. It's a great smile. The cutest.

"Hey, sweet girl." Harley sits down next to her. "Thank you, Selene. Go do whatever it is you were doing. I've got this."

Selene passes the plate of food she's feeding Calista to Harley. "I have a piece to get back to. Nice seeing you again, Rome." She squeezes my arm before she walks out of the room.

"You too, Selene. I'll be back."

She giggles, leaving me alone with Harley and my daughter.

My daughter... who would have thought?

I slide into the seat on the other side of Calista. Her eyes zero in on me but instantly go back to Harley, peeking at me every few seconds as though she's checking that I'm still there.

Great, I'm freaking out my own baby.

"Calista," Harley says, not giving her any more food as she gestures to me, "this is Rome."

"Daddy," I correct.

"Rome." Harley squares her shoulders.

"Daddy." I smile and inflect my voice with happiness.

Harley gives up. "She doesn't even understand the meaning of the word."

"Doesn't matter. I'm her daddy."

Calista's head shifts from me to her mom and she laughs, stopping us both from arguing. I don't want her to think I'm an evil monster to her mom.

"Let's take her to the park after she eats," I suggest.

"Wee!" Calista smiles and rocks to get out of the high chair.

"Not yet." Harley directs her stone-cold stare at me. "Rome just doesn't know we finish all our lunch before we say words like that one."

"Words?" I look at Calista and point at myself. "Daddy."

Harley rolls her eyes. "The place with the swings and the slide."

"The park?"

"Wee," Calista says, rocking again, her small fingers moving to her belt.

"Not yet," Harley says in a sweet voice I'm sure I'll never hear directed toward me.

"What's wrong if she's excited about going to the park?" I ask.

"Wee!" Calista screams, growing upset that neither of us has let her out.

"Nothing is wrong, but as you can see now, she's not eating."

"Let's just bring it with us. She can eat on the way."

Harley pinches the bridge of her nose but leans back while I unstrap Calista from her high chair and pick her up. Yes, I am her favorite person right now. The king saving his princess from the evil mother dictator.

"She'll need a nap too." Harley follows us out to the foyer.

"Didn't she just wake up?"

Harley rolls her eyes as my hand moves to open the door. "Coat. She needs a coat!"

Selene comes out of her studio, her fingers doused in yellow paint. "Everything okay?"

"We're taking Calista to the park and maybe for ice cream," I say with a smile.

"Yum yum," she says in my arms, patting my jaw like she did Harley last night.

"Calista..." Harley's tone is one of warning.

The word no is not in our vocabulary today. If I didn't think Harley would lose her shit, I'd suggest I take Calista out by myself, but that would go over as well as me trying to seduce her into bed again. And I like my balls, so screw that.

"I don't have a stroller," she says, reaching into the closet for Calista's coat.

"Good thing you got me." I flex one arm.

She rolls her eyes again. I'm starting to think that maybe Harley has some rare condition that causes her eyes to constantly roll. She should get that looked at.

"You realize that the first time I met you, you never rolled your eyes."

She worms Calista's arms into her jacket and grabs a hat for her. "I guarantee I did."

"Nope. You were all dreamy-eyed and gaga over my abs."

"Either the blackout you experienced that night is fading or you're making crap up." She lightly pushes my shoulder.

"Hey, I got a baby here." I pretend to stumble and wobble.

Calista laughs, her head falling back, and I quickly straighten. Whoa, that wasn't funny. Her head was, like, an inch from the coat hook.

Harley stares at me for a moment with an "I told you so" expression and opens the door. "Let's go wee."

"Your baby talk is impressive. For future reference, I'm not much of a baby talk kind of guy in the bedroom." Why is it so fun to get a rise out of this woman?

"The kind of talk you like in the bedroom should never be spoken in front of those little ears." She follows me out the door, shutting it behind her.

The air is a little warmer than when we were out in the backyard, and I look forward to the nicer weather. I kind of hope Harley sticks around for Founder's Day. Especially since Calista is a Bailey.

Whoa... she's the first in the next generation of Baileys. The awestruck feeling is mixed with longing because Mom and Dad will never get to meet her.

I should stick to the here and now, set aside my thoughts about the future and the past. I'm not a grudge-holder. I've always been more of a process-and-move-on kind of guy. So I'm not surprised that once I made the deal with Harley to keep her in town for a week that I'm going all out here. Being responsible for another human being before they're at least eighteen years old scares me. But it's not so much Calista as it is the cold-shouldered mommy walking next to me. I'm surprised at how natural the idea of being a father feels. If you'd asked me last week what my reaction would've been if a virtual stranger had shown up claiming I was her baby's daddy, I would've told you I'd be sailing down the river of denial.

"What do you do for a living?" I ask.

"I bartend. Same place as two years ago. Oh, but you probably don't remember." She puts on a saccharine smile before straightening the purse on her shoulder.

"I get that you're insulted I didn't remember you at first, but don't think of it as you weren't memorable."

She stops dead and bores her eyes into me. "I'm not insulted. I couldn't care less."

"Then why do you keep bringing it up? I told you it's coming back to me slowly."

Calista runs a hand down the scruff on my face. "Ow." She yanks her hand back.

"I know, Daddy hurts," Harley says to our daughter.

"I'll shave tomorrow, sweetheart." I kiss Calista's palm,

but she places it back on my cheek, poking me with her finger.

We have to walk through town in order to reach the park. Which means eyes and ears will all be in our direction. Should I prepare Harley or just let her experience it without a warning? Hmm. Let's see how well she does on her feet.

"We have to cut through Main Street to get to the park on the other side of the library."

"I had no idea Selene was this close to downtown."

"When you drive, you practically have to go around the entire lake, but we can cut through and walk the path beside the lake."

"Um... how do you expect us to get back? She's going to be tired. You don't take a baby out all day, especially in this weather."

I wave off her concern, but from the evil look she's sporting, she doesn't much care for other people taking charge. Which oddly enough is *not* the memory coming back to me. I have a vague memory of her enjoying when I told her exactly what I wanted her to do. Especially when she undressed in front of me.

"It'll be fine."

She raises her eyebrows. Her hair is cute today, pulled back in a ponytail that swings as we walk the path. And no, I'm absolutely not thinking about how much fun it would be to wrap my hand around that ponytail while I took her from behind.

"Wa wa." Calista points at the lake.

"Water. Yeah. You're so smart." I poke her stomach and she giggles.

Is she this welcoming to everyone or am I doing something right here?

"I bet most women would beg you to sleep with them after watching you with her." My head snaps to Harley, who raises her hand and covers her mouth, eyes wide. "Shit. Did I just say that out loud?"

"You did." I laugh, which makes Calista laugh, which makes it appear as though we're both laughing at Harley.

"That was an internal thought, and for the record, I'm *not* one of those women." She speeds up and walks in front of us on the path.

"I think Mommy finds Daddy attractive," I say.

"I do not," she says over her shoulder.

"Do too," I say right to Calista and tickle her tummy, which spurs another round of the most adorable giggles.

"Get off your high horse."

I catch up to her and we walk in silence for a couple of minutes.

"So bartending, huh? Rough hours when you have a baby to care for."

Harley glares at me and speeds up again so she's in front of us. "Some of us don't grow up with privilege."

"Are you suggesting I did?"

"Well, I heard all about 'the Baileys.'" She puts the Baileys in air quotes. "Town saviors." She shakes her head.

Her ass must've been a huge selling point for me because damn, my hands are itching to grip it.

"No wonder you're a manwhore who sleeps with anyone with a pu—"

"Judge much? First of all, I used my college money to go to culinary school. Everything I have now I made and earned and invested myself. Okay? But I know to you it must look like a lot."

She whips around so fast, the end of her ponytail hits her face. "Don't go assuming you know anything about me."

Yeah, I might've stepped over the line on that one.

"I apologize, but don't go judging me like my life is some fairy tale either."

"Fine. I won't." She puts her hands on her hips.

I lead us up the path toward Main Street. We couldn't have picked a worse moment because G'Ma D is walking directly toward us.

"Fuck," I murmur.

"Fuk," Calista says.

Harley blows out a breath. "Nice. Literally, like what? Ten minutes?"

"Oh, believe me, you'll be saying it in a second too."

G'Ma D looks up from the piece of paper in her hand and our eyes lock. It all happens in slow motion. Her eyes move from me to Harley to Calista. Baby-snatcher eyes ignite, and she walks toward us as though she's on a mission.

"Buckle up, the ride's gonna be bumpy," I say.

"What are you talking..." Harley stops speaking when the little blue-haired lady stops in front of us with her hands out for Calista.

Yep, this'll be interesting.

NINE

Harley

"Give me," the old woman says.

I remember her from the restaurant when I confronted Rome. Her eyes were fixated on Calista the entire time, as though she had some magical power and could figure out whether my daughter was her grandson's.

"Um." I slide my hands under Rome, the back of my hand grazing his strong chest.

An unbidden memory from the night we were together flashes through my mind. How is that even possible? The man is wearing a light jacket.

Go figure that a night I haven't been able to forget for two years, Rome has no recollection of. I think he's humoring me with his newfound clarity.

Once Calista's in my arms, she stares at the blue-haired woman in front of us. The one who is pouting.

"You can't just take her," Rome says to his grandma.

"She's my great-granddaughter. And I'm your grand-mother, so watch your tone." Her hand falls between us. "I'm Dori Bailey. Your soon-to-be grandma-in-law, but I hate that whole in-law thing, so let's just stick to grandma."

"We're not getting married," Rome deadpans. "Mind leaving us to our business since this is my first day with my daughter?"

Dori waves him off. "You'll have many more years than me. I'm old and could be dead tomorrow." She moves her gaze to me. "I'm the sweetest. Mother of this one's dad and grandma to all nine of the Bailey kids. I'm a card-carrying American Red Cross CPR-certified member. Let's see what else." She looks at Rome. "You should be boosting me up here. You know I don't like to brag."

Rome rolls his eyes and she hits him in the stomach. "Hey," he says.

Calista's eyes are wide, watching it all unfold. "Ow."

"Abusing me in front of my daughter. Great example you are."

Dori turns her back on him. "Anyway, I'm Dori and you are?"

"Harley."

"I'm sorry for my grandson's manners with the whole knocking you up and leaving town thing."

"I didn't know she was pregnant," Rome says with exasperation.

Dori puts her hand up in his face. "He's a bad seed. Well, they're both bad seeds. Him and his brother Denver. Those two never grew up. I'd tell you to run for your life if I didn't love him so much." She turns around and pinches his cheek. "Other than his commitment-phobia, he's fun. Which I'm sure you know, hence this little one."

"G'Ma D?" Rome mouths "sorry" to me from behind her.

I hold Calista out between us. "Would you like to hold her?"

Rome's eyes widen in surprise. Hell, I'm surprised myself, but something about her spouting off a resume just to hold her great-granddaughter softened me. I want Calista to have the one thing I didn't have growing up—a family and a support network to love and be loved by.

"Here." She shoves her bags into Rome's stomach.

He fumbles but catches them. Her wrinkled fingers stretch a few times before she picks up Calista and props her on her hip like a pro.

"You are so cute." She tickles Calista's stomach, which Calista loves so she giggles, spurring Dori to do it again.

Rome smiles at me, admiring the way the two interact. Shockingly, I don't feel one ounce of jealousy or fear. I'm not scared this woman will take Calista away from me.

Dori turns and walks down the sidewalk, and all that peace shatters like crystal.

Before I can react, Rome meets her pace. "G'Ma D?"

"I thought we were going to the park."

Rome looks at me. I wave it off.

"Wee," Calista says.

"That's right. Wee. Do you like the swing?" Dori asks.

"Wee," Calista says again.

"*Rome!*" a man shouts from behind us.

He and I turn, but Dori doesn't stop. I watch her back, although she's still moving at a pace I can easily match.

"Colin," Rome says to the guy, "What's up?"

"The fridge. It's about as warm as a summer day in Florida." He raises both eyebrows.

The guy looks at me, smirking as if someone told him a

secret. Maybe I should walk around town with a sign around my neck that says Rome Bailey's Baby Mama.

"Crap." Rome looks at Dori and back at me.

"Go," I say.

"But..." He wavers, putting all his weight on one foot then the other.

"Seriously. We'll see you at the park. I'm fairly sure your grandma isn't going to let us sneak away."

"I'm Colin." The blond-haired guy puts out his hand. He's cute in that boy-next-door way.

Too bad I've always been more into the bad boy type. My eyes instinctively find Rome, who's still looking unhappy.

"Harley." I shake Colin's hand.

"Okay, I'll be there in a few, but..." Rome reaches into the diaper bag and takes my cell phone from the front pocket.

My gaze slides to Dori, and I see that someone has stopped her on the sidewalk. Another older woman with stark red hair that she obviously dyes. At least she's still in my line of vision, though God only knows what she's telling that poor woman.

Rome's phone rings in his jacket pocket a second later.

"This way we have each other's phone numbers just in case." He tucks my phone back into the bag.

"Great."

He winks and steps forward, his hand ready to land on the small of my back, but I step back. "Yeah, okay. Meet you at the park."

He jogs down the street toward his restaurant, Colin leisurely walking behind him and saying hello to everyone he passes.

During the daytime, downtown Lake Starlight is quaint

and cozy. With all the shops, bakery, diner, and restaurants mixed in with the insurance, veterinary, and medical offices, it gives the impression of a movie set.

"Oh, here she is," Dori says, waving me over when she sees me coming.

"Hi," I say to the red-haired woman.

"Harley, this is my dear friend Ethel. She's yet to be blessed with a great-grandbaby." Dori pokes Calista again, but Calista squirms and reaches for me.

"And Rome is the father?" Ethel asks. Closer now, I can see her layers of makeup and bright red lipstick.

"Yes," Dori answers for me. "Speaking of which, where did he go?"

"Emergency at the restaurant. He's meeting us at the park."

Calista continues to squirm, and Dori finally gives up the fight and hands her to me.

"Oh yes, we're going wee," she says to Calista with wide eyes. "Talk to you later, Ethel."

"Are we still playing Mahjong tonight?" Ethel asks.

Dori gives her a bland look. "Be realistic, you think I'm giving up my title?"

I laugh.

Ethel glares at me for a fraction of a second before putting on a welcoming smile. "See you then. Nice meeting you, Harley."

"You too," I say, catching up to Dori, who's decided she's done talking to poor Ethel. Relief falls over my body when the park comes into sight. "You play Mahjong?"

"Gotta keep the mind sharp. Me and the girls try a new game every eight months."

"Eight months?" That seems like an arbitrary amount of time.

"We're old, so it takes us at least two months to stop arguing and understand how to play in the first place. Gives us six months to master the game. Mahjong was my pick." Her tone is filled with pride.

I have to say, I might like Dori. "I think that's great."

"Don't mock me. I understand it's completely ridiculous for a bunch of old women in their seventies to play a game in a different language." She waves to someone eyeing Calista and me with curiosity. "Don't mind them. Lake Starlight is nosy, you'll have to get used to it."

"I don't plan on being here long, so…"

She nods. "I'm born and raised in Lake Starlight. I get why some people don't like it. I mean, people are in your business all the time. There's this gossip blog called Buzz Wheel where anything you do can end up for all the residents to read. And add on that you're a Bailey—"

"I'm not a Bailey."

"She is." She nods to Calista as I put her in the swing.

I refrain from mentioning that Calista's birth certificate says my name—Sullivan.

"It must be hard to raise her all by yourself. Do you have family that helps?" She pushes Calista.

Calista's dangling feet excitedly move back and forth while she giggles.

"I have friends." I lean my shoulder against the wooden post holding up the structure. Attendance at the park is sparse with there still being clumps of snow on the ground. Wasn't this Rome's idea and now we're the ones out in the cold?

"No family?" Dori asks.

I might as well lay it all out, because this woman isn't someone I can guide into another line of conversation. She's going to pry as though I'm an oyster and she wants that pearl inside. Besides, I made peace with my childhood, or lack of childhood, a long time ago.

"I was left at a fire station when I was younger. I bounced around from foster home to foster home until I was eighteen."

She pushes Calista, her eyes not meeting mine. "I'm sorry. That's hard." It's the first time I've heard concern out of Dori's mouth. "I wish my ungrateful grandchildren knew how good they have it."

"I'm fine."

"Sure, you are, sweetie." She smiles, a fake one.

She's not worth proving wrong, I remind myself. Being a foster kid doesn't define me.

"You said you're not staying long. Where are you from? Seattle?"

Calista's head droops, the swinging and fresh air tiring her out already. I really wish I would've brought my stroller.

"I am. That's where we live."

Dori nods. Slowing the swing, she picks up Calista. Her eyelids flutter for a second before falling completely closed, her head on Dori's shoulder. Without a word, Dori walks over to the bench and sits.

Calista is such a traitor. Why can't I have that daughter who clings to me and wants nothing to do with strangers?

"Do you have a job there?" Dori asks.

I shrug. "I'm a bartender, but I'm going to school."

"School? For what?"

"Massage therapy." I sit down next to her, watching Calista's mouth fall open. She's so off her schedule, tonight will be a nightmare.

"Oh, I've had a massage before. My grandkids thought it made a good Mother's Day gift. But let's be real, no one wants to give a woman in her seventies a massage. I went anyway because being old means you don't really give a shit either."

I laugh.

"My massage therapist was telling me that she moved up here from the lower forty-eight because they get paid more in Alaska. I mean, the cost of living is more expensive up here, but she said it was double. That's amazing, right?"

Go figure. The trade I'm learning has to pay double around here. And add on that Dori knows that fact? Bonus.

"I still have to finish my schooling. I have one more class."

"Oh. Only one class away?"

"Yeah. Calista had some health issues, so I needed to take some time off because between working and doctor appointments..."

This woman was a mom. She'll understands what that means.

Her forehead creases. "What are Calista's health issues?"

There's no sense in keeping them to myself. I have a feeling this family shares everything with one another. Or with Dori at the very least. I explain Calista's condition and how it affects her. Dori's frown grows deeper.

"That's why I'm here, for Rome to take a DNA test. With me having no idea where I came from, I at least want her to have the information from her father's side."

"Well, lucky we ran into one another. You need to come down to my place. I'll show you the long line of people Calista comes from and I can tell you all about what diseases they suffered from."

"That's kind of you, but I really only need his DNA. That's all."

She's quiet for a second, her hand rubbing Calista's

back. "Once you get his DNA, you're heading back to Seattle?"

I put my finger under Calista's open hand on Dori's shoulder, staring at my daughter. "Yeah, but Rome asked that I stay for one week. Then he'll take the test."

She smiles. "Rome is my smartest grandchild, did you know that?" She winks.

She thinks Rome will convince me to stay permanently somehow, but they still don't know about Shane. One of my friends is more than a friend.

TEN

Rome

I stop at the corner, waiting to cross the road, heaving for a breath since I jogged as fast as I could. Who knows what will come out of G'Ma D's mouth?

Man, I'm so out of shape. I need more cardio in my life. And now I'm a dad. I refuse to have the dad bod. Time to ramp up the workouts.

G'Ma D, Harley, and Calista are on a park bench, Calista's head draped on G'Ma D's shoulder while the women are in a deep discussion.

I knew leaving them alone was a shitty idea. What did I hire Colin for if he can't handle a fridge not working? Thank goodness Jack at Hammer Time Hardware has connections, so a guy will be here within the hour to fix it.

Do I have time for Calista and Harley in my life right now? Hell to the no, and repeat that twice for effect. I'm two weeks away from opening my restaurant.

Stupid me decided Founder's Day was the ideal time to open, as a tribute of sorts to my parents. Now all I can think of is how I can convince Harley to stay a little longer.

She mentioned spending adolescence in foster care, which might mean no parents or family to speak of. What a shithead thought. I'm sure she's got friends and a life in Seattle. I can't assume she'll pick up and move here.

Finally there are no cars, so I jog across the street, catching the last bit of conversation between G'Ma D and Harley.

"Rome is my smartest grandchild, did you know that?" G'Ma D asks.

"Oh, G'Ma D, I love you too." I kiss her cheek, staring like a jealous boyfriend at Calista sprawled across her shoulder.

"You get it from me." She winks. "Well, I should go now." She hands Calista her to Harley, who looks dumbfounded at me while trying to soothe my baby girl back to sleep.

"That was quick." Though I'm not complaining. I thought G'ma D would be superglued to our sides all day.

"What? I can't sit around here forever, things to do." Grandma leans into me. "Was I the first though?"

I feel the crease form between my eyebrows. "The first what?"

"The first Bailey to hold her." She's already wearing a prize-winning smile as though there's a board with rankings and her name will be under the number one.

"Um... yeah. Except for me."

She pats my arm. "Good. I have to go practice. I have a big game tonight." She kisses Harley on the cheek then Calista on the head. "We'll see each other again soon."

"Okay," Harley says, clearly confused. "Good luck at Mahjong tonight."

"What?" I say.

G'Ma D disregards me and waves. "Oh, I don't need luck, but thank you."

As she walks away, I sit down in the spot she left.

"She's fun." Harley rubs Calista's back.

"You can say she's batshit crazy. I won't take offense." I stare at Calista, surprised at how easily she fell back asleep.

"Your fridge?"

"Repairman will be there in an hour."

She nods. "When are you opening?"

"A little over two weeks." I fiddle with the hem of my jacket.

"That's great. I mean that you own your own restaurant. That's a big step."

I glance at her. "Yeah, baby daddy and restaurant owner in one month. Big changes for Rome Bailey."

Her shoulders falter slightly.

I shift on the bench to face her. "That wasn't a dig."

"I wouldn't blame you if it was, but I'm not sure how I would've found you. I bribed a friend I worked with to look up any Denvers flying to New York that next morning, but she couldn't find one, so I figured I had wrong information."

"Hey, let's just forget it. I don't hold a grudge. We had a one-night stand and produced a beautiful baby. I'm cool with just moving forward. That's why I can't hold you hostage here for a week."

As I waited for word from Jack, I went over the agreement I made with her in my head and it's not fair. Besides, do I really think she'll fall in love with Lake Starlight in a week? Hell, I grew up here and even I know Lake Starlight is an acquired taste.

"What do you mean?" she asks.

"I made my appointment for two days from now. If you want to go back to Seattle, you can go."

She thinks hard. "So you don't want to be..." She clears her throat. "Okay, okay." She stands and positions a still-sleeping Calista on her shoulder. "Could you point me to where I need to go to get back?"

"I'll walk you." I stand.

"No. You have the fridge, your restaurant, and your life. I'm fine."

She's clearly not. Her wobbly stature and tight voice alerts me that something is wrong. Like G'Ma D said, I'm the smart grandkid. It doesn't take long to figure out that she's assuming I'm giving her a pass to go back to single motherhood in Seattle.

"Harley, what exactly do you think I'm agreeing to?"

"Oh, don't feel bad. I mean, I threw this all on you, and I kind of prefer it just being me and her. I mean, I was getting a little protective when she went to your grandma with no problem. I just... I let my mind wander. It's fine."

I touch her arm and wait for her eyes to meet mine. My hand runs down the back of Calista's head. "I'm her father. I *will* be part of her life. We'll have to come up with a visitation plan, and I want to start paying you each month for her expenses. But it was wrong of me to blackmail you into staying here for a week, to hold that test over your head. I want you to stay, but I'm giving you an out."

A tear slips from Harley's eye, and I see more waiting to fall. The way she straightens her back and inhales deeply, I'm fairly sure that'll be the last one she'll let slip though.

"Do you not want me to be a part of her life?" I ask.

She shakes her head. "No. That's not it."

"Then why are you upset?"

"You want her?" she asks.

"Of course I do."

She nods, and her gaze shoots to the left of me. "Then we're here for the week. You can take the test whenever you want, but I give you my word we're here for the week so you can get to know your daughter. We'll have to figure something out after that. I really can't afford to stay at the Cozy Cottage B&B for an extended length of time."

My stomach bubbles with excitement like I'm a fucking girl. "Really? You're going to stay. For me? Why?"

More tears fall. She digs into her diaper bag but apparently finds that difficult with Calista, so I grab her and quickly turn her around to lie on me. We need to get this girl a stroller.

"She has a dad who met her less than twenty-four hours ago, and he's willing to up-end his entire life to include her. I can't take that away from her. I know what it feels like not to have that." She wipes her tears with a Kleenex.

My heart goes out to Harley for the upbringing she must have had, but I know she doesn't want my pity, so I try not to let it show on my face. "You thought I'd be content with never seeing her again?"

She shrugs.

"I think not only do I need to get to know Calista, you need to get to know me." I put my arm around her shoulders. "First way to do that is that I get to feed you."

She laughs. "Feed me? I doubt you have anything in that fancy restaurant I'd like."

I huff. "Such little faith. I hope you're hungry, but first things first. If you're staying here for a week, we need a stroller."

I direct us toward Sweet Home Baby Boutique, where I proudly get to make my first purchase for my daughter.

An hour later, Calista is in a high chair with Harley at the front window of my restaurant. Calista's eating some mac and cheese I made as I try to assemble the damn stroller.

"No, the instructions say to put Part E with part—" Colin wiggles the instructions in front of my face, and I rip them from his grip and toss them on the floor.

Fucking hell. I'm not even sure I'd feel safe with Calista riding around in this thing once I'm done.

"Why don't I help?" Harley moves to get up from her chair.

I put my hand up to stop her. "Nope. I got this."

As if I need more spying eyes, two jackasses walk into the restaurant.

"We're closed," I say, looking at Colin. "Show them the door."

A look of fret crosses his face because Colin's not exactly a big guy. He's kind of scrawny, but the guy's got crazy knife skills. That's why he's my sous-chef.

"We're family." Denver sits across from Harley, next to Calista, and picks a noodle out of the baby's brown hair.

"Only one of you is," I remark, snapping on a piece of plastic. "Fuck me."

"Fuk," Calista says.

Harley glares at me, releasing a long, annoyed breath.

"Are you really telling me you've never sworn in front of her?" I ask.

Harley sips her soda, saying nothing. The smile teasing her lips says Calista might have known the word well before me.

"We didn't properly meet. I'm Denver." He extends his hand over the table.

Harley shakes it, studying his face. This is a common occurrence. She's looking for some way to tell us apart. Denver has a small scar under his chin from when we were six and he fell in the shower, trying to be Spiderman. Other than that, my mom used to say my nose was slightly wider, but truth be told, I've never noticed.

"I'm Liam." Our buddy puts out his hand.

Harley shakes it, looking at the big mass of a man. Calista's eyes widen as her own head keeps tilting up. It's cute. Like he's a real-life giant. She pokes a tattoo on his muscular arm and flaps her arms up and down.

"You're brilliant. Yes, a bird." Denver ruffles her hair, and she smiles at him.

We really need to teach her stranger danger. Although I can't really blame her on the whole Denver thing. She probably thinks it's me.

"Nice to meet you both," Harley says.

"You're putting that together all wrong," Liam says, sitting next to me and taking the part out of my hand.

"Have at it then."

I sit next to Harley, putting my arm around the back of her chair, but she side-glances me, so I move it to my lap.

"Hungry?" I ask my brother.

"Always," Denver says, picking up a fork and stabbing a piece of mac and cheese out of Calista's bowl. "So," he mumbles over his chewing, "what do you do, Harley?"

"I bartend, and I'm going to school for massage therapy."

Denver's lips tip down, and I know that on the count of three, he's going to fucking embarrass me. "Massage therapy? Not one of those happy-ending massage places, right?

Is that how you two met? Did you practice on Rome? You know one way to tell us apart is below the belt."

"Yeah, I'm bigger." I grin.

Denver laughs.

"Tell me, Denver, how many happy-ending massages have you gotten over the years?" Harley quips.

He holds up his hand. "None. I don't need to pay for those."

"But you know of places that supply them?" She crosses her legs and rests her elbows on the table. I keep seeing reasons why I slept with her. Her wit is damn sexy.

"Everyone does." He shrugs.

"I don't." Her eyes widen and she glances at me. "Rome?"

"Nope." I shake my head.

Denver leers at me.

"Liam?"

We glance over to find he's halfway finished putting the stroller together. Damn show-off.

"Never. I strictly go for the neck and back pain I get from being slouched over doing tatts all day. I've never heard of a massage therapist's hands roaming where they shouldn't." He doesn't look up as he reads the instructions. The fact that he can listen to our conversation, respond to a question, and still put together that stroller grates on me.

"Whatever, you guys." Denver takes some more mac and cheese, but Calista's arms stretch out and she grabs the bowl, bringing it to her chest.

"Mine!"

"Man, I don't get any love in this room." Denver pretends to pout, and Calista watches him carefully for a moment before sliding the bowl back his way. He smiles at Harley then me. "Well, shit, I love her already."

"She," Calista says, and Harley throws her hands in the air.

"Here you go," Liam hops up from the seat, pushing the stroller back and forth a few times.

"Who the hell are you? Galileo?" Denver asks.

We all gasp.

"You know Galileo?" I ask.

He shakes his head and unstraps Calista. "Just me and you, girl." He dances with her around the restaurant. "Screw all them."

Calista touches his face and smiles at him as if he's the funniest guy in the world. Harley turns to me briefly, no smile or anything on her face, and goes back to watching them. There's so much love here for Calista. I wonder how much there is back in Seattle.

ELEVEN

Harley

Rome has spent every day this week with Calista and me. We've gone to the park, visited Grandma Dori where she lives, seen the house he grew up in, and been to his parents' burial plot. Most of his time with us is spent with Calista in his arms and me pushing the expensive empty stroller he purchased. Every day I see him growing closer to her and her to him.

We ended up putting off the appointment at the lab until later in the week, but today he's picking me up to go with him to get his DNA test. I have Calista's sample to bring in, so we're going alone, leaving Calista with Selene since we don't know how long it will take. I'm not even sure why I'm accompanying him. There's no real reason I need to be there. But he asked if I'd join him and I said yes. This whole exercise feels like a finality. The last checkmark on our weeklong list before I go back to Seattle.

Speaking of which, Shane texted me last night. Our situation is so complicated, I have no idea where to begin. He finished his big case and says he's looking forward to seeing me. He's going to pick us up from the airport in Seattle.

Rome's truck pulls up outside, and I rush to grab my coat and tell Selene we're leaving.

"Have a nice trip to Anchorage. Enjoy the drive." Selene holds Calista on her hip.

Another nice part of being here this week is Selene. She's watched Calista a couple of times, which has given me time to look online for classes here to finish up my massage therapy license. It's nice having people around to help. Selene feels like a pseudo mom—not that I'd know what that feels like.

"Thanks." I kiss Calista. "Be good for Selene."

Calista tugs on Selene's hair and looks at her. Yep, we're both growing attached. This isn't good.

Rome knocks on the door, and when I open it, he's there, just like every other day this week, but I swear he grows hotter every time that door swings open. Today, he's in jeans, a sweater, and a jacket. His hair is gelled back instead of the loosely ruffled waves it usually has, and the bad-boy vibe has been replaced by some good-guy feels. I need to contemplate which look I prefer, because they both work for him.

"Da!" Calista says, and both of our heads whip around.

"What?" Rome barrels past me and holds his hands out to her.

Calista leans forward, and Selene passes her to him.

"Da! Da!" Calista repeats.

Rome holds her out in the air like she loves, swinging

her around. "That's right! Dada." He points at himself, pulling her into his body.

Selene steps back, giving us some space for this newfound classification my daughter has discovered. Not that she knows what the word means, but Rome's been in her face every day repeating it. It seems to have stuck.

Rome holds her, his hand on the back of her head, his lips at her ear, looking at me over her shoulder with the widest, cheesiest grin. One that says, "I'm never giving her up." I can't fault him. I never will either.

"Dada has to go somewhere with Mommy, so you stay with Auntie Selene, okay?" He lifts her up, staring into her eyes while he talks to her.

He swivels her around, lays her tummy over his hands, and acts like she's an airplane landing into Selene's arms. Cheesy as hell, but cute as hell at the same time. I never thought I'd see a man like Rome baby-talking and making our daughter into an airplane.

I never thought I'd feel guilty when she calls him Dada either, because two days from now, it'll be me separating them when I take her home.

"Now you two get going. You know, traffic." Selene winks and shoos us out the door.

Rome kisses Calista on the head then opens the door for me.

"There's traffic in Alaska?" I quirk an eyebrow.

"Hey, it's a popular place to be." Rome ushers me out with his hand.

"Bye, Selene. We won't be gone long," I say. I know Selene can be trusted, and I've had to leave Calista with daycare personnel for my job and schooling back in Seattle, but there's always that fear in the back of my mind that when I return, she'll be gone.

I blow a kiss to Calista, who quickly realizes what's going on. Her bottom lip dips.

"Take her, Rome," Selene says, realizing what's about to happen.

Calista's wailing begins as Rome shuts the door behind us. I reach for the doorknob but stop myself.

"What are you waiting for? Go get her. We'll take her with us," Rome says, concern lacing every syllable.

I look at him. I've been there—the edginess of his tone, the spastic way he's ready to bulldoze past me to reach her. I lean in closer to the door and hear Selene singing. Calista's cries die down, and I take my hand off the doorknob.

"What am I missing?" he asks.

I touch his forearm and nod toward the walkway. "Let's go. She can handle her."

Rome stands on the porch, wavering on whether to believe me or bust through the door. Thankfully for all of us, he follows me to his truck.

Soon we're on our way to Anchorage. His rock music is at a low enough volume that we could talk, but what is there to talk about?

Yeah, okay, you got me there. We could literally fill an entire ocean with issues that need to be resolved. Right now is as good of a time as any, so I turn and face him.

His thumbs beat on the steering wheel to the drum rhythm. He really is devilishly handsome. It doesn't matter, I remind myself. Nor should I care.

"You sure you're okay doing this?" I ask.

He nods and smiles, his strip-the-panties-off-any-woman smile. "Anything for Calista. Shit. Speaking of which." He grabs his phone from the console, presses a few buttons—careful to keep his eyes on the road—and hands it to me. "Have you heard of the Buzz Wheel blog?"

"I've heard you all groan about it." I glance at the screen and see the Lake Starlight Buzz Wheel blog website, cute blue-and-black logo and all.

"Think of it as a rite of passage. The headline today is about us. I wanted you to know in case people in town give you looks or refer to you by name."

I cringe, looking at him before reading the latest blog entry.

BABY DADDY FOUND

The new girl in town with baby in tow is Harley Sullivan. The baby girl, Calista. The baby daddy? None other than Rome Bailey. I know, I would've sworn it was Denver's too. Although I did hear a rumor about a mix-up over who the father might be, so who knows? Our two new Lake Starlight additions have been spotted all over town, Rome acting as their tour guide. Could this little darling be the one to lock down one of our crazy bad-boy Bailey twins? I think I speak for all of us when I say a resounding YES! Regardless of Mama and Dada getting together, it's a time for celebration because the Baileys have a new generation to welcome. WOO HOO!

My eyes scan down the page.

In other news, I guess the apple really doesn't fall far from the tree. Karen Radcliffe, Holly Radcliffe's (soon-to-be Holly Bailey) mother, and Brian Canmore were caught playing with the whipped cream in the backroom of Lard Have Mercy last night. I speak for all of us when I say, I'll still take the pecan pie but hold the whipped cream. The Radcliffes must have something for public sex. Holly and Austin can't seem to keep it in the bedroom either.

All that follows is an email to send stories or pictures to.

"What is this, high school?" I place his phone back in the center console.

"Yeah, kind of, but in this weird way, it brings the town together too."

I keep my mouth shut, but I can see the fascination with it. "Tell me, how much of a bad boy are you?"

He chuckles, turning us out of Lake Starlight and onto the highway. My stomach clenches as Calista gets farther and farther away from me.

"It's a smaller-ish town, so most of it's hearsay. Plus, the town can be boring. Denver, Liam, and I tend to find our own fun."

I turn toward him. His long fingers are still strumming on the steering wheel. "You didn't answer the question."

His lips turn up in a "you got me" expression. He shrugs. "What's your definition of bad boy?"

"No way. You're not throwing the question back my way to dodge answering."

He chuckles again, the sound filling the entire cab of the truck and wrapping around me like a warm blanket. Is this why I slept with him years ago? Was his flirtatiousness this alluring then too? Probably.

"If your interpretation of bad boy is sleeping with a different woman every night, then no, I'm not a bad boy."

I huff and roll my eyes.

"I'm not saying I'm a saint. When I sleep with women, I don't want a relationship out of it, so it's strictly about the sex. But I'm not down at Lucky's every night, picking up women." He glances at me before passing a semi. "I get that's hard to believe, given our history. I usually seek out female companionship when I'm pissed or upset."

"Female companionship?"

"Would you rather me say fuck buddy?"

I shake my head.

"Don't worry, I'm not a head case. I'm fully aware of my reasons for doing it."

"Which is?"

He glances over, easing back into the right lane. "Women tend to help me forget what I'm upset about. It's really that simple."

"You don't have sex when you're happy?"

"Depends where I am. If I'm with my brother or Liam, we tend to do stupid shit when we're happy. Stupid shit that involves the sheriff."

"Yeah, you might be pretty high on the bad-boy spectrum."

I try to let the majestic view of the mountains push the thought that men like Rome Bailey aren't ones to settle down from my mind. Throughout the years, there have been more men than I can count who I thought I could change. I won't add Rome to that list.

That's why Shane is so easy. He knows what he wants and wears his feelings for anyone to see. He's stable and good. Predictable.

"What about you?"

"What?" I push Shane out of my head for now.

"You slept with me that night. Are you a bad girl?"

"I learned a long time ago that sex is sex. I think I have every right to enjoy it with whoever I want. There don't have to be strings attached."

"And here we are, two years after our no-strings-attached one-night stand, with a thick bungee cord attaching us. Calista will always bond us together."

What Rome knows as truth I only came to realize a few days ago. The closer I saw him and Calista become, the more I realized that he can't remove himself from her life. My little girl deserves her father. She deserves to have everything I didn't get.

"True." I glance out the window, wondering what the future will bring. How will we manage the distance? Co-parenting? Finances?

Rome surprises me by almost reading my mind. "Let's get this test over with, then we'll head to a restaurant and talk about our plans."

I can't keep living in limbo. I have to get back to school and work before I don't have either one left. I have to get back to my *real* life.

TWELVE

Rome

I order for both of us at my favorite seafood restaurant that looks out over the Gulf of Alaska. It's a no-frills, plastic-tablecloths-on-wooden-tables kind of place where they drop crab legs on the table, along with plastic cups of butter and cocktail sauce.

"I should call Selene." Harley reaches for her phone.

"I texted her while you were in the restroom. Calista is sleeping."

She inspects her phone and nods. "Naptime."

"Yeah." I don't know our daughter's schedule as well as Harley, but I'm starting to.

She concentrates on the few fishing boats coming in and out of the port. "It's really beautiful here."

I look at her. I could be cheesy and do the "she's the beautiful" thing, but I don't think she'd respond well. Plus, it's clear that if I want this co-parenting thing to work out, a sexual relationship isn't the best place to start.

But it's easy to see why I slept with Harley that night. She's gorgeous in a girl-next-door-with-an-edge way. She tucks her feelings twelve layers deep. I don't think she'd ever admit she's hurting, and to hell with anyone seeing her vulnerability.

The past couple of years couldn't have been easy for her. I'm struggling to keep up with the restaurant and they've only been in my life a week.

"So the massage therapy thing? How much longer do you have to earn your degree?" I straighten in my chair.

Her eyes find mine, leaving the scene of the hard-working fishermen anchoring their boats to the pier. "I have one more class, but when Calista got sick, I had to push it aside."

"I'm sorry."

She shakes her head. "Don't be sorry. It's not your fault."

"Still." I straighten my silverware on the table. I desperately want to tell her about the research I did, but I'm not sure how she'll react.

"The shitty part is my friend, Miranda, just graduated. She's already working and I'm kind of jealous, you know?"

"I get it. I have a friend who's a top chef in a renowned restaurant in New York. I took the long route of touring Europe, learning and refining my culinary skills, while he practically jumped out of culinary school into this spot. Then here I am, opening up a restaurant in Lake Starlight. But comparison is the thief of joy, as they say."

She nods. "I tell myself that. I would never change anything. That night. Not Calista. She truly is the best thing to happen to me. It's just..."

"What?" I lean in closer, because the more she shares, the lower her voice becomes, and I don't want her to stop talking. I love that she trusts me enough to let me know what she's thinking.

"Getting my massage therapy certificate can change our life. I could be home more nights, we'd be able to move out of the tiny apartment we're in and maybe rent something better. I feel like my life has stalled."

I can't relate to that. I've been go-go-go my entire life. Mostly because settling down is boring. Returning to Lake Starlight was a tough decision, because I knew wherever I opened a restaurant, it would mean becoming a permanent resident. I finally concluded that if I was going to have a permanent residence, I wanted to have it in my hometown with my family.

I decide to go with my usual philosophy in life, which in a nutshell is *fuck it.*

"I looked up local massage therapy classes." The words tumble out of my mouth.

Her face twists and she picks up her water, her cheeks indenting from her deep suck on her straw. She's not making this easy on me, is she? "Why?"

"Because I want you to stay here."

There. I threw it out there. I'm not opposed to being vulnerable. And I don't think it makes me less of a man to admit that I want my daughter in my life. I want her to grow up in Lake Starlight.

"Rome," Harley sighs. "We have a life—"

"What kind of life? You can bartend for me, and if you don't want to do that, then I'll find you something else. You can finish your classes in massage therapy. I have eight siblings and a town filled with people who would help. What's in Seattle that's not here?"

She twists to stare at the fishermen again. My eyes stay on her. A rush of emotions flit over her face, and I bet she has no idea how transparent she is. I'd bet Terra and Mare that she thinks she masks all her feelings, but I see them.

"There's something you need to know. Something I haven't told you."

My gut twists as her head slowly circles back my way. It's clear that whatever she's about to tell me will change this newfound relationship of ours.

"I have... there's someone... I'm dating a guy back in Seattle."

Whoosh. I swear a tsunami just slammed into me, leaving me gasping for air. How did I not consider that? I may not be dating anyone, but that doesn't mean Harley is celibate. She's beautiful, of course she's found a guy.

"Oh," is all I can say.

She leans forward. "I mean, it's not serious, but it's not casual either."

"He knows why you're here?"

She nods.

"Does she..." My voice cracks. "Does Calista think of him as her—"

"No." She shakes her head and leans over the table with pleading eyes. "It's not like that. They've met, and you know her, no one is a stranger."

Sourness fills my stomach, and I swallow back the bile rising up my throat.

The waitress comes over and dumps crab legs in the middle of the table. She politely smiles and asks if we need anything else. Harley shakes her head, her lips tipping down. I stare at the plastic tablecloth, trying my best to wrap my thoughts around this boyfriend thing. I thought I had a good case to keep her here. I realize now that I have nothing.

"Can he give you a good life back in Seattle?" I ask, pushing aside my jealousy over his relationship with Calista.

"He's a lawyer."

"Of course he is." The words come out before I realize it.

"What does that mean?"

"Nothing."

"Please understand—"

I pick up a crab leg and crack it open. "I do."

She leans back in her chair. "I didn't think it pertained to you. I mean, that's my life. and we're still finding new ground here."

"And in the last week, you didn't think to tell me you had a boyfriend? Someone permanent in Calista's life?" Even I hear the bitterness in my tone. Where is this jealousy coming from? This is about Calista, not Harley. Not about us becoming a family, it's about me being a father. I sure as hell can't do that with her in Seattle and Calista seeing some lawyer douche more than me.

"Rome, you're being immature about this."

I pull out a large piece of crab and place it on her plate. "You'd be okay if I had a girlfriend and hid it from you?"

Yeah, okay I can see that I'm being a jackass. We've known each other a week. I need to tamp down the shit-talking.

"Never mind," I say. "Let's just eat and figure this out. So I can't very well convince you to stay here to finish your degree... when do you plan on going back to lawyer boy?"

"Rome," she sighs again.

"Sorry. Seattle. When are you going back?"

She picks at the crab, dipping it into the melted butter. "In two days."

My stomach sinks to my toes. Everything I conjured up in my mind over the last few days flies out the open window like a pile of papers. "And you probably don't plan on coming back?"

"Maybe at some point, but it's not like I have a job with vacation time."

"Yeah, I get it." I stare at my plate. "I'll figure out a way to get to you, but can we at least promise to FaceTime a few times a week?"

It feels like such a cheap substitute compared to the week I've gotten to spend with my daughter.

"Definitely. I don't want to strip her from your life. And Shane—"

I quirk an eyebrow. "The lawyer?"

She nods. "He's not her father, nor does he act like one. There are no worries there."

"Okay." He might though—someday.

She buries her head in the crab, every once in a while glancing up to check that I'm okay.

Yeah, I'm doing great over here. I've been introduced to and had my daughter ripped away from me in the span of a week. Shit is just stellar.

My leg shakes under the table, trying to relieve some of this pent-up frustration. I need to get away from Harley and find a place for these feelings. How can I be jealous of some guy I've never even met? Why do I care?

Calista. This tornado of feelings is only about my daughter.

Yeah, I'll keep telling myself that. Sooner or later I'm bound to believe it.

THIRTEEN

Harley

The doorbell of the Cozy Cottage B&B rings. Since I hear "Heart of Gold" by Neil Young coming from Selene's studio, I'm guessing she's pretty busy making her art, so I pick up Calista from the pile of big blocks that Rome bought her a few days ago and carry her to the door.

After peeking through the peephole, I bite my lip and open the door. "Hi."

"Come." Dori plucks Calista from my arms and points at herself. "Grandma Dori."

Calista, who's already familiar with her, touches her blue-tinted hair.

"Yeah, you're the only one I'd allow to touch my hair after seeing my hairdresser." She smiles at my daughter as though she's loved her since the day she was born.

That's the oddest part of all this—these people love my daughter because she shares their DNA. I get that she's a child and not hard to fall in love with. But I swear they all feel bonded to her. I can't help but love that she'll have the one thing I didn't have growing up—a family who appreciates and, most of all, wants her.

Except they'll be thousands of miles away. That thought makes me frown.

"Listen, I was going to kidnap you—" Dori starts. My eyes widen and she puts up her hand. "Not kidnap really. But I was going to get you in my car and take you somewhere."

"I think I'll take Calista back." I hold out my arms.

She pushes my arm down. "Rome told me you're leaving tomorrow, and Calista really hasn't had a chance to meet her aunts. You can thank me for that, because I threatened them with dismemberment if they harassed you to see Calista. You and Rome needed time to sort through everything first. Anyway, I was going to trick you into going over to Holly and Austin's for brunch. But Savannah said that was no way of staying in your good graces, so here I am, being upfront and honest."

"And it looks like you're highly annoyed by that?" I giggle.

"I like to do things my way, but Savannah had a point." She leans forward as though Savannah is nearby. "Never tell her I said that."

"Okay."

"Okay, you'll come? Willingly?"

I shake my head. "No. We're not going."

"See, this is why I should've tricked you. Listen, you'll have fun, and it's a small break before having to go back to Seattle where you're with Calista twenty-four seven. We have some wine, and Holly's a decent cook. She's not me, but I'm here to get you, so I couldn't do both. Please? These are her aunts." She shuts the door behind her, following me into the living room.

"Doodoo." Calista pats Dori's head.

"No Doodoo," Dori says.

I bite my lip to keep from smiling.

Calista lays her head on Dori's shoulder. "Doodoo," she says softly.

"Why is she saying that? Did she go to the bathroom?" Dori peeks into the back of her diaper. "Nope."

"Um."

"Doodoo!" Calista says, more excited now.

"No Doodoo!" Dori says, looking baffled.

"I think she's calling you Doodoo because she can't pronounce Dori?"

Her mouth opens, and she stares at me. "Oh, no. I already have people comparing me to that damn fish. I will not let my first great-grandchild call me Doodoo." She points at herself. "We're changing gears. Nana."

"Doodoo!"

Dori points at herself again. "Nana."

"Doodoo." Calista wiggles in Dori's arms, ready to get down.

"Okay, just for that, you're coming with me." She grabs my jacket off the hook and throws it at me.

"What happened to staying in my good graces? You've lost all your manners with me."

"Then you should feel honored because I'm treating you like family." She grabs Calista's coat, sets her on the floor, and bends down to put it on her. "*Nana* is going to put on your coat."

She emphasizes Nana as though that'll make a difference. Calista is as stubborn as me and that name isn't going to change until she's older.

"I don't have a car seat. We'll have to walk."

"Oh, no. I have my car, and I bought us a car seat."

"Us?"

"Yeah." She opens the door, and I see a huge, older model Cadillac in the driveway. Something like Elvis drove once upon a time. "Mum is the word, because I'm only allowed to drive until dusk."

"Who told you that?"

"Sheriff Miller. We have an understanding." She winks.

Great. I'm going to put my daughter in harm's way.

"Maybe I could drive? I mean, you can tell me where to go and I'll drive. I really missed driving this week."

She narrows her eyes. "I'm a good driver."

I wave off her words. "I know you are, but this way you can sit in the back with Calista and keep her busy."

Her eyes light up. "Perfect."

She hands me the keys and I'm shocked it was as easy as that. Maybe Dori's right about this tricking people thing.

"I'm just going to scribble a note for Selene." I head into the kitchen and jot a quick note for her and put it by the teapot.

"It has to be getting costly staying here," Dori says as we walk down the path to her Cadillac.

"Yeah. If I come up again, I might need to figure out something else."

I've yet to pay the final bill, which will take my last paycheck from the bar.

"I'd love to have you, but Ethel would complain about Calista staying in the senior center. She's such a pain in my ass."

I inspect the back seat, where a new car seat is waiting.

"No worries, Kingston installed it. He does the safety checks to help the fire department when he's not jumping out of planes. That kid, I swear he'll give me a heart attack."

Kingston. Kingston. I'm not sure I remember which one he is.

I put Calista in the car seat and secure the straps. Dori climbs in next to her, and I throw the diaper bag in the passenger seat before arranging the mirrors and seat to fit me. When I turn over the keys in the ignition, Elvis blares out of the speakers.

I glance in the rearview mirror as I lower the volume. Calista has covered her ears.

"That's the king, baby girl. You never cover your ears when he's playing." Dori pries my daughter's hands off her ears.

"You never know, he might be watching from the forest," I joke about the rumor that he's really alive somewhere.

"Yeah, he might," Dori says, no humor in her voice.

Okay then. No jokes about the king.

***

Don't even ask how we got to Holly's in one piece. I mean, I made so many sharp right and left turns because of Dori's last-minute directions, cutting people off, I'm sure they thought it was Dori driving.

I park outside a nice log-cabin-style house with a three-car garage. It's secluded, with a long, winding driveway. There are no neighbors to be seen unless you're counting wildlife. I'm not sure this is for me. Might as well ask for a bear to visit you for breakfast.

Three cars are already parked in the wide paved area in front of the house. It looks like they're used to always having company and have sectioned off part of what would be their front yard for their guests' vehicles.

"This was Rome's parents' house. Austin, his older brother, and his fiancée, Holly, live here now."

That article I read on Buzz Wheel comes to mind. Karen's daughter, Holly, is the person it was talking about.

"It's very nice," I say as we approach.

Dori opens the front door, the diaper bag on her shoulder, leaving me to hold Calista. "We're here!" she screams, not waiting for me as she walks into the house.

I shut the door, not sure whether I should wait or what.

But by the time I turn around, one of Rome's sisters (I assume) is there. She's tall with blond hair, and she's wearing a pretty navy pantsuit. She looks completely put together and in control of her life, and it makes me feel a little like a hot mess given the situation and the messy top knot in my hair.

"Hi. We haven't properly met. I'm Rome's sister Savannah." She holds out her hand.

"Hi. Harley and this is—"

"Calista." She doesn't try to take her but smooths her hand down my daughter's hair. "She's beautiful."

"Thank you."

"Come. We're just opening the wine, and Holly made these awesome sandwich things. She has some stuff we think the little one can eat too."

The kitchen is buzzing with women talking. Karen and another woman are behind the counter, moving from the fridge to the food. They work well together, and that's when I realize the other woman must be Holly.

A blonde and an auburn-haired girl slide off their stools at the breakfast bar, walking toward me.

"Juno," the auburn-haired one says. "Auntie Juno," she says to Calista, touching her arm.

"Brooklyn," the blonde introduces herself. "Number-one auntie," she whispers to Calista, holding up her finger.

"Oh." The other auburn-haired woman behind the counter wipes her hands on the small apron wrapped around her waist. "I'm Holly, welcome." She doesn't shake my hand. Rather, she pulls me into a hug and kisses Calista's temple. "I was able to scrounge up a high chair and I have a small area blocked off in the circular gate for her to play. We have two dogs, Myles and Daisy. Austin is walking them to get rid of some of their energy. Myles is a tad..."

"Spastic." Brooklyn cringes.

Holly shakes her head. "No, he's just easily excitable."

"He's tried to eat Wyatt's balls, like, three times." Brooklyn sips her wine with her eyebrows raised.

"It's only him. Probably smells his money or something." Holly laughs, waving off her comment like a joke. "Come in and make yourself comfortable."

I sit in the seat they pat for me and prop Calista on my lap. She peers around the table, unsure of who to focus on. Brooklyn's obviously the most eager for her attention because she starts playing peek-a-boo.

"Oh, she loved playing that with Brian at the diner," Karen says, patting my hand. "Welcome." Her smile conveys a message—you're safe here.

I still have that kindred feeling with her, like she knows what I might be going through.

"May I?" Brooklyn asks, standing and holding out her hands. "We'll just play over here. We each brought her something."

I nod, and of course Calista has no problem going to her. Her fingers immediately entwine in Brooklyn's hair. Tears prick my eyes, but I suck them back. All these people unconditionally loving my child and wanting to be a part of her life feels overwhelming. Buying her things to make our life easier. I never in a million years thought me coming up here would turn into this.

"So you're going back to Seattle tomorrow?" Savannah asks, picking up a sandwich.

"Yes." I look around, wondering where Grandma Dori went to.

"She'll be back. This is her MO. She tricks you, then goes MIA. Don't let your guard down. Next thing you know, a priest will be at the door with Rome." Savannah laughs.

"She usually goes directly to the Bailey child though. Tracked Austin down." Holly smiles from where she's assembling food at the counter.

"She went to Wyatt for me," Brooklyn says from the family room. "Meddling woman."

"Yeah, we apologize ahead of time. But thank you for coming over and spending some time with us." Savannah smiles and pulls up her phone again.

For the next ten minutes, Juno tells me about her matchmaking business while Holly and Karen joke about the Buzz Wheel articles. It isn't until the man I believe is Austin comes in with two dogs, one jumping up and down on his leash, that all of this feels like déjà vu. I've never been here before. Why does this feel so familiar?

"Don't let him off," Holly says, but Austin's fingers have already unclipped the leash.

Myles barrels into the family room and gives Calista one long-tongued lick up her face.

Her face scrunches like it does right before she cries. I

stand to go over to her, but the front door opens and slams, drawing all of our attention.

"This is the last straw!" Rome's voice booms through the house.

He stops at the entrance of the family room, sees Brooklyn with Calista, and beelines over. Rome picks Calista up out of his sister's hold and brings her into his chest. He inspects her as if Myles mauled her then stares down his family.

"You have all crossed the line." He looks around. "Where is she?"

FOURTEEN

Harley

"She's gone." Juno points at the window.

Sure enough, we all see Dori's Cadillac fishtail down the driveway.

I take Calista from Rome and wipe the one tear that leaked down her cheek.

"She's going to get herself killed," Austin mumbles. "Does this mean I get a sandwich?" He kisses Holly's cheek and runs into the kitchen.

"No!" she screams, chasing him. "They're for our guests."

He grabs one as she catches him, and he holds it above her head. "Surely she can't eat all of these," he says, his gaze directed at me, waiting for my agreement.

"Have at 'em, big guy," I say and kiss Calista on the cheek. She seems better now.

"Your mutt is a problem," Rome says.

"He licked her." Austin's eyes are focused on his fiancée, laughing as she attempts to get the sandwich. Her boobs are bobbing up and down. "Rome, go into the other room. You don't need to see this."

"Nothing I haven't seen before," Rome says, picking up his own sandwich and holding it out to Calista. She nibbles on the edge of the bread.

Sometimes I'm surprised at how instinctive being a parent seems to be for Rome. I feel as if I'm failing every day and he's like Clark Kent, changing quickly between one identity and another.

"You haven't seen hers, so leave."

"Fine." Rome nods toward the other room.

I follow but glance over my shoulder to find Austin stuff the small sandwich into his mouth, grab Holly's ass, and hoist her into his arms. Man, that's sexy as fuck. She playfully swats at him when I'm fairly sure she's probably thinking, *take me upstairs.*

When I pull my eyes off of them, a tingle ignites between my thighs. It's been a long time since I felt as though a guy wanted me like that. Shane is a considerate lover. He makes sure I come before him and he has no problem with going down, but everything feels like it's a list and he's crossing off the steps as we go. There's not much passion or spontaneity in our sex life.

Rome sits on the floor, pushing Myles back with his forearm.

"Woof," Calista says, reaching out to pet the dog.

"Bad dog," Rome scolds.

"Give Myles a break." Brooklyn buries her hands in the husky's fur, petting him until he lies down beside her.

Calista crawls out of Rome's lap toward the dog.

"Oh no, you don't," he says, but she keeps up with the

wiggles. He looks at me and I nod. "It's on you if something bad happens."

Calista toddles over and sits next to Brooklyn, her small hand reaching out. Brooklyn keeps petting Myles, and Calista slowly moves her hands over the spot Brooklyn shows her. It's so cute how she stares at Brooklyn like she's eleven years old and Brooklyn's Taylor Swift.

"Why would Dori bring us here and leave?" I ask.

Savannah sits on the couch next to me, Juno in the chair by Rome.

"She's meddling. Told us all it would be a chance to get you to stay in Lake Starlight. She even brought these brochures." Savannah points at the table, where there are some massage therapy pamphlets.

"But why would she leave?"

"Be thankful you didn't have to hear any stories about her and our grandpa." Austin comes in.

Holly places a plate of crackers and cheese on the coffee table then sits close to her fiancé. Watching them together would make anyone believe in true love, that's for sure.

"I'm so confused," I say.

"She's trying to smother you with Baileys," Rome says. "Thinking if you meet all of us and see what we can offer you, you'll stay. She's an old bird who can't keep to herself."

Austin smacks him on the head. "Respect."

Rome grabs the back of his head and nods.

"She means well," Austin says. "She's always felt like she was our mother, father, *and* grandmother after our parents died. I have no complaints about her meddling."

He and Holly look at one another, and my stomach clenches. What must it feel like to know someone loves you that much?

I pick up a pamphlet and read it. When I look over the

top of the paper, I find Rome's gaze on me. Our eyes shift to Calista, who's playing with Brooklyn, then we lock gazes again.

"The next session starts in three weeks," he says in a low voice.

"How do you know?" I whisper.

He shrugs. "I looked it up. I could watch her while you have class."

I scan the room. Everyone is distracted, but talking about this with other people around feels weird. "I need a minute. Holly, where's the bathroom?"

She stops flirting with her fiancé for a second and looks at me. "Oh, down the hall to your right."

"Thanks."

I glance one more time at Calista, but Rome is here, and he might be more protective over her than I am. My little girl is more than fine here.

Why does that make me sad?

Oh yeah, because we're leaving.

I open the bathroom door to find Rome there with his hand extended, asking permission to lead me somewhere.

"What about Calista?"

"My sisters have her. Remember, there's nine of us."

I nod.

"She's good. I promise."

I lock my hand in his. A flood of emotions rush over me. How can this man I really don't know at all make me feel so safe?

We walk out the back door and down the stairs of a

balcony that overlooks a fire pit and a wooded area. Following a trail, Rome doesn't say much, and I have to wonder what he's trying to do right now. When we come upon a small lake surrounded by woods, he guides me to a bench on the side. I sit, and he slides in next to me.

"I really wanted you to come to this realization on your own, but I fear you won't. So I'm just gonna do it."

"Do what?" I ask, worried he's about to pull out a ring and drop to one knee or something equally crazy.

"Lay my cards out."

"Okay," I say tentatively.

"I want you and Calista to stay in Lake Starlight. I want you to finish your degree here. I can watch her, and if I can't, I have plenty of family who will help us. You'll get your degree faster, and I'll be able to have my daughter in my life."

I sigh and walk toward the water's edge. With warmer temperatures the last few days, the last snow piles are dwindling to nothing.

"It makes perfect sense. I get that you have the lawyer back in Seattle."

"Shane."

Rome nods. I fear he doesn't say Shane's name because that would make him too real. "Come on. I wasn't there for the first eighteen months or during the pregnancy. Let me be there now."

I have to admit, it's tempting. All the relationships with family members that Calista could form is an added bonus.

What do I really have in Seattle? Shane and Miranda. Miranda has her own life. And Shane? I haven't had a real conversation with him since I've been here. It's all been through text. But he is nice and there could be a future there.

"I have nowhere to live."

"You'll live with Savannah," Dori's voice comes out of the woods.

I gasp, startled by her appearance. "What the hell?"

"G'Ma D?" Rome asks, looking behind us and finding her on the bench now. "Are you a witch?"

She laughs. "No. I came back after dropping Ethel's dentures off at the home. I was holding them for her earlier today and forgot to give them back."

Rome massages the bridge of his nose. "I don't even want to know."

"Probably not, dear," Dori says.

"What are you doing out by the lake?" he asks.

"This was your grandfather's and my spot. I come here when I miss him."

I look at Dori with sympathy. "I'm sorry."

She waves me off. "He's been gone a long time. Anyway, you two get back to what you were talking about."

Rome looks at me with pleading eyes. "You're going to ruin it. I almost had her."

"You think so, huh?" I ask.

He nods. "Definitely. It's too good of an offer." His tongue skates over his bottom lip.

He's right. If anything, I'm looking for excuses to stay, but they might be for the wrong reasons. This thing between the two of us is developing, and I want to know what that means. But I can't get involved with this man and ruin my daughter's hope of a future with a family who loves her. Especially when they're my entire reason for staying here to begin with.

"And the job at the restaurant? It's mine?"

"Definitely." He nods, a hesitant smile in place.

"I'll go tell Savannah," Dori says before her footsteps can be heard stepping on twigs.

"Rome, if I do this, I'm uprooting my entire life."

He nods. "Trust me."

"Trust you?" I stare at the lake, wishing it could grant me some guidance.

I've gone on my gut my entire life. I've never had parental guidance. Sure, there were counselors, but they wanted to make sure I was good enough to transition into society. As long as I wasn't abused or malnourished, they thought they were doing fine. Every once in a while I'd come across a fresh-faced counselor who still had hope, but eventually they all waved the white flag. Asking for my trust is like asking for every foster kid to live in a caring home with people who are in it for the children and not the money. Impossible.

My hands fall to my stomach. *Tell me what to do.* What's best for Calista and me?

Rome steps up to the water's edge, his shoulder rubbing across mine, and a flush of warmth spreads through my body. My gut screams at me to stay, so the words fall out of my mouth before I can stop them.

"I'll stay."

He leans closer. "Tell me I heard that right?"

I giggle like the schoolgirl he makes me feel like. "We'll stay."

He picks me up and swings me around. "I promise you won't regret it. I'll give you all the good shifts. Savannah will love having a roommate. And all my sisters and Holly, hell, Denver will love to babysit Calista." He lowers me to the ground, my body slowly pressing against his on the way down. His large hands land on each side of my face. "You won't regret this."

Then his lips land on mine.

For a moment, I don't move. I stay there, knowing I should pull back, stop this, but my body literally loses all signal from my brain. He pulls me into his chest, his hand venturing up my back and past my neck, holding my head to his. His lips are soft and inviting. His smell exhilarates every sensitive spot on my body. I want to scream, "Take me."

Instead, that transmitter between my brain and my body reconnects and I step back. "We can't." My hand covers my lips as I hope the taste of him will vanish in the cool Alaskan air.

"Yeah, sorry, overreaction. I was just excited." He shifts and holds up his hands. "I know you have the lawyer. I shouldn't have done that."

I nod, wondering how long we were pressed against one another. It felt like an eternity, but it was probably only a second.

"Shane." I wish he'd been what was on my mind while Rome tried to kiss me.

"Yeah, right."

We walk back up the trail without touching, an awkward silence settling between us. I close my eyes and inhale a breath.

Please tell me I'm not letting my va-jay-jay lead me instead of my gut.

FIFTEEN

Rome

"I don't understand how I got roped into this." Savannah stands in her doorway with her hands on her waist.

"Mind moving?" Liam says, not waiting for her to actually move.

She gives him a scathing look. If she was a witch, he'd have disappeared by now, but she steps aside when he nudges her.

"It's not forever and you have the room. The apartment above Terra and Mare is a hazard for Calista right now. Austin and Holly are newly engaged and fuck nonstop. I really don't want my daughter repeating panting and moaning sounds."

"What about Liam? He has more bedrooms than he needs," she says.

"Liam's a bachelor. The same reason applies to him as it does to Austin and Holly."

"What are you saying about me?" She follows us upstairs, one painful step at a time as we maneuver the crib box.

"That you don't get laid," Liam says.

"You have no idea how often I get laid."

"How long's it been?" Liam asks. The man likes to push her buttons more than Calista does her fake toy telephone she can't seem to part with. "And vibrators don't count. Neither does that suit you were dating last summer."

We finally reach the landing. As I try to figure out how to maneuver the box into the spare room, Liam and Savannah look as if they're having a staring contest.

"Why would he not count?" She comes back at Liam like I knew she would.

Liam scoffs. "Please, I'm sure that guy knows how to get a woman off about as well as a thirteen-year-old boy."

"That's unfair. I'll have you know—"

"Let's go." I pick up my end of the box, stopping their stupid fight.

Liam picks up the other side, and we're able to figure out a way to get it into the room. Calista will sleep in here, and Harley will stay in Savannah's guest bedroom. It all works out perfectly.

Liam uses his pocket knife and opens up the box. I spot the instructions inside and pull out the sheet of paper to have a look.

"What the hell is this? It looks like a jigsaw puzzle." I glance at all the parts and metal pieces Liam is already arranging on the floor. *We're screwed.*

"Oh, just let Liam do it." Savannah waves off my concern.

My jaw hangs open. She just complimented Liam? We

might have to go back to 2011 for the last time that happened.

Liam says nothing, but his shit-eating grin as she scans through the directions is enough to piss off Savannah. She stomps out of the room.

"I think this is entirely unfair," she says.

I follow her. "Oh please, it'll be good for you to have some company. Harley's awesome, and who couldn't love my daughter?"

She blows out a frustrated breath when she reaches the guest room. She takes down the pictures on the dresser—one of her at graduation with our parents, another of my mom holding her as a baby.

"You can keep your shit in here," I say.

"No, if she's staying here, I'm not going to let her feel like it's not her space. She needs to fill it with her own things so it's home to her, not a stranger's house." She continues plucking anything personal off the furniture.

I lean my shoulder on the doorframe. "Thanks, Savannah. I really appreciate this."

She nods and looks at me from across the room. "Can I ask you a question?"

"Sure." I shrug.

"What are you hoping happens with her staying in Lake Starlight?" She grabs a storage container from the closet and sits on the edge of the bed.

I swear, she's the only person I know who has empty storage bins on hand "just in case."

"I don't know, but I don't want to miss any more of Calista's life, and I invested all my money, plus some investors' funds, into Terra and Mare. I can't run away from that."

Last night, I stared at my ceiling asking myself the same question. That kiss with Harley at the lake behind my parents' house was over before it began, but it gave me a taste of her. Of how her body molds to mine, how it feels to have her in my arms. The fact that I already enjoyed her once and all I remember are bits and pieces eats me up inside. If I had her now, I'd take her slow, explore her body like an adventurer of Harleyland, mapping it for the first time ever.

But she was quick to step back, quick to say no, and I can't say she's wrong. I can't promise her much more than a night or two. The last serious relationship I had was, well, never.

"This whole thing could blow up in your face," Savannah says, picking a piece of lint off the pale blue comforter. "You could lose them both."

"How so?"

"I see it. The way you look at her. I see when you check her ass out or how your eyes zoom in on her cleavage when she bends down to get Calista, but it's the way you look at her when she's mothering your daughter that has me wondering. When she holds your daughter, you look at her like you could love her and maybe a small piece of you does."

"What are you smoking?" I push away from the doorjamb.

She shrugs. "You asked, and I'm just being honest."

She's so wrong. "Maybe I'm staring at Calista like that because I love *her*."

She picks up the box off the bed. "Okay, maybe I'm wrong, but maybe I'm not." She shoots me a tight smile and passes me, walking to her room.

I shake off Savannah's comments and head back into

what will be Calista's room. Liam's got half the crib up already.

"What the hell? When did you become Mr. Fix-It?"

He gives me the finger. "Just because I chose not to go to college doesn't mean I'm an idiot."

His massive forearms flex as he uses the wrench. At least I know Calista will be safe in this thing with Liam in charge of assembly.

"I'll go grab the mattress," I say, backstepping.

"She's right, you know," he says just loud enough for me to hear.

"Who?"

"Savannah."

I stop and circle back around. "I should email Buzz Wheel and let them know you two have both complimented each other in the last half hour."

"Yeah, keep that to yourself." He stops, drops the wrench, and looks at me. "But don't do what Rome Bailey does this time, okay?"

"What does that mean?" My forehead creases.

"All I'm saying is, don't jump in with two feet only to swim to the other side and sneak out of the water."

"When have I ever done that?"

He raises his eyebrows like "do you really want to rehash your past?"

Bring it. I'm not the type of guy to do that.

"I could name about five instances, but this is your daughter, man, and her mom. These two women will be in your life forever. Don't fuck it up. That's all I'm saying."

"Fine. Thanks for the vote of confidence." I leave the room, ignoring Liam's advice too.

When have he and my sister been on the same page —ever?

I grab the crib mattress from my truck, and I'm heading back up the stairs when I overhear Liam and Savannah talking in normal tones. And they say I'm the fucked-up one. So hot and cold, those two.

I lean the mattress against the wall in the hallway and hear a knock on the front door downstairs. I head back down to see Harley there with Calista in her stroller.

"Hey, you," she says.

"Hey. I'm still putting the crib together."

She reaches under the stroller. "I got a thank you gift for Savannah."

It's a pie from Lard Have Mercy.

"What kind?"

She cringes. "Hopefully Karen was right... lemon meringue?"

I nod. "Only Savanah could love something so sour."

I peek into the stroller to find a sleeping Calista.

"The fresh air always gets her."

"Come in." I hold open the front door so Harley can maneuver the stroller into the foyer. "Come upstairs and see your new digs."

She leaves Calista in the stroller and follows me upstairs. I take her to Calista's room first and surprise, surprise, my sister and best friend are back at each other's throats.

"I think you have it wrong," Savannah says, pointing at the instructions.

"I don't," Liam responds.

"You do!" Her voice grows louder.

"I don't," Liam responds in a monotone voice.

"Hey, look who's here."

Savannah turns around and smiles. "Hi."

"Thank you so much for letting us stay. I promise we

won't be too much of an inconvenience, and once I'm on my feet, I'll look for my own place."

"No worries, Harley. Savannah could use some happiness in her life," Liam says.

Savannah huffs, then her jaw does that clenching thing it only does when Liam's around. "Come and I'll show you your room."

The two leave, and I follow them. After Harley's seen the room, Calista starts crying.

I turn to go get her, but Harley stops me. "I got her."

Savannah follows her downstairs. I overhear them go into the kitchen, and I hear the silverware drawer opening. Yeah, lemon meringue pie is Savannah's weakness.

"So what exactly did you mean earlier?" I ask Liam, holding up a piece of the crib while he screws it into place.

"Come on, man, you know. Any girl you've ever gone after, as soon as they wanted you and the chase was over, you left, weren't interested anymore. Hell, everyone was shocked you picked Lake Starlight to start Terra and Mare because you're not a stay-in-one-place-for-long kind of guy."

"And you are?"

"Smokin' Guns has been open for six years. I've lived here my entire life. I'm not just talking about relationships, Rome. I'm talking about a commitment to anything."

"I'm a fucking chef."

He shrugs like "so what?"

So what? It took a lot of fucking commitment to become a chef.

"How many chefs in Europe did you work under?" he asks.

I try to do the math in my head then give up. "I was traveling to learn different types of cuisine, asshole."

"Okay," he says, seeming placated but I know better than that.

I'm beginning to understand why my sister's always so pissed with him.

I know I'm doing the right thing with Harley, and I commit to plenty. I don't need his approval or his warning.

"All I'm saying is that it'll only take you hurting her once before she's gone for good."

"I would never hurt Calista." See? He's so wrong about everything.

"I'm not talking about Calista."

And with that, the bastard turns his back to me and goes back to assembling the crib.

SIXTEEN

Harley

My hands tremble as I press Shane's number on my phone.

"Hey, babe," he answers. "I can't wait to see you tomorrow. Sorry about your flight being canceled. I hope you found out before you got to the airport."

Don't judge me for lying. This is hard for me. I'm not used to hurting other people.

"Hey, about that..."

"What's wrong? Shit, hold on." He puts his hand over the receiver. "No, I said I needed Colt versus Ferguson. Please start writing this down."

I hear someone say something muffled, then his hand moves away from the phone.

"Okay, I'm back."

"You're working late," I say because it delays me having to say the hard part.

"Yeah, I got another big case. I can still grab you and Calista tomorrow, but then I'll have to go back to the office. I'm sorry, I really wanted to take you to that Thai place you love."

Fact—I don't love it, he does. Calista despises it. But at least he was thinking of us, I guess.

"Actually, you don't have to worry about that because there have been some developments here." God, why can't there be a service you can hire to break up with people? This is horrible.

"Are you okay? Calista?"

"Yeah, we're good, um..."

"Did that bastard not give you the DNA test? Because I have attorney friends in Alaska who would be happy to help you."

"Shane, I've decided to stay here. I'm sorry, but I owe this to Calista. There's a college where I can finish my course, and her dad has eight siblings who will help with the baby."

Silence.

"Shane?"

"Are you getting together with him?"

"No," I rush out, although I'll keep that impromptu kiss to myself. "It has nothing to do with him. You know how I grew up, and for Calista's sake, I can't walk away from these people. They're her family, true family, and I want her to have relationships in her life that I never did."

"Okay, but certainly those relationships can still grow with you in Seattle with me."

I hear someone say something in the background, and this time he doesn't bother to cover the receiver before he yells, "Jesus Christ, Bonnie, this isn't rocket science. Go down to the file room!"

I hate when people go from one to ten in a millisecond. It triggers my flight instinct.

"I'm sorry. I really am, but I have to give this to my daughter. I have no idea how long I'll be here, so I'm breaking it off with us because it wouldn't be fair to you—"

"Fair to me? Fair to me would be you coming home. We have something good going. I get that the trauma from your childhood is telling you to run away from something as great as you and me, but you need to ignore those insecurities and come back home. I'll find you a nanny and you'll get your massage therapist license. I have the means to give you whatever you want if you'd just accept it."

Shane's argument holds weight. There's no question. He's always been open with his feelings and telling me what he wants. Hell, he would've moved us in on our second date—without ever even meeting Calista—but I wasn't going to live off a man. Where would that leave me when he decided he didn't want me anymore?

I hate having to rely so much on Rome when it comes to me staying in Lake Starlight, but I'll do it for my daughter. She needs these relationships. She deserves to be around family who wants her, so I'll suck up the free lodging at Savannah's and the job at Rome's restaurant to make it happen. One day I'll pay them back for their sacrifices, even though they seem to give freely and want nothing in return.

Shane is a whole different story. I've always felt like all his promises come with strings, but the stability he offered seemed like a fair trade.

"I'm sorry, but I'm not coming back. I wish you a lot of luck. You're a wonderful man and you're going to make someone very happy."

Silence continues over the line.

"I really think you're making a rash decision here."

"I don't," I say. "I'm going with my gut."

"If you went with your head, you wouldn't have an eighteen-month-old daughter and you wouldn't have to venture up to some jerkwater town in Alaska to find her father."

I lean back on the couch. This is a very different Shane than I have ever encountered. I mean, it's not like I've never heard him say mean things to his assistant, Bonnie, but never to me.

"I guess you're right, Shane. But then again, I went with my gut when I started dating you, so I guess I should've used my head instead because then I wouldn't be breaking up with you right now. Have a great life."

Click.

Damn, that's a relief.

<hr>

Terra and Mare will be the most upscale place I've ever bartended, and I find I'm a little nervous as I walk through the doors, finding the place practically ready for opening. Rome has decided that the day after the Founder's Day parade will be opening day because he wants to spend Founder's Day with Calista at the carnival after.

"Rome!" I call.

"Hey." He comes out of the back, wiping his face with the bottom of his white tee, revealing a set of abs so lickable, a shot of lust locks me in place. "The fucking fridge is out again."

I have to get rid of this attraction to him. Nothing good can come of it.

"I think you got a lemon." I drop my purse on a table

and follow him into the kitchen, thankful I no longer have to pretend not to be looking at his washboard abs.

"Where's Calista?" he asks.

"At the park with Karen and Brian." I've yet to really admit it to anyone, but it's nice having help with her.

"This fridge is pissing me off, but in better news…" He picks up his phone and slides up to sit on the counter. "I am the father." He says it as though he's Maury Povich and holds out his phone, showing me an email.

"Did you doubt it?" I raise an eyebrow.

He laughs, wiping off more sweat, but thank God he uses his sleeve instead of the bottom of his shirt. "Not once."

Our eyes lock.

"Does it feel different with it in writing?" I lean against the counter and cross my arms.

His gaze dips to my chest for a second. "No. But I did call to make sure everything was sent to your doctor in Seattle. We'll have to get her medical records transferred to a doctor up here so that everyone is aware of her condition if something happens."

I nod. With everything going on, I almost forgot how important that is. Especially with other people watching her now. "We need to brief everyone that if she gets hurt, they need to take her to the emergency room right away."

"Here." He picks up his phone and messes with it for a second.

An alert vibrates on my own phone in my back pocket. I pull it out to find I've been added to a group text titled "Bailey Crew."

Rome: *FYI if you watch Calista and she gets cut or anything that involves blood, you need to take her to the ER stat. Call Harley or I second.*

Three dotted rows appear, and a string of texts commence. I have no idea who is who, but one common theme in all their responses is, *what's wrong? Did something happen? Why?*

"Way to make them panic," I say.

He shrugs. "Believe me, that family text message string will save you a lot of headaches. So much easier than sending eight separate texts." He slides off the counter.

The door chime rings a second later.

"Rome!" a man calls from the front of the restaurant.

"In here," he says.

The man who gave me the directions to Rome's restaurant my first night in town comes into the back.

"Hey, Jack. This is Harley. I don't think you guys have met."

"Actually, we have. Sort of. Nice to officially meet you though, Jack."

"Likewise," he says, placing his toolbox on the floor. "Harley came into the hardware store looking for directions."

"Gotcha." Rome places his hands on his hips with a frown and looks at the industrial fridge. "Think I should just send this back?"

While the two of them talk refrigeration, I hammer out a quick text in the group chat to let everyone know that Calista is okay and healthy, but I explain her condition and what risks it poses.

Another row of messages come in. *Thanks Harley, Oh my poor niece, What can we do to help*, etc. Eventually they all put their names with their numbers, and I program them into my phone. By the time I get to the last one, Bailey looks misspelled because I've been staring at the word so long.

"I'll be at the bar," I say to Rome and Jack, though I'm not sure they even remember I'm in the room.

I glance around the dark wood bar at the bottles lining the glass shelves. Rome spared no expense. His wine selection is exquisite, and he has most of the high-end brands of hard liquor. I wonder how much business a restaurant like this can do in a town like this. Not that it's a poor town, but everyone I've met seems more like a diner-type person versus fine dining.

I make note of the positioning of the coolers, the ice bucket, and glassware so that next week on opening night, I don't make it a disaster by being unable to keep up.

Rome comes in. "Hey. Everything look cool?"

"You did a great job. Did you ever bartend?" I inspect a few more bottles.

"No, but I've worked in enough restaurants to know what the musts are. If you need anything added, let me know."

"I think this should be good."

He slides into a chair on the other side of the bar.

"What's your drink, Rome?" I ask, leaning over the counter. His eyes fall to my cleavage again, so I stand up straight.

"You don't remember?"

"Well, that night you took about four shots of Jack as a starter and drank beer the rest of the night."

He nods. "Sounds like my MO. I'll just take a water."

I reach under and grab a water bottle, unscrewing it for him.

"I set up some interviews for you tomorrow. I can watch Calista."

"Interviews?" I tilt my head.

"You can't tend bar every night. You have school, and then there's Calista."

I tilt my head even more, trying to understand what he's talking about.

"You're the head bartender, so the decision of who to hire is yours. I did scour through the applicants first and there's one guy I already hired. Asked him to come in too, to get your approval. If you don't like him, I can send him packing."

"Head bartender? No, Rome." I shake my head.

"Yes. You're the most qualified person I know. It's perfect."

"Perfect? You didn't even know I was coming here. What was your plan before me?"

He chuckles., tipping the water bottle back, his eyes never leaving mine. "I didn't have one yet. Hence why your timing was perfect."

I lean against the edge of the bar. "Are you doing this because I'm Calista's mama?"

He laughs again. "No. I'm doing it because you're experienced. If you think it's too much, let me know."

I decide to take him at his word, which is *not* easy for me. "No. It's fine."

"Good." He nods, guzzles his water again, and finishes off the bottle in record time before crunching the plastic and setting it on the bar. "I'm glad that's settled." He stands from his chair. "If I don't figure out this fridge though, there's not going to be an opening day."

"All right. I'll leave you to it. I'm going to go grab Calista."

"Give her a kiss for me." He heads to the back.

"Hey, Rome," I say, and he stops and turns back to me. "Congratulations on officially becoming a father."

A slow, satisfied smile parts his lips. "Thanks." He winks. "I'm pretty stoked."

I smile back and watch him disappear through the swinging door to the back.

My hand goes to my stomach in an effort to stop the caterpillars from morphing into butterflies. Butterflies are not allowed where Rome is concerned. There's too much to lose.

SEVENTEEN

Harley

Founder's Day is not at all what I expected.

Rome really wanted me on the Bailey float, whatever that means, but I refused. I'm not a Bailey. Calista is.

That said, my nerves are on high alert as I stand on the edge of Main Street, waiting for them to go by. In the past few weeks, I've found myself trusting not only Rome but his family. But something about my daughter being on a float makes me extra nervous.

"Hey," Holly interrupts my jumbled thoughts, coming to stand alongside me.

"What are you doing here?" I ask.

"I'm not a Bailey yet." She puts her hand on a woman's shoulder who is standing behind her. "This is Francie and her husband Jack."

"Hi, Jack. Nice to meet you, Francie." I squeeze over to make room for them.

The dark-haired woman smiles and shakes my hand. "Are you enjoying Lake Starlight?"

"I am, thank you."

"Rome tell you we got the fridge working?" Jack asks.

I nod. "He did. Good work."

Francie beams at her husband.

"I didn't realize you knew Jack," Holly says.

"Small towns. You know how it is."

Holly nods, but Jack looks at me and winks, keeping the fact that I was originally looking for Denver to himself. I smile at him in appreciation for his discretion.

Holly knocks me with her elbow. "I heard Calista's on the float."

"Yeah, hopefully nothing happens."

She swings her arm around my shoulders. "It won't."

I slide out from under her touch, but she doesn't notice because two lines of muscle cars drive down Main Street with "Shake it Up" by The Cars playing over the speakers. Everyone on either side of the street sings along and dancing.

"Did I just enter a movie set?" I ask.

Holly's dancing next to me like she's at a sock hop, putting her weight on one foot then the other. I don't have the heart to tell her she's in the wrong era. "I know, right?"

Francie's head bobs back and forth. No wonder they're close—they're both confused about the music. Maybe I should do the Twist.

"Liam always picks the best songs." Jack holds his wife and twirls her out and back into him.

What kind of town did I move us to?

"Did you hear they changed it up this year?" Francie says to Holly.

Wyatt approaches from behind us with an older woman by his side. "I figured I'd find you guys."

"You're not on the float either, huh?" Holly continues to dance while talking to him.

"You're engaged. I'm still just the boyfriend." Wyatt laughs and the older woman slides her arm through his. "This is my mother, Eva."

We all wave and say hello to her.

"The 'Sea of Love' is coming right before the Baileys' float," Francie says. "It's my favorite part." She looks at Jack and he twists her out again.

Liam winks at me from the lead car, and the two rows of cars turn the corner.

A float appears right after them, the soft music of a love ballad taking over. There's a man in a suit singing into a microphone and a woman in a bridal gown seated on a chair, looking at him with lovesick eyes.

"I'll let Francie explain this to you. She's the romantic." Holly slides over.

Francie loops her arm through mine. "Okay, so Mr. and Mrs. Bailey, Rome's parents, had 'Sea of Love' by the Honeydrippers as their wedding song. Since they passed, the town has done this tribute to them each year. The high school drama department is in charge of the float."

I nod and look around. Everyone is swaying back and forth, singing along. Francie starts up louder than everyone.

Seriously, I moved to Corneyville, USA.

As the float grows closer, Francie covers her mouth and gasps.

"Yeah, they may have recruited my help this year," Holly says as we see a huge blown-up picture of Mr. and Mrs. Bailey dancing at their wedding.

Rome's parents.

I saw one picture of them hanging on the wall at Austin and Holly's, but it was years after this one was taken. They already had their own children and no longer looked like a set of kids with doe eyes and their entire lives stretching out in front of them.

All the boys look more like their dad and the girls their mom, with the exception of Phoenix and Sedona, who have dark hair. But the man staring at his wife could be Rome—their resemblance is that uncanny.

Francie swipes some tears. "I miss them so much."

Holly takes her by her shoulders and moves her over to Jack, coming back to my side. "Everyone says they were remarkable people, but I guess they had to be to have the children they did, right?" Her eyes water as we watch the float go by.

It's not even past the corner before cheers erupt.

"Is this the theme from *Golden Girls*?" I ask once I hear the song blaring from the next float.

Holly laughs as they come into view. She nods. "Yep. Rome's pick. He's not really the sentimental type." She must see my confusion. "Every year, one of the Bailey kids has to pick a song that they all sing to the crowd. It has to be thanking them or something like that. This year was Rome's pick."

"And he chose this one?"

"Like I said, he's not sentimental."

Holly sings along with Francie and Jack. Even Wyatt and his mom sing right behind us.

The float comes into view and I can't fight my smile. Calista holds prime real estate right next to Dori, one level higher than her dad. My heart drops to my stomach until I see that she's in a car seat that's not moving at all. Not sure what he did to secure that, but it looks steady.

"Don't worry, I bolted it myself." Jack touches my shoulder.

"She's not going anywhere," Francie says.

"Thanks."

Rome finds me in the crowd and winks. All the Bailey siblings sing the song with what appears to be enthusiasm. Calista is smiling and waving, laughing and playing with her feet. Her eyes are wide, taking in everything going on around her. I catch Rome looking over his shoulder to make sure she's okay.

At some point, she sees me, and I wave and blow her a kiss. Her hands reach out, trying to get out of the restraint. Dori tries to tickle her, but Calista's having none of it, swatting her hands away.

"No, Doodoo!" I think Calista says, if my lip-reading skills are on point. "Mama!"

I wave again and clap as if she's doing a great job.

"Uh oh, I think she's about done now," Holly says next to me.

Dori tries to tickle her again, bending down and kissing her head, but Calista smacks her. The crowd laughs and Dori's face turns red.

"Tell me that didn't actually just happen." I bite my lip.

"Oh, it happened," Wyatt says with a chuckle.

Rome's on it. He hands his mic to Denver and unbuckles Calista before picking her up. He holds her to his chest and the crowd cheers louder, clapping.

"I know you have no idea, but this is a big deal in this town. The first Bailey grandchild." Holly squeezes my hand. "I know you might feel overwhelmed by the attention. I did at first. If you ever want to talk about it, I'm here."

"Thanks," I say, still not sure what to think of all this.

Rome doesn't sing for the rest of the song, but instead

holds Calista to his chest. Her head falls to his strong shoulder, her tears drying as her eyes close. Her thumb finds its way into her mouth and he sways as if he's been doing it since she was born.

"Oh, he's rocking her to sleep," Wyatt's mom says from behind me. "How precious."

The rest of the crowd must agree because cheers turn into "aww"s, and now tears prick my eyes.

My baby girl is with her daddy.

I never thought this day would be possible. I never truly wanted it to come, but now that it's here, I can't deny how happy I am.

Everyone in this town sees what a caring and good dad Rome is, and I commit the scene to memory. No matter what paths our lives take, I need to remember this moment because it solidifies that they belong together.

My phone vibrates, and I see it's a message from Holly. I look at her before I pull up her text.

"Speaking as a girl who doesn't have a dad in her life, you need to snap these when you get a chance." She smiles.

I open her message and find a picture of Calista's arms wrapped tightly around Rome's neck, as if she's scared he might leave her.

Don't worry, baby girl, I vow to never take you away from him. No matter what.

"Thanks," I croak, blinking back tears.

Rome looks at me with a cocky expression as if he wants to say, "See? I got this."

And he so does.

And it's *so* damn sexy.

EIGHTEEN

Rome

The float stops at the end of the parade route, and all my siblings hop off. Denver gives me a hand since Calista is stuck to me like a baby koala bear.

"Well, that was interesting," G'Ma D says.

"Sorry, she was tired, and she saw Harley," I say.

She kisses Calista's forehead. "It's okay. I forgive her, but if this town starts calling me Doodoo..." She shakes her head and swings her arm around Juno's. "Take me to the library."

"Colton, we're taking Grandma to the library," Juno yells.

Since he knows the drill and has been waiting here the entire time, he jogs to catch them.

I'll never understand that friendship.

"Austin!" Holly screams through the crowd.

He walks toward her, swinging her into his arms the minute she's within arm's reach. "I told you you should've been up there."

She touches his cheek. "When I'm actually a Bailey."

"You are," he argues.

She giggles and raises to her tiptoes to kiss his cheek, but he switches gears and captures her lips. A pang of jealousy hits my gut as I watch my brother look so fucking happy he might burst.

After he thoroughly kisses her in front of witnesses, he rests his forehead against hers. "Memory lane ride on the Ferris wheel?"

Holly bites her lower lip and nods.

Jesus, these two. Remind me never to go on the Ferris wheel again. God knows what they're doing.

"Thank goodness Calista is sleeping!" I say.

Austin flips me off as they walk away.

"Look, Sav, you're rubbing off on everyone," Brooklyn says with a chuckle.

Harley walks up with Wyatt and his mom. Wyatt kisses Brooklyn much more conservatively than Austin did Holly, but his mom is standing right there.

Harley places her hand on Calista's back and looks at her drool on my shoulder. "I was a tad worried there for a second." She laughs.

I join her because it was a shitshow when Calista smacked G'Ma D in the face. "Yeah, she was done. I saw her rubbing her eyes a block before, should've clued in."

I'm still getting this father thing down. I really hope Harley isn't about to yell at me for having her on the float in the first place or for taking her out of the car seat. It was dangerous, but I'd never let her fall.

"You both stole the show." She rises on her toes and kisses Calista's forehead. "But I'm not sure you're gonna be able to show her the carnival. She's sound asleep."

"I left the stroller at Terra and Mare. Let's go get it."

"Okay," she says.

We walk away from the rest of my siblings as they scatter to do whatever they want for the rest of the day now that their family obligation is over. One block over, at Terra and Mare, the grand opening sign with tomorrow's date hangs below the awning.

"Nervous?" she asks me as I dig out my key and hand it to her.

"Yeah." That's an understatement. I don't think my restaurant will bomb, but can it sustain itself? I won't have that answer for another six months.

We walk in, and I lower Calista into her stroller before strapping her in and reclining the back. We put the blanket stored in the bottom over her.

"Come on. I have Founder's Day to show you."

Harley opens the door, and I push the stroller through.

"Is it hard?" she asks on our way down the now desolate sidewalk. Everyone's already down at the carnival or by the lake.

"What?"

"Being a Bailey in this town. You guys are, like, the most popular kids in this place."

I laugh. Being a Bailey has its perks. I've tested how far those perks could get me before being pushed back. But I regret that now that I'm older. It was wrong of me to take advantage.

"After my parents died, it sucked. That would've been the case with any family in this town, but for us, the mourning just never stopped. Every anniversary of their death, the cemetery gets inundated with flowers. It was just one of those small-town nightmares that was felt so deeply it was hard to get over." I'm trying to give her the polite answer. No one wants to hear how horrible it was during those first few years.

"I don't remember my parents. I was two when they gave up their rights. Well, my mom did. I never knew my dad. There's no name on my birth certificate. So it's hard to relate to you. I've never lost anyone I cared about, but that might be because I don't have a lot of people I care about."

Her words slice me open fast and deep. Here she is divulging something so raw, and I gave her some politically correct response about how my parents' deaths affected this town.

"I run," I say, trying to match her honesty.

"I hide," she says.

"As soon as I get close, I pull away."

"I bottle up."

"I disappear."

"I stay, but I'm not really invested," she says. "Anything's better than being alone."

Well, shit, aren't we a pair.

We walk to the carnival, but I lead us to the path around the lake because the loud noises of the rides and the laughter will wake up Calista.

"Being a Bailey in Lake Starlight can suck sometimes," I tell her. "People used to have all these expectations. Like when Austin was in high school, they assumed he was going to go pro for baseball. Savannah would be president one day. Then my parents died, and everything just crashed. We all did too."

She puts her hand on mine on top of the stroller.

"I never thought I'd feel normal again. I did whatever I could to cause trouble to make sure this town would think I was a fuckup who didn't deserve their sympathy. I was sick of their pitying eyes. I just rebelled."

"It's understandable."

"Yeah well, my reputation in this town isn't stellar."

"I think you're wrong about that." She bumps me with her shoulder.

"Wait until you're here longer."

We walk along the paved path on the lake's edge. It's nice to be alone with her. We've barely talked like this since she got here.

After a couple minutes, she breaks the silence. "Thank you."

"For what?"

"Everything. Welcoming Calista into your life when you have so much going on. Convincing your sister to let us move in with her. The bartending job. You're a great man, Rome. That warning you've labeled yourself with isn't working." She smiles at me.

My gaze falls to her lips. I catch my neck bending, wanting to capture them, but my self-preservation kicks in right before I do. "I'll disappoint you, I'm sure of it."

She shakes her head and places her hand on the stroller, forcing me to stop. The sunset reflecting on her skin makes her look like a dream. "Don't do that. Not with me. Okay? Be the man you are with Calista without any apologies. It's okay to be a good guy, and if people feel sorry because you lost your parents so young, let them. It means they care about you."

I stare at her. She really is amazing. How did I not see

this that night? How was I only consumed by the curves of her tits and ass and not her kind spirit and mushy center under that hard exterior? Even after the rough life she's had. A helluva lot rougher than mine. She never had parents to lose, and that's so much worse.

"Okay," I say, unsure what she expects me to say. "But you agree to do the same? Open yourself up for people to see you? This town might have its downfalls, but you can trust my family. That's one thing I can guarantee. They'll never disappoint you."

"And you?" She steps closer. "Will you disappoint me?"

I blink a couple times and fixate on her teeth pressed down on her bottom lip. "I..."

I should kiss her and deal with consequences later. Maybe we can give Calista the all-American nuclear family.

"Dada," Calista mumbles, stirring under the blanket.

"Saved by your daughter," Harley says, moving away and picking up the blanket to reveal a smiling little girl.

"Mama," she says.

Harley unbuckles Calista and pulls her from the stroller, bringing her to her chest. "Hey sweet girl. Look." She turns around, and Calista's eyes widen when she sees me.

"Dada," she coos but doesn't try to leave her mommy.

I don't blame her. I'd love nothing more than to have my head pressed up against Harley's chest right now too.

"Carnival? Cotton Candy? Wee?" I ask my daughter.

Her eyes grow bigger with each word. She kicks to get down, but Harley carries her while I push the stroller back toward the neon lights filling the sky of Lake Starlight as the sun descends.

Thank God Calista woke up, because I was about to do what Liam told me not to. I was going to jump into the deep end, hoping Harley would jump in with me. But what if Liam's right and I find myself swimming to shallow waters once she's invested? I could ruin everything. She could uproot Calista and move back to Seattle.

If I could trust myself, this whole situation would be a lot easier.

NINETEEN

Harley

Three weeks have passed, and I've started my final class for massage therapy up in Anchorage. Dori was nice enough to let me borrow her Cadillac, though I catch Sheriff Miller double-checking it's me almost every time I cross city lines.

Tonight, I work at Terra and Mare, which now has reservations booked for a month out. The bad part about that is Calista and I have limited time with Rome. Luckily, the restaurant is closed Sundays and Mondays, so we have those days. I mean, she does.

I'm behind the bar, filling the drink orders for the early tables who are already seated, when Rome steps out from the kitchen. He looks hot in anything, but a chef's coat is like game over, ovaries explode, heart eyes, wet panties. His name is embroidered on the top right, and when he wears a bandana to keep his hair back, I want to beg him to lay me down on the bar top and take me right there.

"How's it going?" He leans along the back of the bar, looking at his customers.

"Good." I place two wine glasses on a tray.

The door opens and a rush of air floats in. We both look up, and my jaw drops as the hostess greets Shane. As in, my ex Shane.

He's in a suit with his tie undone and hanging around his neck. The jacket is wrinkled, and he has no luggage with him and, oh my God, what the hell is he doing here?

"Give this guy a drink on the house. He looks like he's run a marathon to get here." Rome continues to lean on the counter, not noticing my freak-out.

"Um..."

Shane and the hostess turn in my direction. My heart-beat pounds as he smiles and approaches the bar.

"Harley, hey," he says.

"Shane, what are you doing here?"

"Shane?" Rome bolts up, crossing his arms and standing at attention as though his drill sergeant scolded him.

"Can I talk to you?" Shane asks me.

"I'm working," I say.

It's been almost a month since I broke it off, and we haven't spoken. I can't imagine why he's here.

"After work then. When do you get off?"

"Um..." I glance at Rome, whose eyes are on Shane. "Not until late."

"You can take your break," Rome chimes in from behind me.

Whose side is he on?

"I don't have anyone to cover me," I say.

"I'll do it. Colin's in the kitchen. He can handle it."

Why is he doing this?

"Please, Harley," Shane pleads.

I attempt to untie my apron, but the double knot grows tighter and I can't loosen it. Rome comes up behind me, his strong chest inches away as his fingers work out the knot and graze my ass with every pull. I swallow the saliva pooling in my mouth.

"Take a seat at that table. I'll be right there." I point at a vacant table.

Shane does as I say.

"You're still with him?" Rome asks, his breath hot and heavy on my neck as he continues to fight with the knot.

I never told him we broke up because it didn't matter. Me breaking up with Shane had nothing to do with me and Rome. "No, we broke up almost a month ago."

His fingers slide the strings to get me out of the apron. They're so close but so far away. I want them to explore me more than I want to breathe right now. His hands touch my hips, and I still. Is he feeling what I am? Is he ignoring the charged energy that's constantly between us?

"Go remind him that you're staying in Lake Starlight," he whispers, and a shiver runs along my spine. Then he steps back, crosses his arms, and takes his usual casual stance along the back counter of the bar.

I hesitate with each step but eventually slide into the chair across the table from Shane. He tries to take my hands, but I tuck them under the table.

"I'm working," I say.

"I know. I'm sorry, but your boss seems cool."

This would be the time. The time to tell him that my boss is Rome, Calista's father. But it's not his business anymore.

"I have five minutes. I can't lose this job."

He nods. "You wouldn't need the job if you'd come home with me. I miss you. I miss Calista."

I glance over my shoulder to see Rome's gaze steady on us. "I told you, I'm staying here. It's important to me that Calista get to know her dad. He has a really big family and they all love her."

"So you're sacrificing the love you could have with me for her?" he asks.

"No. But I would. In a heartbeat. I like it here, and you know the way I grew up. It's important that Calista has family surrounding her."

"I can be her family. Miranda told me you barely talk to her anymore."

"That's not true. Obviously she's the one who told you where I work, so..."

"Well she said you've been too busy to talk much," he amends.

"I had to enroll in school. Get my transcripts sent over. Transfer all Calista's medical records. I started this job."

He leans back, unbuttoning another button on his shirt as though it's stifling hot. Something doesn't add up here.

"It's been almost four weeks since we broke up. You're just now missing us?"

"I had a big case. You know how they consume me and everything outside of the case disappears."

I do know. I realize now that it's probably what made us work. As soon as he'd start smothering me, something would come up at work and I'd get some relief. Which always made me feel guilty, but Shane could suffocate an affectionate puppy. Which isn't a bad quality, but I'm not a new puppy filled with hope for attachment. I'm the five-year-old dog that's bounced from shelter to shelter.

"Well, I still stand by what I said. I'm staying here,

which means it's not going to work out between us. There's no hard feelings—"

I stop when he slides out the chair and lands on bended knee beside the table, digging through his pocket.

"What are you doing?" Then it dawns on me. "Get up, Shane," I whisper-shout.

"What I should've done before you left to come up here. I had it all planned, but then that case landed on my desk."

I look around. The ohhs and ahhs are already starting. I can't even look at Rome, but I wonder what he's feeling right now. He's probably worried I'll accept and take Calista to Seattle.

The better question is why do I want to look at him and see jealousy in his eyes? I shouldn't hope for that reaction, and since I doubt that's what I would find anyway, I concentrate on the man in front of me. The man who obviously cannot take no for an answer.

"Get up, Shane."

"Harley, I think we have something special. I should have sealed this deal before I let you fly away. Will you marry me?" He opens the box.

Inside rests the biggest diamond I've ever seen in person. It's a pear-shaped solitaire with small diamonds along the band. The ring is beautiful but not at all my taste. Just another confirmation that this isn't right.

I finally find the nerve to look at the bar, but it's empty and my heart cracks a little.

What was I expecting?

My mind goes into overdrive, sorting through all of my internal struggles. I swore I wasn't going to fall for Rome. It could be disastrous for Calista. Ruin everything we're building. This co-parenting thing has been smooth, and the transition was easy.

So why does my heart decide to slide in and take over? Why does it think it gets a say in this? I'm going with my brain this time around.

"Har?" Shane says, and I look down, realizing he's still on bended knee.

Shit. I sit up in the chair, take the box from him, and shut it. "I can't."

"You won't." He takes it off the table and tucks it back into his pocket while I ignore the blatant stares from the nearby tables.

"Yes. I won't."

"Why?" His face is red, and he takes his seat back across the table from me.

"Because I don't love you and you don't love me."

"You don't know that."

"I do, and if you think really hard about it, you do too. I think you're probably more upset about losing in general than losing me specifically."

He blows out a breath. "You have no idea how good you'd have had it. I loved your daughter like my own. I was willing to give you a life like you've never had before. You'd never have to worry about money. You'd have anything you wanted."

Anger replaces my guilt for not accepting. "I don't need a sugar daddy."

He stands, his eyes narrowed, and I guess he's going to try to cut me with his words again. I'm familiar with that look. The one of shock and surprise when I don't want what they're offering me. It reminds me of my foster dad at fourteen, when he tried to sneak into my bedroom and told me that if I made him happy, he'd take me to the mall the next day. Yeah, I reported him the next day instead of going to school. What did I have to lose? I was used to bouncing between homes.

"Have a nice life in this shithole town. Don't come crawling back when you realize how big you screwed up here tonight." Shane shakes his head at me as though I'm an idiot then huffs and leaves.

The sweep of fresh air that floats in after his departure feels nice.

I sit there staring out the window for a second, absorbing what happened. I spot Juno as she hops on Colton's back on the sidewalk, the two of them playfully messing around. They're cute together, but I thought they were just friends?

"Harley." Rome's voice pulls me from my thoughts, and I turn to face him.

"Hey. Sorry, I'll get back to work." I press my palms on the table to get up from the chair.

"Not yet." Rome falls to bended knee next to me. "I have no ring, but marry me instead."

My ass falls onto the hard wooden chair with an oomph. This time the ohhs and ahhs are louder.

Of course, because a Bailey just proposed. That's big news in Lake Starlight, even if the Bailey in question is delusional.

TWENTY

Rome

S he leans over the edge of the table and whisper-hisses, "What are you doing?"

"Marry me. Forget him and marry me. Stay here in Lake Starlight. I know I can't offer you what he can—the money, the big house, and I don't even have a ring." I shake my head. "But I'll be good to you and Calista and I'll make you laugh every day. Even if it's just because I'm making a fool of myself."

"Like you're doing right now?" She widens her eyes.

"Just say yes."

"Get up," she says between clenched teeth.

"Not until you say yes." I unbutton my chef's jacket. It's getting hot in here.

"You want to marry me?" She leans back in her chair, crossing her arms.

I nod. "Yes."

"Why?" She's so cool and calm.

A crease forms between my eyebrows. "I just told you."

"No, you told me what you had to offer."

I wipe my forehead and notice that all the people nearby are staring at us. "Okay." I try to swallow even though my mouth is dry. "I love that you're hard-headed and stubborn."

"Really?" She laughs.

"I love the mother you are to Calista."

Her head moves right then left though she's weighing that one, then she focuses on me, waiting for more.

"I love the way I asked you to stay and you did. I know it's not easy for you to accept help, but you did in order to stay."

She smiles. Maybe I'm winning her over. Hopefully wherever that lawyer guy is, he knows I won this. I want to stand up, rip my shirt open, and say she's mine. *They* are mine.

"And you love me?" she asks.

Shit. Why is she asking me that?

"I..."

I could lie. I mean, I love her as a person and as the mother of my child, but love love? I'd love to fuck her, but I don't think that's what she means. Do I even know what love is? I've never stuck around long enough with anyone else to know.

I see the way Austin looks at Holly and the way Wyatt looks at Brooklyn, but I don't think I look at Harley that way. They look like a lost puppy who found its owner. I look at Harley as though I'm a stray dog who got served a big juicy steak on a silver platter. I'm not sure they're the same thing.

"Yeah, that's what I thought." She walks away, but not behind the bar. She heads toward the kitchen.

"You're saying no?" I follow her.

"Of course I'm saying no," she says, bypassing Colin and heading right to my office.

"Why?" I stop, but she continues until she's at my office door.

She spins around on the balls of her feet. "Do you really have to ask? I asked you if you loved me and I'm pretty sure you had to swallow down the bile rising up your throat." Her hands are on her hips and her eyebrows are so high, you'd think she painted them on.

Colin looks at her and me and back at her.

Jesus, I'm not having this conversation in front of him. "Colin, give me ten minutes."

I do what she wants me to do and I go into my office and shut the door.

I'm not even behind my desk before she opens the door back up and peeks her head out. "It'll only take two minutes." She spins around and closes the door again. "Rome, do you really want to marry me?"

"Yes." I nod emphatically. She can't take my daughter away from me.

"And if I told you that I declined my first offer of wedded bliss today?"

Oh, thank fuck. Relief washes through me and my muscles that were coiled so tightly begin to relax.

"Would you still want to marry me?"

"Well…" It's not the worst idea. We have the chemistry. I have a feeling our bedroom would never grow cold.

"Exactly. Oh, you irrational man." She chuckles, rounds my desk, and leans her ass against the edge. I've yet to sit down, so my eyes fall over her short skirt and nylon-covered legs.

"I couldn't have you marrying him."

The jealousy that surged through me when he got down on one knee was almost too much to bear. I came to my office and paced until I came up with my plan to beat the guy at his own game.

"Well, no worries. I told you I won't take Calista away from you and I mean that. So no need to act so impulsive." She smiles at me.

My gaze falls to her slender neck since her hair is up. A few blond strands have fallen out and I want desperately to tuck them behind her ears.

"Harley," I say, stepping closer.

"Nope." She puts up her hand. "You were only worried about Calista leaving Lake Starlight. Do not transfer that onto me. You're confusing the two."

I take her hand and lower it to the desk. "What if I'm not?" I whisper.

I can hardly believe it myself. No, I don't want to marry her, but shit, I think I might want to do something. I definitely want to sleep with her, but Harley's not a fling. Not with me anyway. If I cross that line, I have to be prepared for either the fallout or the follow-through.

"You are. Trust me." She looks away and stands. "I need to get back to work." She rounds the desk and her hand is on the doorknob before she turns back to me. "Do me a favor and don't ever propose to a girl again if you don't love her. The love part is the sticky stuff that binds a marriage together. Without it, there's no chance for a happily ever after."

I say nothing as she leaves my office, shutting the door.

I fall into my seat and run my hands through my hair. What the hell has happened to me?

***

Harley comes into the kitchen as Colin is finishing washing the dishes and I'm cleaning up the stove and floor.

"I put up the closed sign," she says.

"Thanks. Who has Calista?" I'd been hoping to get out of here early tonight, but after the whole proposal fiasco, I did what I do best—I poured myself into cooking so I didn't have to think about what is or isn't happening with Harley.

"Brooklyn and Wyatt are at Savannah's. She had that business meeting in Idaho."

I nod, vaguely remembering something being mentioned. Harley's the one in control of Calista's schedule, even telling me when to come by.

"All done." Colin dries his hands and stares between us for a second. "Okay... well, I'll see you two tomorrow."

"Bye," I say. "Thanks."

"Bye, Colin." Harley's finger runs a figure-eight on the stainless steel counter while she bites her lip.

After Colin leaves, the energy in the room feels charged and somewhat awkward. I need for it to disappear if only to clear my head for two seconds.

"Are you hungry?" I ask.

"I'll grab something at home."

"Here, I have some leftover pasta. I can heat it up quickly. I haven't eaten either." I open the fridge, thankful it's working so it can reduce the heat level rising inside me.

"Rome," Harley says, but she's closer now. "This whole awkwardness between us... I hate it."

I shut the fridge door to find her leaning against the counter, having slipped off one shoe and running her foot along the other leg. Is she trying to seduce me?

"You're the one who told me I was confusing my feelings." I place the pasta on the counter behind her and step to her side.

"I know. I should go relieve Brooklyn and Wyatt." Her eyes dip to my lips, but she doesn't move.

"What are we doing?" I ask, my neck bending ever so slightly toward her.

"Something really stupid," she says, leaning forward a bit.

"This could destroy everything we've built."

Her lips are millimeters from mine, and I can smell the lemon she always adds to the water she drinks during her shifts.

"It could. It probably will." She nods.

I stop before breaching the final distance. "Is that a no?"

She sighs. "I'm not sure."

I pull back and grab the pasta to plate and heat up. "Then we're not doing it."

"What? I thought we were speaking our minds, putting our worries out there?" She comes up behind me. Her chest presses to my back, her hands sliding in front of me, stopping me from putting the pasta on plates. "If we do this, is it a one-and-done for you?"

I'm not sure I'm in any frame of mind to answer. My dick is a straight rod in my pants, begging me to put my conscience aside and fulfill its wish of coming deep inside her.

I turn and place my hand on her cheek. "No, but I also don't know what will happen. I mean, I can promise you the world right now, but I've never had a relationship. I've never even tried to have one. Usually I lose interest, or I'm too scared to care."

Her hand covers mine on her cheek. "That makes two of us. I had Shane and a few boyfriends over the years, but no one who could destroy my life as much as you could. I mean, we have a daughter. That means this has to be about more than just sex."

"But?" I say. There has to be a but, because there's one for me.

"Is there a but for you?"

"I asked first," I say.

She laughs, her head falling back and my thumb tracing down her neck. I can't wait to lick that soft skin. "But I do want to give it a try. I've spent the entire shift debating it in my head. I was ready to say good night and leave, but then I looked at you and it was game over."

I lean down to seal our declarations with a kiss. Neither of us knows what we want after this, but we're definitely on the same page for tonight.

"Wait. What's your but?" She rears back, dodging my lips.

"My but is that I want you so fucking bad and more than any other woman who's ever been in my life. I can promise you this—I'll be honest with you. I won't run."

"Okay," she says, looking at me with heavy-lidded eyes.

"Okay."

And finally, my lips descend and I get to taste her again. All those worries vanish and it's just the two of us, like it was the first time.

TWENTY-ONE

Harley

The kisses I shared with Rome two years ago have lingered within me. I tried to forget the way he perfected the soft and gentle touch mixed with firm lips. I knew then that I was one of many in his life because a guy isn't born knowing how to kiss like that—he learns it from practice. But the minute his lips hit mine, I don't feel like one of many—I feel like his.

He pushes me back toward the counter, his thigh separating my legs, sliding my skirt higher up my thighs. My fingers fumble with the buttons of his chef jacket. He tastes like the bourbon sauce he kept sampling through the night, and I deepen our kiss. Rome doesn't hold back, gripping my hips so hard he might leave a mark. I revel in his touch, every finger indent a small indication of how much he wants me.

My mind transports me back to that night outside his

hotel room, when he stopped us before sliding in his keycard. My back was planted against the wall and his thigh was exactly where it is now. There have been times when I've walked through a cologne section of a department store and his smell wrapped around me, stopping me in my tracks. That night was one of pure passion like I'd never—still to this day—had with anyone else. Thoughts of his hands, his lips, his tender touch and demanding tongue, all of it would rush to the forefront of my mind, demanding attention.

This isn't like then though. Back then I had no strings, no attachments to him and I thought that's what I loved about it. A stranger in bed who would disappear the next morning. Until the plus sign showed up on the stick two months later.

Now he's the father of my daughter. My boss, and for some reason, it all feels like too much...

"Stop thinking," he murmurs along my lips, his hand brushing the hair off my neck.

"Are we being stupid?" My head rolls back when his tongue slides up my neck.

"We're human." His mouth takes my chin and his thumb caresses my jawline.

He's different tonight. I need to stop comparing this to the last time I had him. Our relationship is different now. This isn't a one-night stand, this is... well, whatever it is, I'll be seeing him tomorrow morning and every day after that.

Rome is right though. We decided to do this, and it all feels too good to turn back now. Damn the consequences. We're adults. We'll handle it.

He picks me up and puts me on the counter, his hands running up my inner thighs and parting them for him. Finally, I have all the buttons on his chef jacket open and I slide the fabric over his shoulders until it falls to the floor. I groan, seeing him still in a white shirt, which only makes him laugh. He grabs the hem and pulls it off his body.

My mouth salivates as I watch each ab in his stomach contract with his movements. Without warning, he rips open my blouse and his lips crash to mine.

Oh my God, that was hot.

"Screw this." He tears his lips from mine, slides me off the counter, and takes me to his office, kicking the door shut.

My skirt is up around my waist now. "I know. I need you right fucking now."

Keeping me in his arms, he takes one hand and swipes everything off half his desk, his computer still sitting in the opposite corner. He unbuttons his pants, his eyes smoldering like kindling before the log pops and explodes. His pants stay open and he molds his hand on my cheek, his thumb brushing my bottom lip. "Undress for me?"

I smile, my fingers pulling my ripped shirt farther apart. I lick my bottom lip and he takes the opportunity to push his thumb into my mouth. I twirl my tongue around it, showing him exactly how I'll suck him off when the time comes.

I let the fabric of my shirt fall down my arms and his gaze dips, his hand sliding down my body until he pulls down the cup of my bra, his wet thumb running a circle around my nipple. Reaching behind me, I unclasp my bra. The straps fall down my arms until it lands in my lap.

Rome pushes his pants down, steps out of them, and sits on his office chair.

Our eyes haven't left one another for a second as I slide off the desk, unzipping my skirt from behind and letting it fall to the floor with his pants. I remove my nylons and I'm about to have my panties follow, but Rome wheels his chair closer, stopping me.

"I'm barely hanging on. If you take those off now, it's over."

I smile, loving the effect I have on him. He's not shy to reveal his desire and that's making me wetter.

"Straddle me, baby." He taps his legs.

I slide my legs on either side of him, his boxer briefs and my silk panties the only barrier to keep him from sliding into me. He wastes no time taking my nipple into his mouth. I use his shoulders as an anchor and arch my back to give him full access to my breasts.

A moan escapes as he kneads and sucks the flesh into his hot mouth. His hands explore, his thumb running along my throat, his tongue following every nip and bite to my eager breast.

I grind against the rigid length beneath me and my body wants my hand to descend to get me off, but I don't because I know Rome will get us there. We've been here before. I'm growing impatient as his tongue glides across my skin and his groans and growls set fire to my libido because he can't get enough of me. Me. This gorgeous man wants *me*.

My gaze catches his as he looks up at me, sliding his tongue along my peaked nipple. I'm done. It's over. I'll never recover from him this time. It's ten times better this time around because I know him. He's not the hot guy at the bar who turned me on with his alluring eyes and flirtatious smirk. He's Rome. The father of my baby. The chef who took a chance and opened a fancy restaurant. The middle Bailey child who lost his parents too young. The crazy twin whose rebellious teenage self left a lasting impression on everyone in this town. A reputation he seems to want to dispel. The man who moved back here to be close to his family.

"Please," I moan, and his hands slide to the nape of my neck, pulling me down to him.

"Top drawer," he says right before he catches me in another soul-searching, suck-all-the-air-from-my-lungs, leave-me-gasping kiss.

I mindlessly open the drawer with his lips still attached to mine and feel past pens and note pads and a ruler. Hmm, that could be fun. Another time. When the foil packet slips between my fingers, I want to sing halleluiah.

I draw back and Rome plucks it from my grasp. "Let's hope it works how it's supposed to this time around." He laughs.

My forehead lands on his as I watch him pull himself out of his boxers and sliding the latex down his hard length.

"We have a failsafe this time," I say.

He looks up at me, clearly confused.

"I've been on the pill since she was born."

"Double protection. Perfect." He shoots me that panty-disintegrating smile and I could just melt into a puddle right here and now.

His masterful fingers slide aside the fabric of my soaked panties and I rise up to get him underneath before slipping his length into me. We both groan from the pleasure of him filling me.

"Shit. You feel so fucking good," he says, brushing my hair from my forehead.

How can he be so tender and so demanding all at once? Like he's got the whole thing under control and all I have to do is follow his lead. He glides his hands down the sides of my ribcage and goose bumps follow their path like an avalanche.

"You okay?" This time he tucks my hair behind my ear.

"I'm perfect."

His lips take mine once again, but they're slow and methodic and dare I say, loving. I rise up on his length and his hands run up and down my thighs, his thumbs sliding along my inner thighs while I shift my hips. The friction across my clit is amazing. His thumbs grow closer to my core every time I move until they're there, lightly brushing my clit each time I come down.

Our kiss ends and our foreheads rest on one another's as we focus between us, watching me move over him. His hands skim over my skin until he grabs my ass, widening me, and he slowly takes over the rhythm, increasing the pace until we're panting and our bodies are slicked with the sheen of sweat.

With him taking control, I pull my hands off the arms of the chair and wrap them around his neck. Our eyes lock, and all that desire and heat swimming in his sweet brown eyes drowns me. I match his speed as he expertly draws me up his length before slamming me back down.

"Fuck, Rome." I pant, anchoring myself to him so he can keep doing what he's doing. "Never stop."

"Never," he says, sweat coating his forehead and dripping down between us.

I'm so close. So close.

"I can't," I say, because my orgasm is dangling like a ripe fruit from a tree but just out of reach.

"You can." One of his hands controls the rhythm while his other circles my clit.

A second later, all my nerve endings commence into a ball of energy and explode outward. My sex clenches him as if I don't ever want him to leave my body. I try to stay upright, but he has other plans anyway.

He picks me up, careful to get my legs out from under the arms of his office chair, and puts me on the edge of his desk, pounding into me fast and hard.

"So wet," he says then grabs one of my breasts and props one of my legs straight up on his chest while he dominates me.

His gaze falls to me, and I watch his orgasm overtake him. He pulls out, ripping off his condom and letting his cum spray all over my chest.

And I'm ready for round two already.

TWENTY-TWO

Rome

"Sorry," I say, but looking at her with my seed all over her stomach is doing something to me. I like it. It's like she's mine. Although she's not. Well, she kind of is. What did we agree to right before we had sex?

She giggles and grabs a few Kleenex from the box and hands them to me. "You made the mess, you have to clean it up."

I take the Kleenex and wipe her down. Her body is perfection. I can't even believe she had a kid. That's when I see a faint line along her lower abdomen.

I run my fingers along her C-section scar. Having eight siblings, you tend to know about birth stuff no matter how many times you cover your ears and shake your head.

"You never told me about Calista's birth." I help her up, throwing away the tissues and grabbing more for myself.

"That's not exactly a 'let's get to know each other' question." She collects our clothes into a pile, putting my pants on the desk.

"I guess not, but tell me. I want to know."

She shakes her head. "Nothing like a post-sex 'how did the baby come out of you' convo. So sexy." She turns and grabs the extra shirt I keep for myself off the hook on the back of the door.

I tuck my dick back into my boxers and put on my pants, realizing that my shirt is still in the kitchen. My stomach rumbles as a reminder of what I was up to before I was distracted by sex.

"Hungry?" I ask.

She glances up from buttoning the shirt. "I should get home to relieve Brooklyn and Wyatt."

"Then I'll take the pasta with us and we can heat it up there." I pat her ass as I walk by her into the kitchen, but I'm not even out of the office when she calls my name. I turn, and from her downturned eyes, I already know what she's thinking. Yeah, an actual conversation without the sexual energy swirling around us like a tornado would've been better *before* we had sex. "Yeah?"

She raises her eyebrows and I cut a path to her then run my thumb along her cheek. She's so gorgeous.

"We're going to give this a try."

She nods. "Just jumping into the cold water, huh?"

I laugh, pulling her against my body. "You're worried?"

Her arms rest on my shoulders and she looks at me. "Just do me one favor. No matter what happens with us, don't ever leave Calista."

Her seriousness throws me back a few steps. "I would never."

"I could never forgive myself if I was the reason she didn't have her dad in her life, okay?"

I nod. "Hey." I lean down, moving my head around until I have her eyes locked with mine. "She's my daughter. I'm in her life until I'm six feet under. I promise. Even if you break my heart." I wink and kiss her nose.

"Me break your heart? You're the one who doesn't remember our first time." The lilt in her voice says she's joking, but I hate that I don't have a full memory of that night.

"I was a fool." I slide my hand into hers and pull her out of the office.

"We should clean up."

"Tomorrow," I say, picking up my shirt and throwing it on before hanging my chef's coat on the hook by my office door. "Tonight, we're going home to our daughter."

She smiles and I wish I could put that in a bottle and seal it up on the off chance I fuck this up. Everyone knows I tend to screw shit up.

Harley leaves G'Ma D's Cadillac at the restaurant, and I drive her in my truck over to Savannah's. I'm supposed to watch Calista in the morning anyway, since Harley has a class.

When we walk into Savannah's cute three-bedroom house, a dog barks.

"You let her bring that mutt?" I ask, referring to Brooklyn's dog, Gizmo.

Harley shoots me a "what is wrong with you" look. "Of course."

"What if he hurts Calista?"

"Calista loves dogs, and Gizmo is just her size."

Harley slips off her shoes and I do the same. Savannah's

anal and she'll probably find the one speck of dirt I leave behind and have it tested at the lab to find out whose shoe it came from.

Gizmo runs down the hardwood as if he's a minute from losing his grip and sliding into the wall. Of course, Savannah probably waxes these every day, so it might not be his fault.

"Speaking of," I say.

"Hey, Gizmo." Harley leans down and pets his head.

Brooklyn comes to the archway between the kitchen and family room at the end of the hallway. She's got this weird look on her face. I try to dissect my older sister's expression for meaning, then it hits me.

"You're shitting me, right?" I pull my phone from my pocket and head into the kitchen.

"What is it?" Harley asks, petting Gizmo.

"It's Buzz Wheel." I click on the website and there you have it. "Someone took a picture through the window?"

"Technically it was your back door. You need to be more discreet." Brooklyn grabs her coat.

Wyatt rolls his eyes over her shoulder, helping her get it on. "Don't point fingers."

"They got a picture of us?" Harley comes to my side.

"I have to say, I'm proud of you two," Brooklyn says.

If Harley wasn't next to me, I'd flip her off. But I don't want Harley to misconstrue my meaning.

I press the button, and there's the Buzz Wheel article with a picture of me caging Harley to the kitchen counter right before I went in to kiss her.

"At least they disappear so Calista will never read this," I say, but Harley swipes the phone from my hand. I look at my now-empty hands.

"Get used to it, man," Wyatt says, laughing.

Harley reads it aloud. How kind of her. "'All the single ladies out there? You should be molding yourself after Harley Sullivan because she got proposed to twice tonight. Sadly... well, as a TEAM ROME member, I don't really think it's sad that the guy who flew here from Seattle was denied when he fell on bended knee. The guests at Rome's new restaurant, Terra and Mare, were all ready to clink their glasses when Harley sent him packing. Then Rome himself emerged and fell down on bended knee in the same spot as the mystery Seattle man, but sadly (and this time I mean it), she didn't say yes to him either. Well, at least to marriage. According to a fellow Lake Starlight resident who captured this photo of the couple seconds away from kissing, Harley cried out yes quite a lot tonight. The question remains, will Harley let Rome put a ring on it in the future?'" Her face becomes paler the longer she looks at me.

"It's nothing. No one really reads it," I argue even though I know I'm lying.

"Nice try." Harley hands me back my phone.

"Don't worry, there's more news in there. Supposedly Denver is moving in with Liam because his landlord raised the rent, so now someone in town is upset that Liam's house is going to turn into a brothel or something." Brooklyn laughs so hard she snorts.

I shake my head. Denver and Liam are moving in together? That should be interesting.

"Thanks for letting us bring Gizmo," Wyatt changes the subject. Good man.

"No problem. I want Calista around as many dogs as possible because I want her to be comfortable with them. Who knows, maybe someday I'll get one?" Harley looks at me and smiles.

I want to look away. Is that a question like are *we* going

to get a dog? Pull up the reins on those horses, we're not there yet.

"Yeah, he's doing this weird thing when we leave the apartment where he takes a stuffed animal, and when we return, he's chewed out the eyeballs," Wyatt says.

"Oh!" Harley rears back.

"And he puts them right next to the stuffed animal. It's creepy as hell," Wyatt says.

"Separation anxiety," Brooklyn says. "I talked to Colton about it and he said it's harmless since it doesn't happen every time, but he's probably mad when we leave."

"Hold up. After you leave, he gets a stuffed animal, bites the eyes out, and puts them on the family room floor right next to the mauled carcass?" Harley asks.

Brooklyn nods.

"Why do the two of you have stuffed animals?" I ask the real question I want an answer to.

"Wyatt's a pro at carnival games. I went home with a whole bunch from Founder's Day."

I shake my head.

"That's sweet, he won stuffed animals for you," Harley says with a touch of adoration.

Whatever. I could win her stuffed animals.

"Anyway, we better go and leave you two to do whatever you're going to do." Brooklyn waggles her finger between us.

I roll my eyes for the millionth time.

"Thanks again." Harley's about to see them out, but Calista whines on the monitor. Before we know it, she's saying her goodbyes and headed upstairs.

"So? Are you two a couple now?" Brooklyn asks the question I know she's dying to get an answer to.

I place my hands on her shoulders and turn her toward the door. "Good night."

"Come on. I'm your sister." She digs her feet in. I'm using all my energy to push her out the door. If we were ten and twelve again, I would push harder, wishing she'd fall forward and land flat on her face, but we're adults now. Mostly. "Don't mess this up."

"Bye," I say.

Wyatt stands on the other side of the door with Gizmo in his arms, watching the scene unfold. Thanks for the help, buddy.

"If something happens and they leave Lake Starlight, you do know we're kicking you out of the family, right? Harley and Calista will replace you."

I push her again. "Sure. Whatever. Go home."

She falters forward through the door, laughing. "Bye!"

She wiggles her fingers and I shut the door in her face.

"Not a very nice goodbye to two people who just watched your daughter." Harley comes down the stairs with a red-faced and sweaty Calista.

"What's going on? I had plans to eat pasta off your stomach."

Harley hands Calista to me and she comes easily, wrapping her arms around my neck and nuzzling her head into my shoulder. Her pacifier is going a mile a minute in and out of her mouth.

"Do you ever worry about this pacifier and oral fixation?" I ask, following Harley into the kitchen.

"No. I'm going to cut it off at two." She places pasta on two plates and microwaves it. Not the way I would've done it, but I'm not arguing since I get to hold Calista.

"Shouldn't I get a say?"

"Did you read up on it? Because I have a feeling that

you think that oral fixation means she's going to want to give blow jobs to anyone and everyone when she's eighteen." She raises her eyebrows.

Well, yeah, isn't that what oral fixation is?

She shakes her head and ignores the topic any further.

I sit down, rocking our daughter in her cute yellow duckie onesie, her sweaty brown hair matted to her forehead, and watch Harley move around the kitchen as we talk about the future of our daughter.

Maybe we can do this family thing.

TWENTY-THREE

Harley

On my way to class, I dial up Miranda because Shane was right—we've drifted apart in the short time I've been here. I've had so much to do and get used to, but Miranda has always been a good friend to me. Case in point, she arranged for all my stuff to be put into storage after I gave my landlord notice, and she shipped me all my clothes. I don't want to lose her even if I've moved thousands of miles away. I hit the speaker button on my phone and place it in the console.

"Well, well, well," she says. Although she's trying to sound tough, there's a lightness to her tone that's always present with Miranda.

"Hey." My tone conveys how embarrassed I am about not calling more often.

"I heard Shane came back with his tail between his legs."

How she hears gossip in a city as big as Seattle, I'll never understand. But then again, I could see her taking him out for shots to heal his broken heart. She's that kind of girl.

"Why did he come up here to begin with?"

"Yeah, sorry about that. He came to Wet Sprocket, and I was a little tipsy. Your name came up and I kind of told him about what was happening, and before I could sober up, he was already proposing to you."

"It's fine. Hopefully he has some closure now."

"Still, that's not girl code. I might've been a little pissed that you've been ignoring me. You know how I get mean when I drink." The apology in her tone is sincere, and I wish she was in front of me so I could hug it out with her.

"Don't worry about it. How's it going otherwise?"

"Eh... okay, I guess. I'm not sure I'm meant for massage therapy. I mean, in my mind, I think I figured I'd be massaging a bunch of Bradley Coopers all day."

I laugh because that is so Miranda. "And?"

"And this lady came in the other day. She had to be like two hundred and fifty. No shame whatsoever, which is awesome, own it, lady, but when I asked her to flip onto her back, her boobs were pretty much hanging down either side of the table."

"Are you thinking we'll be immune to gravity as we get older?" I chuckle.

"It just depressed me. All I wanted to do was hold mine up and cry, rock them back and forth, and say no, no, no."

I laugh then sip my iced coffee.

"You sound like you're on your way somewhere."

"I'm finally taking that last class so I can hopefully graduate." I cross my fingers in the air although she can't see me.

"Oh, that's great! So this Lake Starlight is really working out for you. I'm happy, except I do miss my little ladybug."

I smile, remembering Calista lying between Rome and me last night, the two of us watching her sleep. Him picking her up and placing her in her crib and coming back to my room before stripping and sliding into bed with me as though he'd done it every night before.

"Yeah, he's a great dad to her, but she misses you too. Come up and visit. He has a twin."

She giggles and I wonder if she's alone because that's her uncomfortable "don't talk about that now" tone.

"Miranda?"

She giggles again. Though the highway noise drowns out some of the noise on her end, I'm fairly sure she just moaned.

"Miranda!" I scold.

"I couldn't not answer. It's been forever and you're always so busy."

"Bye."

But before I can press End, she responds. "Call me later. I'll check flights. I just might surprise you one day."

"I hope so."

I drive the rest of the way to Anchorage in Rome's truck, since he won't let me drive the Cadillac up here anymore since it's an older vehicle. It was so nice of Dori to lend it to me, but I don't miss the extra scrutiny from the sheriff when I was driving it.

***

L ater that night, I'm sitting in my pajamas, watching Bravo—because really, what other station is there to watch when you just want to unwind?—and my phone dings.

Rome: *Send me a naked pic.*
Me: *Wrong number creep.*

I laugh, dropping the phone into my lap, and resume eating my popcorn.

Rome: *Shit, that was supposed to go to my girlfriend. What do you look like?*

For a second, a red-hot poker jabs into the wound that has yet to heal and was caused by him, but he's probably joking. Just to be sure, I scour online as fast as I can and send him a pic of someone else.

It takes all of a second for him to respond.

Rome: *Nice tits, but my girlfriend's are better.*

I laugh so hard popcorn falls out of my mouth.

Rome: *Open the door, baby.*

My stomach flips a million times over the fact that he's here. Then I look down at myself. Applesauce is sticking to some of my hair, and my shirt looks as if it's been tie-dyed with food stains from Calista's dinner.

I walk over to the front door and look through the peephole. "You said we weren't going to see each other tonight."

"Well, I got horny."

I open the door, cross my arms, and stare at him. He ignores my pissed off expression, steps in, places his hands on either side of my face, and kisses the breath right out of me. He kicks the door shut then back steps us until my back is pressed into the banister. I'm always backed up against something when he's around.

"This is perfect," he murmurs, his hands sliding up under my shirt until each hand has a breast in it. "Tell me you have no panties on either."

I giggle like the hopeful girl who believes in happily ever afters he turns me into. "Find out for yourself."

His hands leave my breasts and slide down my torso into my pajama pants. He groans when he finds that I'm not wearing panties, and he grabs my ass with both hands. "You're killing me."

I swat his chest and slide out of his hold. "I thought you were catching up on paperwork tonight?"

He walks past me and sits on the couch in the living room. Falls into it more accurately, his hand in the popcorn right away.

"Are you hungry?" I ask.

"I'm too tired to cook," he whines.

"Lucky for you, I know my way around a kitchen too."

His head perks up like a dog's at the word "treat."

I head into the kitchen. "No judging though. I didn't attend culinary school."

He drags himself off the couch and slides onto a breakfast stool.

"Is breakfast okay?" I ask.

"Will you serve it to me in the morning too?"

I pull the eggs out of the fridge. "Is that your sly way of asking if you can spend the night?"

He chuckles and shrugs. "Maybe."

"Sure, but when Calista wakes up..." I say, although this morning he was here. But he was watching her, so that's different. I don't want her thinking that every morning she wakes up, her daddy will be here. Maybe

Rome and I need to get out of the express lane and head into the slow lane.

"She'll have no idea if I spent the night here or not."

I crack the eggs into a bowl. "If she starts waking up depressed and crying for her daddy, you'll be coming here every morning."

"I'm pretty sure the party stops once Savannah returns. She can be kind of a buzzkill."

He watches me and I grow nervous under the attention of a professional chef. After grabbing a green pepper, onion, jalapeño, and mushrooms out of the fridge, I pull out the cutting board and a knife. He sits up straighter now, and I just know he's going to tell me how to cut these properly.

I point the knife at him. "Let me do this my way no matter how painful it is for you to watch."

He laughs and holds his hands out in front of him. "I'm just happy you're feeding me."

I slice the green pepper and get the seeds out. He says nothing, but as my knife is about to pierce the pepper again, he stands, rounds the counter, and comes up behind me. His strong chest locks me against the island and his hand covers mine on the knife, his other arm around me, positioning my knuckles on the vegetable.

"Like this," he whispers, his hand dictating my movements with the knife. "Use the tip of the knife."

He shows me and I'm trying hard to concentrate, but all I can smell is him behind me. He must've showered at home before coming here.

We get through the green pepper, but he doesn't leave me, and we move on to the onion. Hey, I'm not complaining. I'm basically doing nothing. We stay like this the entire time he shows me how to properly dice an onion, then the mushrooms. His whispered directions in my ear and his lips, just millimeters from my skin, rack my body in shivers. By the time we get to the jalapeño, my body is as hot as it tastes.

Once he cuts the jalapeño in half and places it on the cutting board, his lips scatter across the top of my shoulder.

"Hey now, aren't you supposed to be careful while cutting?" I say, a little breathless.

He nips my neck, his teeth scraping along my flesh. "I can't help myself. I want you so bad."

He grinds his hips into me from behind, and his hard bulge presses against my ass cheeks. I wanted him before, but now after hearing his breathing and smelling him and feeling how much he wants me, I want to say, "Screw the omelet, eat me, baby."

The knife drops onto the cutting board and his hands slide up my shirt.

"Rome"—I swat them away—"you were hungry."

"I'm hungry for you," he says, turning me around.

His lips land on mine, and no way am I going to deny him.

His hand slides down the front of my pajama pants and my legs part. The second his fingers slip between my folds and hit my clit, my breath labors. I pull down his track pants, thankful there are no buttons or zippers to worry about. I feel guilty that we're about to have sex on Savannah's granite countertops, but not enough to put a stop to this. I wrap my hand around his length, and he growls, his fingers increasing their pace and sliding through my wetness.

We stand in the kitchen, fondling each other, our kisses growing more intense, and the harder I tug on him, the more pressure he puts on my clit. I'm lost in the abyss of his kisses when I register that something doesn't feel right. It's hot.

Down there. Like super hot. I circle my hips to find some relief, but I don't get any.

"You okay?" he asks, kissing my shoulder, continuing to strum my clit.

I fondle his balls a bit, only to be met with another growl. "I'm not sure. It feels hot down there."

He looks at me then behind me at the counter and retracts his hand. "Oh fuck!"

He moves over to the sink to wash his hands. I watch him shift his weight from one foot to the other while the burning sensation between my legs increases. My hand covers my pussy over my pajama pants.

"The jalapeño," he says, drying his hands and going to the fridge.

I jump up and down. "Oh my God, that's a thing?"

"I just touched the most sensitive spot on your body. It's going to sting." He pulls out some milk.

"What the hell is that going to do?"

"It helps when your mouth is burning from hot wings." He pours some into a bowl.

"I am not putting milk near my vagina! A yeast infection won't feel much better!" I run to the sink, wet a paper towel and push it down my pants, applying pressure, but it's not helping.

"Well, then this is for my balls." He cringes and strips off his pants, puts the bowl on the floor, sits in front of it, and dips his balls into the bowl of milk. He tries to cover his junk with his hands. "Close your eyes or something."

I'm still burning between my thighs, but I can't hold back my laughter. I wish I had my phone to snap a picture. "So I have to be in pain while you get some relief?"

"Grab the Greek yogurt," he says, pointing at the fridge.

"I can't, that's just as bad as milk."

"Pass me my phone." I do as he asks, and his thumbs move like crazy over the screen. "Bring me the yogurt with a spoon and lay in front of me naked and spread."

"Is this your kinky version of some sex game?"

"Do you want your pussy to burn all night?" He raises an eyebrow. Obviously the milk is helping him because he's not holding his balls and whispering prayers anymore.

I do what he says, and he applies the Greek yogurt to the outside of my pussy, staying clear of my vagina. Apparently Google agrees with me and says that's a no-no. Relief washes over me right away and my head falls back onto the hardwood. "Sweet Jesus, that feels a little better."

"Yeah, we have about an hour before it totally goes away, I guess."

"Thanks, Dr. Google." I raise up on my elbows. "Shouldn't you have known this?"

"Take it as a compliment. I forgot the first rule to sex post-food-prep—wash your hands." He snaps a photo of me with his phone.

"No way! Give it to me, I'm taking a picture of you."

He tosses me his phone because, let's be honest, he's a guy and this is probably something he'll show his friends. Just as I snap the picture, the front door opens. From where we're situated, whoever it is will have a perfect view of the two of us.

Panic seizes every muscle in my body, and I freeze.

"Holy mother of God, are you two playing some kinky sex game in my house?" Savannah drops her briefcase so loudly that Calista starts screaming through the monitor.

This night couldn't get much worse, could it?

TWENTY-FOUR

Rome

This isn't the first time Savannah's seen me naked, but it is the first time since I hit puberty.

If Harley's eyes could kill, I'd be six feet under right now.

"I'm so sorry, Savannah," she says, getting up and leaving a path of Greek yogurt as she grabs her pants from the floor. She shoves one foot in after the other so fast she almost loses her balance and hits her head on the counter.

I stay put with my hands over my junk because I'm not willing to give up the relief the milk is offering.

Savannah closes her eyes and then, as an extra measure of assurance, puts her hand over her eyes. Harley runs out of the room, the monitor almost slipping from her hands.

"Rome, put some pants on!" Harley yells as if I'm a five-year-old who likes to streak for fun.

She already knows me well. I *was* that kid who didn't care about nudity. Hell, I don't much care now either.

I stand and Savannah peeks through her fingers then slams her eyes closed as if they're shutters.

"Rome!" She uses the mom voice she perfected after my parents' death.

I use a paper towel to dry off the goods before stepping into my track pants. Then I pick up the bowl because I'm nice like that. "Okay, open up."

Not one millisecond goes by before her eyes laser to mine with the same death glare Harley gave me minutes ago. "What are you doing? My house is not some kinky sex room."

"Red room you mean?" I arch an eyebrow.

When Sedona found Savannah's copy of *Fifty Shades of Grey*, she was razzed for an entire year. Then when the movie came out, we all had another good round of jokes at her expense. Fun times.

She flips me off in true Savannah fashion.

"You need a more original move. How about this?" I put my hands by my crotch and keep them straight, hitting my thighs and moving them to the air.

She flips me off again.

I dump the milk in the sink and I'm about to wash the bowl and the spoon I used for the yogurt when Savannah intercedes.

"Throw them away."

I open the trash can by stepping on the button. "You sure? These are nice."

She doesn't even answer, just gives me a murderous look. God help the man who falls for her. He's in for a lifetime of ball twisting.

I let them go, and they crash into the empty trash can.

"I thought you were returning tomorrow morning?" I ask, washing my hands because I'm going to make an omelet. If I'm not going to get inside Harley, I'm eating.

"I wrapped everything up early and wasn't going to spend another night in a bug-infested hotel room."

"Your room had bugs?" I dry my hands, wishing they were on Harley's hips instead.

"They all have bugs." She opens the fridge, takes out a bottle of white wine, grabs a glass from the cupboard, and pours.

"They really don't." She's a delusional germaphobe.

"Talk to me when you wake up with a mysterious bite." She looks at me. "So what's up here? Playing house?"

I flip her off and she twists her face in disgust.

"We're... together," I say, letting the vegetables brown in the pan while I scramble the eggs.

"Really?" Her face is one of shock—wide eyes, mouth ajar, zero blinks.

"What?"

She shakes her head. "Nothing. Listen, why don't you make your dear older sister an omelet since you scarred her for the rest of her life?"

I move to the fridge and grab more eggs. "You think I'm joking?"

Denver, I would've expected this response from. Liam maybe. But Savannah? She's always believed in me. Shit, half the reason I'm a chef is because of her. She pushed me to follow that dream when Austin kept harping on about baseball and college.

"No, I can tell you're serious. I just don't want to see you get hurt." She speaks low, which I'm sure is so that Harley doesn't hear her.

"Why would I get hurt?" I add the eggs for what will be Savannah's omelet, then some salt and pepper.

"What if she leaves? This town can become too much for some people. This *family* can be too much for some people." She sips her wine and stares over at me.

"She wants Calista to have a dad in her life. I'm her dad. We're giving this a shot."

"And what makes her so different?" Her eyes judge me over the rim of her glass.

"She calls me on my bullshit."

She nods. "That puts her on a pedestal?"

"Yeah."

"Can you step down from yours?"

Whoa. Call the fire department, my older sis—who has always had my back—just threw a match at me. What the hell?

"Meaning?"

She presses her lips together. "You like your life. You make yourself a priority. Now you have a daughter who takes top spot and a girlfriend who has to be second."

Her words sear their meaning into my brain. Though I didn't really think of it before, of course I'd put their feelings first. Hello, I'm not selfish. I'm a child of nine. No one can be selfish in a big family.

"Yeah, they're first."

She nods. "Okay, because if they're not, Rome, you'll see their taillights leaving Lake Starlight." She touches my shoulder, squeezes once, and head over to the table, waiting for me to feed her. It's pretty much the pot calling the kettle black, but I'll keep my thoughts to myself.

I pour Sav's omelet into the pan then prepare one for myself.

"Poor girl," Savannah says.

I look over my shoulder to see Harley carrying in Calista. Our baby is much like she was last night—matted sweaty hair, red cheeks, and half-closed eyes, sucking on her pacifier.

"I'm so sorry, Savannah." Harley sits at the table and positions Calista on her lap. Harley's cheeks are flushed, and she looks embarrassed, hardly meeting my sister's gaze.

"It's okay. I'm used to this stuff with Rome."

She's being way too cool about this, which isn't really Savannah's style. Maybe she got laid when she was away. Yeah right, like she'd ever let her genitals touch hotel sheets.

"Grab a wine glass." Savannah nods toward her glassware.

Calista wakes up a little when Harley gets up from the table. "Dada," my daughter coos when she notices me.

"Hey, baby girl, hungry?"

"Yum yum?"

"She shouldn't eat now," Harley says, grabbing a wine glass.

"She's going to grow up as a chef's daughter and chefs have weird hours where you eat at..." I glance at the clock. "Ten o'clock."

Harley brings her to me and I kiss Calista's forehead before she nuzzles back into her mom. I doubt she'll even stay up to eat.

Savannah pours Harley's wine, and Harley sits Calista in her high chair and puts some puff things on the tray. She goes to town as though she hasn't eaten all day.

"You know I can't keep this story to myself, right?" Savannah says. "Care to explain exactly what you guys were doing?" She laughs.

Harley glares at me. This isn't my fault. I didn't... okay, maybe I did. Yeah, totally my fault.

"It's a long story." I plate Savannah's omelet and hold it out of her reach. "Try to keep it to yourself, okay?"

She leans forward, but I bring the plate closer to me. She blows out a breath. "Fine. I'll try."

I hand it over. This story will be like gold in my family. The *Fifty Shades* thing with Savannah is minuscule compared to Harley slathered in Greek yogurt and my balls in a bowl of milk. I've already accepted defeat. If the roles were reversed, I wouldn't bite my tongue either.

"But it's gonna be really hard not to tell anyone. If only I was like Phoenix or Sedona and had my head buried in my phone all the time, I could've snapped a picture." She laughs, cutting her omelet with her fork.

"Yum yum!" Calista says in her high chair, squirming.

Harley gets up and pours a sippy cup full of milk for her.

"How's work going?" Harley asks Savannah as she sits back down.

She shrugs. "It's okay. Busy. Grandma Dori is driving me crazy. One of you two need to get her to watch Calista or something. She's coming in every day, and last time there was this guy from a lumber yard there. He's the son of the owner and we had a meeting to see if we could use them up north."

She takes a bite of her omelet and chews for a minute. "Anyway, the entire meeting, as I'm trying to talk numbers, she's asking the guy why he's not married and telling him how I'm single and that we should go out. That I could use someone like him in my life."

"Was he good-looking?" Harley asks.

I flip my omelet in the pan. My stomach grumbles.

"Yeah, he was."

"What's the problem?"

I'm surprised by how comfortable Harley's become with Savannah since moving in. I think I'd assumed they stayed out of each other's way.

"Even I know I shouldn't be with a workaholic and this man is the guy version of me. Our Sundays would be filled with our computers on our laps and formulas in our Excel spreadsheets or something." She takes another bite of her omelet. "This is awesome, Rome. You still amaze me."

I smile and plate the omelet then turn off the burner.

"Are you looking for someone? Like, do you want to be in a relationship?" Harley's tone is more hesitant now, and I don't blame her. Savannah's love life has always been off-limits. I have no idea the last time she got laid, nor do I really care to know.

Sav shrugs while I slide into the chair on the other side of Calista, cutting the omelet into small pieces and waiting for them to cool.

"Dada!" Calista says excitedly. I'm not sure I'll ever tire of hearing her say that.

"I do, but I'm so busy. My fear is that a man like that is the only man who can handle me because my mind is on work all the time."

Harley's lips turn down and she glances at me. "It must be hard for you to have all that pressure on your shoulders."

Savannah shrugs again and buries her head in her plate.

Harley widens her eyes at me, and I don't get what the big deal is. Savannah likes to be in charge of Bailey Timber. She likes to organize her drawers with color-coded pens. Even her junk drawer has compartments for similar items. That's Savannah. So I have no idea why Harley is conveying to me that she feels bad for Savannah.

"Here you go, baby girl." I put the egg on the high chair

tray and Calista's feet flail. She takes no time at all to pop a piece into her mouth.

Then I hold my fork with a piece of the omelet in front of Harley's mouth. She slides it off the tongs and my dick twitches in my pants. But then she moans at how good it tastes and yeah, full-on hard-on. We need to hurry up this late-night meal and get this baby back to bed because I am starving for Harley.

"And that's my cue to leave." Savannah stands from the table.

"What?" I ask.

"You two are practically eye-fucking each other."

"Fuk," Calista says.

Harley sighs and rolls her eyes.

"We are not." I laugh.

"You were envisioning it." She rinses her plate and puts it in the dishwasher. "I don't want to be up hearing you two screw, so at least keep it down." She comes over to the high chair and pats Calista's head. "Pretty soon Mommy and Daddy are going to give you a brother or sister if they can't keep their hands off one another."

The piece of omelet lodges in my throat. Savannah shoots her eyebrows up at Harley, and they both laugh as they watch me choke.

Great, my sisters have found someone else to join them in tormenting me.

TWENTY-FIVE

Harley

A few weeks later, we're in Rome's truck on our way to Sunday dinner at Austin and Holly's. We have to make a pit stop to pick up Grandma Dori, which I think is actually more of a reason for her to traipse Calista around the senior home and brag about her to her friends.

Once we're parked, Rome grabs Calista out of the car seat, but she kicks him over and over until he places her feet on the ground. Our little girl only wants to walk and never wants to be held anymore unless it's bedtime. I feel bad for Rome, because he missed the time in her life when you could hold her forever.

She runs through the lobby of the retirement residence. Rome jogs ahead of her, egging her on to catch him. They're amazing together. I have a feeling he'll thrive in this newfound freedom Calista's enjoying by being able to move around more. Her climbing needs to stop before she gives me a heart attack though.

Rome stops and positions Calista outside of Dori's door. "Knock on the door," he whispers.

Then he grabs my wrist to keep me against the wall, out of view of the peephole. The man does love his childish games.

The door opens and Calista's looking at us, giving away the joke.

"Calista!" Dori swoops her up and Calista's feet flail. "Whoa. I know it's retired, but great-grandma's love glove can't handle that."

She puts Calista back down just like Calista wants and we all file into the room, finding Juno and Kingston on the couch.

"I have to grab my purse. Be right back," Dori says.

"What are you guys doing here?" I ask them.

"What's up, beauty queen?" Kingston puts his hand up for a high five.

Calista slaps it.

"That's kind of sexist," Juno says, flicking the buttons on the remote.

"Thanks for coming," Rome says to them.

"Sure thing. I love my little beauty queen." He side-glances Juno, clearly not caring what her thoughts are on what he calls his niece, then he picks up Calista and props her on his lap.

She wiggles out from under his arms and her feet are on the floor again.

"She's more active now." I excuse her for not wanting to have anything to do with her uncle.

"She's Rome's kid, so it goes without saying she'll always be running." Kingston laughs and Juno joins in. Kingston picks up a glass on the end table, takes a sip, then looks at Rome. "Hey, bro, got milk?"

Kingston has a milk mustache and I want the earth to swallow me up, knowing what he's referring to. Juno laughs uncontrollably beside him.

Rome shakes his head and rolls his eyes. "How long you been waiting to use that one?"

Kingston laughs and sets the cup back down, licking his upper lip. "Sorry, Harley. Didn't mean to embarrass you, but that one's too good to let pass."

"No worries."

Dori comes in from the back room with her turquoise purse over her arm and a light spring jacket in a matching color. She's very color-coordinated today.

I sit in the armchair. "What are you guys doing here anyway? I thought we were picking Dori up?"

Kingston and Juno look at Rome, and I follow their line of vision to see his classic smirk like "I got one over you."

"You and I are going away," Rome says to me. "I only have Sunday nights and Mondays off, so I figured it'd be cool if Juno and Kingston took G'Ma D and Calista to Sunday dinner, then she'll spend the night with Austin and Holly?"

I sit back in the chair. I can't help but feel as though this is something we should've discussed together, but I do love that he surprised me. I've just never spent a night apart from her. "Um..."

"Austin practically raised us, and Holly, I mean you see how she is with Daisy. They'll take good care of her." Juno sits up, ready to defend her brother and fiancée.

I don't say anything, and Rome sits on the arm of the chair, leaning in close. "We both need a night of just us. She's in good hands."

He's clearly confident about this, and since I've been here, he's been more protective of her than I am. And he's right, I need to release the reins a little. Although our little family of three is working out, it'd be naive to think that Rome and I don't need our own time too.

"We have to go through the directions in case something happens," I say.

He nods, stands, and comes back with a pad of paper and a pen. "You have better handwriting than me."

I prop it up on my knee and write down instructions on what to do should she fall and cut herself or get a bloody nose that won't stop. It's pretty simple—get her to the hospital and tell them she has Von Willebrand disease. Apply pressure to the wound to try to keep the bleeding to a minimum.

After tearing off the sheet of paper, I hand it to Juno, but Kingston snatches it from her hand.

"Hello?" she says.

"I'm a trained paramedic." He winks at me and I'm thrown, realizing for the first time how much he resembles his brother. "Don't worry, Harley, I got this."

Rome chuckles. "Great. Calista!"

She runs out of Dori's bedroom with red lipstick all over her face. I gasp and jump from my chair.

"Oh, my beauty queen," Kingston says with a laugh, carrying her over to the sink where I'm already wetting a paper towel.

"Thanks," I say.

"No problem. I told you. She's safe with me."

I side-glance him, still not sure about this whole going away thing. "I didn't even pack a bag, Rome," I holler through the small cut-out from the kitchen to the family room.

"No worries, I did."

I can only imagine what's in there. "You gave them an extra outfit, pajamas, a couple sippy cups, her blanket—"

"I am her dad, so I do know what she needs." He laughs it off.

Sometimes I wonder what Rome takes seriously in his life.

Shit, that was a crappy thing to think. He's been nothing but stellar since we arrived in town.

"Pacifier?" I ask.

"Two." He comes over to the opening, blows on his fingers, and runs them on his shirt as though he's the shit.

"I guess you're a quick learner."

Calista swats at my hand as I apply more pressure to get the lipstick off.

"Come on. We're going to be late. I have a special guest coming today," Dori says.

I eye Rome, and he eyes me back. The conversation from Savannah's a few weeks ago must run through both our heads. Dori seems to be set on setting Savannah up with someone.

"Who?" Juno asks.

She shoos her away. "Nobody to concern yourself with. Colton will be there for you when you're ready, sweetie."

Juno rolls her eyes. "I'm the matchmaker, what don't you understand about that?"

"You're fine for those other people, but I'm the matchmaker for the Baileys." Dori smiles serenely as though she's not offending Juno in the least.

"You haven't fixed up either one of them." Juno points between her brothers, stands, and turns off the television.

Rome rolls his eyes and leans against the wall, crossing his arms while Kingston blows out a breath. I can tell they're annoyed about the fight brewing. This probably isn't the first time Dori and Juno have had this particular argument, but for me, it says something when people fight.

People fight when they care. It's silence that kills a relationship.

"I don't need to prove my victories to you," Dori says. "Let's go. He can't get there before us."

Taking that as my cue, I say goodbye to my daughter. "Okay, baby girl, Daddy and Mommy are going to go and you're going with Uncle Kingston and Aunt Juno and Doodoo to Uncle Austin and Aunt Holly's house."

Man, that was a jumble to get out. She went from no family to listing five members in one sentence. The thought makes me smile.

"Can we please stop with the Doodoo?" Dori gets in Calista's face. "*Dori!*" She says it loudly with no pronunciation, but I can't say I'd want to be called Doodoo either.

"Sorry, G'Ma D, that's your name from this point on." Rome laughs and fist-bumps Kingston.

"You're going to have so much fun with Daisy and Myles," I tell Calista.

"Woof!" Her eyes light up.

Rome says to Kingston, "Hey, do me a solid and keep Myles back a little. He's so hyper."

"He just loves her." I nuzzle my nose to Calista's, giving her an Eskimo kiss, and wrap her in my arms. "I love you, and I'm going to miss you." I rock her, kissing her cheek. "I'll be back first thing in the morning."

I'm about to kiss her again when she's taken out of my arms.

Rome kisses her cheek, hugs her once, and puts her in Kingston's arms. "We'll see you in the morning, baby girl. Love you." He ruffles her hair and that's it.

My arms are empty, and I want my little girl back.

Kingston stares at me for a moment, probably because he sees the tears filling my eyes. He holds her out to me.

"No, no. It's fine." I wave for him to keep her. This is a good thing, not a bad thing. They can totally handle her overnight.

Rome stares at me like "what is wrong with you, woman?"

I inhale a deep breath.

"I remember when I left Tim alone for the first time," Dori says. "Came back and he had a huge goose egg on his head. I've never wanted to kill someone more than at that moment."

The rest of us stare at her, in awe that she picked that story to share in this moment. It's so absurd, a laugh bubbles out of me, and the other three join in. Even Calista giggles.

"Let's get ready for departure." Kingston looks at Calista, positioning her on her stomach. "Arms out. Legs out."

Calista giggles and follows his directions.

"Next stop, my truck so you can be securely strapped into your car seat." He winks at me, and Juno opens the door for him to fly Calista out of the apartment.

"Go you two. I have to lock up. Ethel is nosey and the one time I forgot to lock the door, I came home to her watching my Netflix account. She watches the stupidest stuff, so now my recommendations all suggest I watch *Our Planet*. Hello, I'm going to be dead soon. Who has time for that?"

Rome puts his arm around my shoulders, leading me out of the room. My eyes are on Kingston as he flies Calista around, and I close my eyes briefly to gather myself.

"Hey, you okay? If you don't want to go, I'll cancel everything," Rome says.

"Everything?" I ask.

"I was going to take you away, but we're going to switch things up now."

I have no idea what he means, but I'm going to let him lead because I can't fault a man who probably underestimated how hard it would be for me to leave my daughter but took the initiative to spend extra time with me. A small part of me has been hung up on the idea that Rome is in this for Calista and I come second. I should come second to Calista, but him taking the time to plan this means I'm a close second. That makes my heart purr, because I feel the same way.

TWENTY-SIX

Rome

I park in the small lot behind Terra and Mare. Though my plans were to take Harley to a cabin down in Homer with a spa, I see now that I'm an amateur and underestimated how hard it would be to separate a mother from her child. In order to salvage the next couple of days, we're going to stay right here in Lake Starlight.

It's cool though, because I've wanted to surprise her with this anyway. Now is as good a time as any.

"Do you have to pick something up?" she asks and steps out of the truck.

"No. This is where we'll be spending the night."

She looks at me quizzically, but I'm not about to tell her I changed our plans because of her reaction. I know her guilt would have her making sure we go down to the spa. Three hours away isn't exactly where I want to be on the off chance something happens to Calista either. Sometimes it's hard to remember Calista has her condition, because she appears so healthy.

"Okay." She smiles, not really caring.

I open the gate to the stairway that runs up the back of Terra and Mare to my apartment. Using my key, I open the door then wait for her to go in ahead of me. She's never been up here because it was a disaster before, and lately my nights have been spent at Savannah's. But I'm sure we're wearing out our welcome over there.

"It's nice up here," she says.

I had to hire some contractors, but the few days and nights I haven't been with her at Savannah's, I've gotten this place together with the help of Liam and Denver. It's great to have bachelor friends who agree to get paid with food.

"There are two bedrooms. I know the living quarters are kind of small." It's a joke how small the kitchen is, but I have one downstairs if I want to make anything big.

I lean against a wall, watching her soak in the place. Her fingers touch the fabric of the couch then trace along the granite breakfast bar that's pretty much the table because there's no room for one. But I have a room full of tables downstairs if we want.

"Go down the hallway," I say.

She checks me out over her shoulder before walking down the hallway. One room is a rosy pink with *Calista* in gold lettering on one wall.

She walks into the empty room and smiles at me. "It's beautiful."

"If you don't like the color, I'll change it."

She shakes her head. "It's perfect."

"Come." I take her hand and take her to the next room.

The master now has a mattress, bedframe, and a head-board. I still can't believe I'm grown-up enough to buy furniture for style rather than necessity. To me, a headboard seems like a waste of money, but my sisters insisted that girls like this sort of thing. Brooklyn decorated the room with light gray paint and a navy-and=gray comforter and curtains, but she added a feminine touch with pink throw pillows. I tried to argue with her, but Wyatt said to let her have her way.

I lead Harley to the mattress and sit her on the bed. "Is it comfortable? Do you like it?"

She laughs, tucking her blond hair behind her ears. "It's your bed."

"Ours."

"Ours?" She shakes her head.

"I get that we're doing everything a little backward here, but move in with me. I understand this place isn't ideal. You probably don't want to live above a restaurant, but just think of how accessible it is for us and work."

She looks around. "I don't know."

"It's only temporary. In a few years, when the restaurant starts making more money, we'll buy a house."

"Rome..." She sighs, standing and looking out the back window that has no view unless you like to see Li from Wok For U throw out his garbage.

"What?" I sit on the bed and wait for her to come to me.

She turns and leans her back to the wall, crossing her arms. "It's all so fast. I mean, you're talking about buying a house in a few years. Don't get me wrong, I love whatever this is between us, but we're not exactly the most well-adjusted couple. I clam up, you run."

"The damage is done. We're a couple, and whether that ends now or ends in three years, Calista's going to be affected."

Harley picks at her nails.

"Come here," I say, holding out my arm. She walks around the bed and sits next to me. I take her hands. "You're scared?"

Our eyes lock, and she nods. "You're a react-now-think-later kind of guy. And it's great. I'm beyond thrilled you planned this getaway for us. This is the part of you that's awesome." She runs her hand down my cheek. "But live together? That is a huge step."

I bring her hand down and kiss the inside of her wrist. "Ever feel like you can never make any headway? Like someone cast you into a role and you'll never prove them wrong?"

Her shoulders fall and her lips dip. "I get it, I'm a foster kid, but it's not that. I just... I know you want Calista..." She looks away.

I put my finger under her chin and turn her head to look me in the eyes again. "And you. I want you too."

She swallows and her eyes grow glossy with unshed tears. "Are you sure?"

I feel as if she slapped me. Is she crazy? Of course I want her. "What are you talking about?"

"Listen. It's easy. We've been thrown together because we share a daughter, but I don't want you to wake up one morning and feel handcuffed to me. It's not like we were a couple before we had a baby." She rises off the bed and I miss having my hands on her.

"You don't feel what I feel?" I ask, a little hurt.

"The sex is amazing."

"I'm not talking about sex. I'm talking about wanting to spend every minute with you. Of course I love Calista and I want to live with her, but I wouldn't make this into a home for us if I didn't want you too. What bachelor agrees to pink throw pillows unless he's falling hard for a woman?" I pick up said pillow and show it to her.

A smile plays on her lips before slipping away. "You're good at convincing yourself of things. We walked into your life as a package, and I want you to know it's not a buy-one-get-one deal. You can have just Calista. We'll share custody, but us living as Mommy and Daddy sharing a bed doesn't have to be part of the deal."

I stand and come up behind her at the window. Sure as shit, there's Li on the phone, throwing out his garbage. My hand slides down her arm, and I link my fingers with hers.

"I want you as much as I want Calista. I'm not doing this as part of some noble quest to sacrifice myself for what I think is best for my daughter. I know I'm not the settling down type, but you've changed the way I feel. Every morning I don't wake up next to you, I count the minutes before I'll see you. And it's not just sex. It's the funny things you say, the way you razz me and fit into my family so well. How you've let down the guard you had when you walked into this town. I mean hell, you're letting Calista stay with my family for the night. I know that's huge for you."

Her head falls back on my chest and she looks up at me. Our eyes lock. All the questions and uncertainty of this decision weigh between us.

"Okay, but—"

I place my finger on her lips. "There's no but, because whatever is after that is a doubt and we're jumping hand in hand into the deep water together."

She turns around and wraps her arms around my neck. A real smile transforms her face. "Okay."

"Okay?"

"Okay." She nods once.

I bend my head down and seal our promise with a kiss. "Let's christen this bed then."

I toss her on the mattress, her body bouncing until it lays flat. Then I strip off my shirt and unbutton my pants in record time. She does the same, and I help her with her shorts. We both seem to need to seal this with more than a kiss. I need to feel her silky skin along mine. To hear her whimper my name as I bury myself inside her.

I crawl up the bed once we're naked, and damn, she feels just like I imagined. "What kind of lotion do you use?" I glide my fingers across her skin as if it's a delicate rose petal.

She giggles. "Never did I think I'd hear you ask that." She kisses me. "I guess you're about to find out."

"Let's make a deal. I get to put it on you every morning."

She laughs again, her head falling back, and I use the opportunity to lick up her neck. Her legs open and I nestle between her thighs, the tip of my dick teasing her entrance as we kiss like we're teenagers in the basement of our parents' house.

Our hands roam and we make use of the big bed, switching to her on top, me on top, facing one another while we explore. I figure out that she loves when I play with her nipples as we kiss. I'll never tire of exploring her body and what gets her off.

"Shit." I strip my mouth from hers. "I don't have condoms." They're in the bag I left in the car for us to go away in.

"Pill, remember?" Her hands run down my cheeks.

"Bareback? You okay with that?" I ask, my dick hardening to epic proportions. I haven't been with anyone but her since my last test.

She nods. "I'm good. Clean."

My dick twitches at the possibility. Never in my life have I had sex without a condom, but this is something I want to share with Harley. Her legs open wider and I slide into her wetness.

Fuck. I'm about to embarrass myself.

"Um... Rome?" Her fingers run through my hair.

"Give me a sec." My head falls to her shoulder. Shit.

I shut my eyes and think of the recipe for baked Alaska, one of the hardest desserts I've ever had to master. The perfect meringue on top is what makes it so special.

She moves a little under me and I swear I almost come.

"You feel... I don't even have words." My hips move, and I rise up on my elbows.

Our eyes swim together, desire increasing as we make love. I've never made love before, but I never want to stop looking at her or feeling her body connected to mine. Something is shifting between us.

"Me either." Her arms tighten around my neck and she rises, capturing my lips in another kiss.

One of the many things I love about Harley is that she takes what she wants without apology. It's sexy as hell. I hope this really does work out long term for us, because I'm not sure how I'd survive without her.

TWENTY-SEVEN

Harley

Sitting on my new couch with a sheet over me and a fork full of orange chicken while I watch *The Dirt* on Netflix is amazing. A naked Rome snuggled in next to me levels it up to awesome. I'm still a little shocked that I agreed to move in with him. I must be crazy.

"You like the food?" he asks, holding up a fork wrapped with noodles.

I open my mouth and eat them, nodding.

After we christened most of the apartment—with the exception of Calista's room because that's all types of wrong—my guilt over my initial reaction set in. I've been trying to come up with a way to talk to Rome about it, but he's not exactly the type of guy who wants to talk about feelings and warm fuzzies. He's a let's-eat-Chinese-food-naked-watching-Netflix-and-then-go screw-some-more kind of guy.

With my daughter's heart on the line though, I feel compelled to discuss my issues. Not that I'm a head case or anything, but I didn't leave foster care without any lasting effects.

"Hey," I say, setting down my container of orange chicken and facing him.

"All energized up now?" He has that gleam in his eyes that I think of as his sex twinkle.

"Can we talk?"

His face falls, telling me all I need to know about what he thinks about my idea compared to his. He'd rather take a fork and jab his eye out. I should let it go. I mean, I've been good so far and we've already talked a little about it. Living together shouldn't change anything. I already work side by side with him at the restaurant, and he sleeps at Savannah's almost every night. This is the same thing but more convenient.

But it's not, and I know it's not.

"What's up?" He places his container down, doing everything a boyfriend should.

How did he go from manwhore bachelor to caring boyfriend in only a few months? Maybe it was always in him.

"Earlier when I gave you such a hard time…"

He shrugs. "No sweat. I'm used to it."

"Why?" I've heard the jokes about him running around when he was young or that he's not one to take life seriously. But here he is, in Lake Starlight, building a restaurant.

He looks at his lap and grabs my container of orange chicken. "I'm kind of a fuckup. I mean, not entirely. I got my shit together after high school. Went to culinary school, toured Europe and mentored under some amazing chefs, but people always think of me as a fun-loving guy. And I am, but that's not *all* of me. I understand the seriousness of our situation. Calista is our priority." He smiles. "It's one of the things I like about you. The way you always put her first."

I twist the sheet in my fingers. "You underestimate yourself. You're not a fuckup."

"You didn't know me in high school. Even now, I mean, I think half this town thinks I'll abandon everything and leave."

"Do you feel like they root for you to fail?"

He shakes his head. "No. They just expect me to."

I frown. "Then why did you come back here?" I would've left and never come back.

"Because my family is here. And I like to prove people wrong." A cocky grin finds its usual spot on his lips.

He's so gorgeous. I can't believe he's mine.

"Why do you think you rebel?"

He quirks an eyebrow. "You psychoanalyzing me?"

I laugh, realizing I'm peppering him with questions. "No, I'm just curious."

I've met a lot of rebellious people in the foster care system. A lot of them were afraid to land in one spot for too long. I get his parents' deaths could've been the cause, but he returned, which is different.

His eyes lock with mine. "You're intuitive."

"Comes from a lot of watching and listening." Which is what you do in foster care. Sometimes speaking up draws attention to you and that's the worst thing you can do.

"I guess for you to understand, I gotta rip out my heart and lay it out for you."

I pick up the remote and pause the movie. Sliding closer, I nuzzle into him so I can still look at him but comfort him in case he needs it. "Don't think of it like that."

He brushes my hair off my shoulder. "Everyone assumes I wanted to leave because of my parents' deaths, which fucking sucked, but that's not why. Don't get me wrong, I wanted to leave town so badly the minute it happened. Everyone always prying and asking how you're doing with their sad fucking eyes."

I've noticed that Rome curses the more he has to talk about his feelings, but I say nothing and let him continue.

"Everyone thinks my parents had this perfect marriage. Nine kids who all get named after places you conceived them in? Sounds like a damn fairy tale."

"Really?" I repeat their names in my head and nod. "I never realized."

"Yeah. Lame, but whatever." He rolls his eyes.

"Wait!" I tilt my head, thinking of him and his twin brother.

He must read my mind. "Layover. They stopped in Denver on their way to Rome."

I smile and nod. Makes sense.

"Anyway, what people don't realize is that my mom sacrificed her career to have this family and so my dad could take over the family company. What travel writer wants to write part-time and take on only a few assignments a year?"

"But—"

"They'd fight about it sometimes."

I shrug. "Parents fight."

"Yeah, and most who do end up divorced."

"Actually, it's when the fighting stops that you have to worry."

He smooths my hair away again, watching his fingers flow through it. "I guess so. But I didn't want to be like my mom and end up with regrets. I know she loved us, don't get me wrong, but that's why I swore I would live my life to the fullest."

I get up on my knees and tuck the sheet under my arms. "Rome, kids are game-changers. Think of Calista. Look how much you're changing right now. Do you resent the changes in your life since she's come into it?"

His eyes fall to his lap, and I hope it's because he's seeing that his fourteen-year-old self's beliefs don't hold as much weight as him being a twenty-five-year-old father.

"If I'd have come into your life before Calista, you might've disregarded me. Well, I guess you kind of did." I cringe.

He looks up with annoyance.

"We were on the same page, but Calista changed you. Without her, you probably wouldn't have taken the time to get to know me. Wouldn't have fallen for me." Shit. Way to put words into the guy's mouth. I shake my head, trying to take it back. "I mean—"

His hand lands on my cheek. "I have fallen for you."

"See!" I cover his heart with my hand. "Calista did that. You having a daughter did that. I know that if I'd insisted on returning to Seattle you would've forfeited your own dream for your daughter."

He inhales a deep breath.

"Maybe your mom's life goals changed. Hell, I was going to move right before I found out I was pregnant. But I stayed in Seattle because I had Miranda and a few other friends. There were times I thought 'what if,' but in the end, Calista trumps all."

He stares at me as understanding dawns on his face. He gets what I'm talking about. I hope he sees that his parents might've argued like any couple and spoken words out of anger, but that his mom didn't regret putting her career on hold to be a mother.

"Maybe you're right."

"Do you feel like you're sacrificing?" I ask.

He leans forward and kisses me. "No. I'm so happy right now."

I smile. "Then I'm sure your mom didn't either."

He shrugs. "I hijacked this conversation with my issues. What did you want to talk about?"

My fingers twist in the sheet now that the spotlight is back on me. "I don't trust easily, and it was wrong of me to think you only wanted me for Calista, but although I've worked hard to heal my wounds, the scars are still there. Sometimes I'll go months without opening up a wound, but then one day I'll be going about my life and bam, there's a jagged edge that cuts me right open, reminding me that I'm flawed."

"I get it. This is fast, and to everyone but us, I'm sure we seem crazy."

"Just be patient, okay? When people tell you your entire life what a waste you are, you tend to believe them. Believing that someone wants you to live with them and be their partner is harder to believe and feels a lot like a fairy tale to me." I place my hand on his cheek. "I don't want to lose you because of my insecurities. So be patient. I'll come around."

"I'm not going anywhere," he murmurs against my lips. My back falls to the couch and Rome doesn't miss a beat before climbing on me. "You're stuck with the fuckup from Lake Starlight."

"Well, you're stuck with a girl with abandonment and trust issues."

He shelters me with his hands on either side of my face.

"We're the comeback kids." I laugh and he kisses my fore-head, then the tip of my nose. "We're going to prove everyone wrong."

The conviction in his words is enough for me to believe we can do this. We know each other's issues and we got this.

Nothing will come between us.

TWENTY-EIGHT

Rome

I haven't had a guys' night since Harley and Calista arrived in town. It's been a month since Harley and I officially moved in together and I have no complaints, other than a schedule that leaves me dog-tired almost every night. But the restaurant is picking up and business is better than I predicted it would be at this point.

"Shit, you should've seen it. This girl had on the shortest skirt," Denver brags as I down my beer. "She actually put my hand on her ass." He shakes his head and downs his shot of Jack. "I'm not used to that kind of forwardness, but hell if I'm complaining."

We left Lake Starlight so we wouldn't run into any of our siblings. Actually, Denver's reasoning is that all the girls are the same at Lucky's Tavern and he needed to venture out of town for some fresh faces.

Based on their stories, they've been doing a lot of that since he moved in with Liam.

Denver smacks Liam's back. "Tell him."

Liam shrugs. His mind has been somewhere else all night.

"Liam brought this girl back last weekend and she wouldn't leave. It was the craziest thing. She stuck around and watched baseball with us the next day. She had great cooking skills, but she couldn't take the hint. And when Liam finally left the house, saying something about an emergency at Smokin' Guns"—Denver eyes him—"which, by the way, I know was complete bullshit."

Liam shrugs, but the tilt of a smile tells me that Denver's right.

"She came on to me. I mean, I don't get it. Like I'd screw a girl my buddy just did the night before?" Denver is in a hyper state that's annoying the fuck out of me right now.

Why? I have no idea. Maybe because he's living this life of girls, sex, and drinking and Calista couldn't sleep last night because of a tooth coming in, so I'm about to fall asleep on the table.

"I didn't screw her," Liam says in a blasé tone.

Denver's head whips toward him. "What?"

"I didn't screw her." He shrugs, and I laugh.

Denver's jaw hangs open. "Why the hell not?"

Another shrug.

I place my hand on my buddy's shoulder. "What's up, big guy?"

He blows out a long breath. "I'm over this shit. Let's go somewhere else. The last thing I wanna do is pick up a chick tonight." Liam downs the rest of his beer.

"I'm game." I push my chair from the table.

"Whoa, whoa, whoa." Denver holds out his hands.

"You, I get. You sleep with pussy every damn night. But you"—he points at Liam—"you're my wingman, I'm your wingman, we're each other's wingmen."

"Not in the mood. Let's go grab some beer and head to the lake or something." Liam stands and pushes his chair back in.

"Let's go back to your place. I'd love a night of watching sports." I follow Liam out of the bar.

Denver huffs like a toddler and drags himself out of the bar behind us, griping the entire way out the door. "This is unbelievable. You've both become boring as shit. You know that, right? I mean, Rome, when was the last time you even came out with us? And now you finally get a pass from Harley and you want to sit around Liam's house watching ESPN?"

I swivel around in Liam's car to face Denver in the backseat. "First off, I didn't get a pass from Harley. I told her I was going out and she thought it was a great idea."

He laughs. A fake laugh. "Since when does a chick think it's cool for a guy to go out with his friends?"

"You don't even fucking know her."

"I know girls, and by the end of tonight, she's going to be pissed off at you." He slaps Liam's shoulder. "Aren't I right?"

Liam eyes him through the rearview mirror then looks at me. "I think he's jealous." Liam smirks.

I think he's hit the bullseye, which is good because I was ready to climb back there and beat the shit out of my brother. "You're jealous?"

"I am not. Without you, I get more ass anyway." He looks out the window at the darkness while we make our way back to Lake Starlight.

"You are jealous." I chuckle. "Do you miss me, baby brother?" I reach across and ruffle his hair.

He slaps my hand away. "Piss off. You have, like, two minutes on me."

"It's okay, I still love you. Harley hasn't taken your spot."

He rolls his eyes. "C'mon, guys, we can't use a night out to just go home."

"Well, I'm not into watching you pick up chicks all night either." I sit forward, glancing at Liam for any ideas.

"We could do stupid shit like we used to in high school?" Denver sits up straighter, eyes so wide he can hardly contain them.

"Sure." I shrug, the guilt of my twin brother thinking I'm done with him enough to make me pull some pranks.

"I'm game." Liam makes a quick right turn. "Gotta go to the store."

We go to the late-night grocery store on the way back into Lake Starlight. It's the only place where you can pick 'up beer and a bunch of crap to prank people with on a Sunday night. While we're there, we put all the shopping carts around the other lonely car in the parking lot.

We do stop at Liam's, because all good pranks take time and preparation. Otherwise you end up with stupid shit no one laughs at.

"The cockroaches. We got to do that one." Denver pulls out the black construction paper and scissors, cracking open a beer.

"Whose car do we cover with Post-it notes? I'm not sure we should do the cotton ball one because that fucks up a paint job," I say.

"I'm doing the wiper blade one. I just have to figure out whose car." Liam pulls out some eraser tips.

The three of us work on our pranks while drinking beer and taking shots. Well, Denver and I do. Liam has decided to be our designated driver in what he's calling a twin bonding night.

"You're really into her, huh?" Liam asks midway through our case of beer.

I forgot how fun it is to laugh with my buddies and do stupid shit just to blow off some steam. Damn, I hope Calista takes after her mom, not me.

"I really am." I smile, thinking of the woman I get to return home to.

"Why?" Denver leans back on the two back legs of his chair, sipping his beer. "What makes Harley so special?"

He's not being a dick. I can tell he truly wants a reason and I can't give him one. I could list the reasons I love being with her. The word love has been on the tip of my tongue, but that's full-on game-changing lingo, and I'm not even sure how Harley would take it. She probably wouldn't believe me, or it might make her panic and want to run.

"I'm not sure. She just is." I shrug.

My brother stares at me for a moment, drinking his beer. "So you're completely off the market?"

Liam throws a beer can at him and Denver wobbles but recovers. "He moved in with her, douche."

Denver's chair falls down to all four legs. "Yeah, but I mean, are you gonna marry her?"

I shrug. "I just moved in with her."

"You already have the kid," he reminds me.

"We're backward, but I'm not gonna marry her yet."

"Why not, if you love her?" Denver's much like me. He's go-big-or-go-home. He'll probably marry whoever his future wife is two weeks after he meets her.

"I never said I love her."

Liam smirks then concentrates on his stupid pencil eraser prank.

"What?" I glance between them.

"You don't have to say it. Rome Bailey doesn't ditch his friends and move a chick into his apartment without loving her. Plus, I mean, damn, the way you look at her when you guys are in the same room?" Denver shakes his head and his whole body convulses in disgust.

"What do I look at her like?"

"Like no one else is there. Except Calista."

I say nothing.

Denver puts his hands together and stares at the ceiling. "Please, God, do not let me ever fall in love." He winks as if God responded and goes back to cutting up his fake cockroaches.

"One day," I say.

"Never. What about you, Liam?" Denver puts our friend in the hot seat.

He shrugs. His answer for everything tonight. What the hell is up with him?

"Should we all just shrug?" I ask, eyeing him for a better explanation.

"It's nothing. Let's go." He stands, collecting all his crap off the table.

Denver and I each chug two more beers and take two shots because we can't have an open container in the car. Liam drives us downtown where it's dark and desolate. Everybody's already in for the night, except for a few people at Lucky's. Smokin' Guns is closed, though we do take the time to head in and put an air horn under one of Liam's employee's chairs so it'll go off when he sits. Denver and I each drink another beer, because Liam can't come in here and not do something work-related, so we have to wait around for a bit.

"Where to next?" Denver asks as we leave the tattoo shop, another beer in our hands.

We pass Lard Have Mercy and tape up a sign that says it's National Take Your Pants Off Day and instructing them to take their pants off and have a seat.

Hey, it's an actual thing in some places.

Rounding the corner, I crush my beer can and toss it into the trash. My eyes focus on the dark windows of Terra and Mare, then shift up to the second story where shut blinds show a hint of light behind them. "Harley's up."

"Maybe she left a light on for you, like that motel commercial." Denver puts his arm around me, laughing. "Let's stop in."

"You'll wake Calista with your loud asses."

Denver and Liam talk about what to do next and whose car to Post-it note, although I'm fairly sure I couldn't actually put them on straight right now. My eyes focus on the light. I want to be there. With her. In bed.

"I'm going home," I say, mindlessly walking across the street.

"You're so whipped." Denver's voice follows.

Liam comes up next to me, propping my arm over his shoulder. Apparently I can't walk for myself.

"I'm not whipped. I'm making this decision," I holler back.

We round the back of the building, and I climb the stairs with Liam holding me up. This is not an easy feat.

"Keys are in my pocket," I say.

Liam holds up his hands. "Not it."

Denver huffs but does me a solid and retrieves my keys. He hands them to Liam because well, Liam can actually see the keyhole.

Liam gets the door open, and there's Harley on the couch with a blanket over her and a textbook in her lap. She looks at me, eyebrows raised.

"Well, this is interesting," she says, shutting her book.

I stumble across the floor and fall into the couch with my head in her lap. "I missed you.".

She turns away from me and looks at the other two. "Alcohol does make the heart grow fonder."

"He's like a magnet. He can't stay away from you." Denver sits in the chair.

Liam shuts the door.

"I think I might be sick." I slide off the couch onto the floor.

Denver cracks up, finding my suffering amusing. Harley shifts to get up.

"I got him." Liam drags me to the bathroom.

Then it's all black. The tile is cold against my face and I let myself drift away.

TWENTY-NINE

Harley

L iam returns to our small family room. "He's found his bed for the night."

"The guy is a lightweight. What did you do to him?" Denver looks at me with judgment in his eyes.

"What do I have to do with it?" I put my textbook on the table and rise to grab my impromptu guests a drink.

I haven't spent a ton of time with Liam or Denver. Both work as much as Rome does, and from the gossip amongst the Baileys, they spend any free time out picking up girls and drinking.

"He spends his time with you."

I open the fridge and grab two beers. "I think Terra and Mare is the mistress in this scenario." I hold out the beers and they each take one. "I pretty much only sleep with him."

Denver downs half his beer while Liam sips his slowly.

"He's going to be out for a while," Liam says. "I haven't seen him this drunk since...." He looks to Denver for some input.

"The night he returned," Denver finishes, and Liam nods.

"I thought for sure he'd be gone the next morning." Liam laughs, and Denver holds out his beer to hit his.

"The boy can't sit still for more than a few months. I'm guessing the restaurant will keep him here," Denver says.

My gut twists in my stomach.

"And you of course." He smiles. "And Calista."

I nod, almost rocking in place to get rid of the ailing feeling that one day he'll want out of our little situation.

"He's here for the long haul." Liam looks at me, and his face looks serious as if to make sure I believe him.

I nod. Not really sure what to say.

"When our parents died, Rome went stir-crazy. He wanted out of this town." Denver continues.

I'd rather talk about which teams will make it to the World Series. Anything other than this. I already freak out enough about my future with Rome. I don't need his brother confirming that those fears could become a reality.

"You did too," Liam says, shooting him a warning glare.

Denver shrugs. "I talked him out of running away."

"You would've been found even if you had." Liam continues batting away anything Denver tries to put out there.

"We're pretty resourceful when we're together." He leans back in the chair, eyeing me.

Liam glances from me to Denver. "Cool it."

"I'm not doing anything," Denver says loud enough to make sure I can hear him.

Liam says nothing. It's easy to see he's the sober one of

the bunch. Well, too bad for Denver I'm not one to sit in a room with an elephant and not address it.

"Just say it, Denver."

"What?" He looks at me as if he hasn't been dangling a carrot, waiting for me to bite.

"We should go." Liam sets down his beer and stands. "Thanks for the beer. Sorry for bringing him home in this condition."

"No." My hand lands on Liam's forearm. Damn, he has muscles on top of his muscles.

He eases back down to the couch. Denver slides to the edge of his seat, holding his beer between his legs. Looks like we're doing this.

"What are you trying to say, Denver?" I repeat my question.

"I'm just telling you how he was."

"Are you warning me?" I ask. "Trying to get me to run off?"

"I figure you're not really the sticking-around type. We should address it sooner than later."

I stare at him. Hearing words like that from a man who looks exactly like the man you love is fucked up. "You know nothing about me."

He shrugs as if he's giving me that one.

"This is ridiculous, he's just jealous. Before you, Denver was Rome's Saturday night date," Liam tries to joke, but neither of us laugh.

"I didn't get myself pregnant," I say to Denver.

"Never said you did. I just find it convenient how you come to town asking for a test, then it doesn't take a lot of convincing for you to stick around. I wonder if Rome being a Bailey and starting his own restaurant had any influence in that decision."

"Denver!" Liam warns like a father who just disrespected his mother.

"Come on. I can't be the only one who's thought it."

I stand from the couch, closing my eyes briefly on the way to the fridge. My sharp tongue is going to give Denver a lashing if I don't rein in my temper. I could very well say things I can't come back from.

After grabbing a beer, I take off the cap, throw it away, and walk back to the family room. "I don't have to defend myself to you, but just so you know, your brother is making his own decisions. I told him I would never keep Calista from him. That we'd make plans and figure it all out. I don't want his money. I don't want his status in this town. So don't worry."

"I'm sorry, he's drunk. We should go." Liam stands again, but this time Denver stops him. Liam eases back down to the couch but sits on the edge.

"I've never seen my brother give one shit about a girl—other than maybe how many times he can get her off in a night."

Nausea rolls in my stomach.

"But you're different. If you're only here for a sugar daddy and you hurt my brother, I'll help my brother sue you for parental rights."

"Okay." Liam looks at both of us, placing his hands in the air, but I smack them down.

"Fuck you, Denver. Do you think I wanted to come here and deal with a father for Calista? Hell no. That would mean depending on someone else, and if you knew anything about me, you'd know I don't want to depend on anyone. I thought your brother was a one-night stand I'd have to wrangle to give us some DNA and then we'd be on our way. I never dreamed of finding a man who loves our daughter.

Another fact about me is that I grew up in foster care. I'm going to stay here and give my daughter what I didn't get. If Rome wants her to be part of his life, I'd never deny that. It's one reason I thought we shouldn't get together—because if we don't work out, that jeopardizes my daughter's future. So I don't really give one shit what you think because this is between Rome and me. You might be his brother and you're entitled to your opinion, but we don't have to listen." I tip the beer bottle to my lips and swallow the cold liquid. I need to catch my breath after that rant.

Denver laughs.

What the hell?

"Let's go," Liam mumbles.

I narrow my eyes at Denver, and he holds up his hands.

"You win that round. Good job. You'll fit in just fine with the family." Denver stands and slides between Liam and me on the couch and puts his arm around my shoulders. "Damn, I don't envy my brother when he pisses you off. I actually thought you might jump me."

I glance at Liam then back at Denver as he squeezes me into his side. "Were you testing me?"

"A little. It's more that I'm drunk and jealous that my brother wants to spend all his time with you. That makes me kind of an asshole, but I'm man enough to admit when someone schools me." He rubs his knuckles on my forehead a little too hard. "You're a toughass. Shit. Foster care." He shakes his head. "That must've sucked."

"It did," I admit.

"Does this mean there's no competition on your side?"

"What?"

"Like, I only have to beat out Austin and Kingston for the world's best uncle spot?"

I stare at him in confusion.

Liam must see it because he nods. "Yep, this is Denver. Able to flip a personality switch with one swipe."

He's right. Denver's a totally different person right now than only minutes ago when he was accusing me of being an opportunist.

"Interesting," I remark.

"It's in the bag. I'll be her favorite." And then his head falls on Liam's shoulder and he passes out.

Both Bailey boys are down for the count. Lightweights.

I wake up the next morning with Rome in our bed, fully dressed and smelling like vomit. One hand is on my breast and his hard dick is pressed against my ass through his jeans. I slam my hand on the alarm and he groans next to me, but the monitor says there's no hitting snooze.

After dislodging myself from him, I open the door to go into Calista's room. She's standing up in her crib, happy, with her pacifier moving in and out of her mouth. She's such a morning person. No idea who she inherited that from.

"Good morning," I say, picking her up.

I change her diaper. Once she's done, she kicks me to get down. She runs out of the room and barrels down the small hallway to the family room.

"Ouch!" Denver yells.

Oh shit, I completely forgot he stayed and Liam left. I jog down the hall but stop, watching Calista poke Denver over and over as he pulls a pillow over his eyes.

"You're better off just getting up. She doesn't relent." I walk into the kitchen to get her breakfast going.

"Even if I play dead?" His voice is rough and edged with sleep.

"Up! Up!" Calista screams.

"Why don't you go wake up Daddy? He's still sleeping," I tell her, and she leaves Denver alone and runs down the hallway.

I start the coffee and pour some milk into a sippy cup for Calista. Denver sits up, rubbing his eyes. Just like his brother, he's fully dressed. His phone dings and he pulls it out of his pocket.

"I'm supposed to apologize for last night?" he asks with one quirked eyebrow.

Will I ever get used to them being twins?

Rome's groan echoes down the hall. "Baby girl, give Daddy ten minutes."

"Dada! Dada!" she says.

I have no sympathy for him. I have a class this morning, so it's all on him. He's going to learn the hard way that hangovers and little ones don't mix.

In response to Denver, I shrug. "Don't worry about it."

"What did I do? I'm sorry. I can be an asshole when I drink."

"True story," Rome chimes in, coming into the kitchen while holding Calista. "Did I get hit by a truck last night and not remember?"

He sits on a stool, placing Calista down on the floor since she views her high chair as an electric chair lately.

"You threw up, which means you're on daddy patrol with bathroom clean-up." I grab a few coffee mugs and place some Advil out for each of them.

Denver joins us at the breakfast bar.

"How were you an asshole?" Rome asks Denver.

Denver looks at me. "I don't know, but Liam told me to apologize to Harley."

Rome's lips fall and his eyes shift between his brother and me then back to his brother. "Harley?"

His tone implies he's ready to ask Denver to step into a boxing ring. It's kind of endearing, though I'm not into that whole alpha fight-for-me kind of guy.

"I don't remember what I said, but I apologized already."

Rome's gaze shoots to me. "What did he do? Did he hit on you?"

"No. Why would I do that?" Denver chimes in before I can say anything.

"Because when you drink, you get horny and —"

"You think I'd hit on your girl? What the hell? I wouldn't do that." He looks at me, confusion still on his face. "Right? I didn't?"

I giggle and pour their coffees. "You didn't." Then I focus on Rome. "He wanted to make sure I wasn't going to hurt you. Just being a protective *little* brother."

Rome has shared with me how much Denver hates being referred to that way.

They down their Advil with the bottles of water I put in front of them. It's kind of freaky the way they screw the caps back on and pick up their coffees at the exact same time.

I'm not sure if some of our conversation comes back to Denver, but he stares into his coffee mug and looks at me a few minutes later. His true sorrow over his actions is clear in his downturned lips and apologetic eyes.

I nod. It's done and under the table. "I have to get ready for school. Have fun with that one, boys."

I ruffle Calista's hair as I walk by and down the hall,

turning around at the last second to see them put their foreheads on the cool granite of the breakfast bar.

"Dada! Dada!" Calista yells.

I laugh because it's going to be one helluva day for Rome.

THIRTY

Harley

Another month goes by, and summer is in full swing with warm weather and long days. I'm still not used to how little nighttime with dark skies they have up here. I'd like to say we've spent the time enjoying the outdoors as a family, but unless Rome makes a trip to the outside patio tables, he's inside Terra and Mare until it closes.

My class finally ended, and now all I have to do is pass my Massage Exam and I'm certified. I pull out my phone to look at my calendar to figure out when I can get it done. It's been crazy lately, juggling my class, Rome's busy schedule, my bartending, and Calista, but somehow, we're making it happen.

It wouldn't be possible without Rome's family watching Calista. None of the Baileys act as if it's a big deal, but to me, it is. I'd never be able to pass that test or work at Terra and Mare without them. Juno and Colton have been our go-to recently, because he's back from vet school for the summer and they mostly just hang out. They don't seem to mind the company of an almost two-year-old.

Calista puts her toy unicorn in my lap. "Mama!" she says, and her head follows suit right after.

I pet her hair absentmindedly, looking at my calendar. Perfect, I'll see if they have any exam openings next week. Speaking of exams, I need to get Calista in for a check-up with our new doctor. I need to refill my pill prescription too. I wonder if I can make that work next week too.

I continue to thread my fingers through Calista's hair, backtracking to my last period to figure out how long I have until I run out of pills.

Wait. Something's not right. I should be having my period right now.

"Let Mommy up." I slowly uncross my legs and pick her up.

Calista's head falls to my shoulder and I look at the microwave clock. It's not even her naptime, but we're not really on a schedule as of late. Holding her, I head to the bedroom, open the nightstand drawer, and open my pill container.

Crap. I didn't even notice I've been taking sugar pills for the last six days. So why hasn't my period showed up yet? They're usually light. Maybe it's coming still.

My stomach turns over on itself and my chest tightens, making it hard to breathe.

"No," I say to myself. There's absolutely no way I'm pregnant.

Calista's head slides off my shoulder. She's going for a nap no matter what.

I push aside the whole idea of being pregnant. I'm sure

the stress of everything going on is the reason I haven't gotten it.

"Night, night," I say to Calista as I set her in her crib. I kiss her forehead then shut the door behind me.

Sitting back down in the family room, I go through the calendar. No matter how I try to spin it, I'm late. Which means I have to address it.

I pull up Rome's contact information and punch out a message to him.

Me: *Do you have fifteen minutes?*
Rome: *Quickie? Love the way your mind works.*
Me: *I have to run to the store.*
Rome: *For what?*

Yeah, I'm not going there until I know for sure. He might actually pass out if I told him. If my stress level is high, Rome's is as high as the Empire State Building.

Me: *It's a surprise. Calista's sleeping. So, can you come up?*
Rome: *Man, you got me all excited for a second. Yeah, give me five.*
Me: *Thanks.*

I put my purse over my shoulders and pace the room. *No way. No way. No way.*

Rome walks in fifteen minutes later because five minutes in his life is never five minutes. At least lately that's the case. He's in his T-shirt and pants, his hair sweaty from being pulled back.

"Sorry," I say.

He wastes no time wrapping his arms around my waist

and picking me up. "No problem. Lunch rush is over, and Colin's got it handled. When did she go down?"

It's not hard to see where his mind is going.

"Fifteen minutes ago," I say.

He kisses my neck. "Perfect."

He sets me down and takes my purse off my shoulder. I should put a stop to this. I should say I have to go get a test because I could be pregnant. We can't have sex because this is what got us into this situation in the first place.

I try to wiggle out of his hold. "I have to go to the store."

"I'll be fast." He toes out of his shoes and shrugs off his T-shirt.

This is us lately, not that I'm complaining. Rome has the ability to clear my mind of anything but him anytime he wants.

His lips brush mine, and like every time, my desire ramps up. He deepens the kiss, his tongue exploring my mouth. His hands pull fabric away so he can feel skin.

There's still that nagging thought in my mind saying no sex. No sex. No sex.

I look at him and fall to my knees, unbuttoning his pants. His fingers thread through my hair, then his thumb runs along my bottom lip.

I love the way he looks at me when he's aroused. Not that it's the only time he has gushy lovesick eyes, but when he's aroused, it's as though I'm the only woman who has the capacity to get him off.

His pants fall to the floor, and I run my hand over the long hard length in his boxer briefs. My bad boy turned faithful lover and wonderful father looks one second away from falling to pieces.

I yank them off him, and he groans, his hands in my hair. With every lick, his fingers grow tighter, the strands pulled tight. I move my tongue as if he's a lollipop, using my hand at the base to pump him.

"Jesus, Har," he says.

I should have him in a chair or propped against a wall, but he doesn't seem to want to press pause. My eyes lock with his as I work him over, and the slurping sounds fill our small apartment. We've learned to be quiet over the past few months. Rome's usually the one having to put his hand over my mouth.

"Shit, baby." He bucks into my mouth.

I increase my speed, already familiar with what Rome enjoys and what gets him to the finish line. Since we're on a timetable, my fingers play with his balls earlier than I normally would. He falls apart, bucking one more time then stilling in my mouth, my hair wound tight around his fist.

Once I swallow, I slowly lean back and lick my lips.

I begin to stand, but Rome has other plans, picking me up and putting me in a chair. He strips off my yoga pants and panties then pushes my legs over the arms so I'm spread wide for him.

He stares at me, sliding his fingers over his tongue before he places them between my thighs. "You're so beautiful."

He maintains eye contact with me as his fingers circle my clit. There's no going slow. He doesn't tease me by kissing my inner thighs. He gets on his knees, both his hands on my thighs to keep me in place, and his tongue laps at me over and over again until he concentrates on my clit.

Just like I do him, he knows how to get me off. It's his fingers pressing into my flesh, the moans that escape his throat as though he can't imagine doing anything else. It's the way he places exactly the right amount of pressure on my clit then blows, eliciting a delicious feeling on my nerve endings. When he sucks on my clit, rolling his tongue around the bud and inserting two fingers into me, stars fill my vision and my back arches, offering me to him as his sex slave.

He always makes sure I ride the wave back down until he slowly withdraws his fingers and places them in his mouth, tasting me as if I'm one of the perfectly prepared sauces he serves downstairs. "Always so fucking good."

He kisses my clit one last time. My thighs close from everything being so sensitive down there, and I run my hand down his face. "You're way too much."

"You know I run on a check and balance. You get off when I get off." He stands and puts on his boxers and pants. "I want inside you tonight though." He holds out his hand, and I allow him to pull me up. "Now go do your errand before she wakes up."

He kisses me hard, leaving me dizzy and finding my legs. I love when we take our time, but I also love this Rome who takes what he wants fast, knowing we don't have a lot of time. It's kind of a necessity with a young child around.

"Okay." I pick up my panties and yoga pants and step into them. "I'll be right back."

I give him a chaste kiss, and he winks. "I hate to see that ass leave, but I do love watching it." He sits back on the couch and presses the button on the remote.

Typical man.

"Ten minutes," I say and run down the stairs.

I rush down Main Street to the drugstore. Inside, I stop in my tracks as I stare at the condoms and pregnancy tests. What am I thinking?

"Harley!" Selene says, spotting me.

"Selene." I hug her. "I meant to stop by this past weekend but..."

"It's fine. I know you're busy. But I'll be at the farmer's market this Saturday, so come by." She eyes the aisle I'm in and looks back at me.

"Definitely. Calista loves the farmer's market." I plant on a fake smile.

We stand there in silence for a moment.

"Everything okay?" she asks.

I bite my lip, and she puts her hand on a box of condoms. I shake my head. Her eyes widen as she places her hand on a pregnancy test. I close my eyes.

"Oh."

"Yeah," I whisper.

I eye the cashier. I don't know him, but he probably knows me. I can just see tonight's Buzz Wheel if I go up there with a pregnancy test.

"Why don't you go pick up all the stuff you came in here for?" She picks up two tests and puts them in her basket.

"Thank you," I mouth.

"I know you have to get back, so don't let me keep you," she says extra loud. "I'll see you Saturday though?"

"Yes. We'll see you then."

I pick up some detangler I meant to get for Calista. Rome was running low on soap the other day, so I grab some of that. By the time I get to the front, Selene is picking up her bags to leave.

I place my items in front of the cashier. "Thank you."

Selene leaves without more than a bye. The cashier is way too enthralled in some show on his phone and probably wouldn't have noticed if I had bought the pregnancy tests, but better safe than sorry.

Once I'm on Main Street again, Selene tucks her bag into mine.

"Thanks," I say.

She nods. "No problem. I'm here if you need me."

She touches my arm, and I nod. *Please tell me I won't need to go back and live with her because Rome freaks out.*

I head back to the apartment, and Rome goes back downstairs to the restaurant. Thankfully Calista stays asleep.

Sitting in the bathroom, I hate that I'm alone in this endeavor again. Just like Calista, this baby couldn't come at a worse time. It's only been months since we moved in together. There's no way we can handle the stress of another baby.

I pee on the stick and set a timer on my phone.

Three agonizing minutes later, I pick up the stick and bile rises up my throat.

Pregnant.

Calista wails on the other side of the wall, as if she knows that she'll no longer be the center of attention.

Throwing it all back in the bag and tying it in a knot, I drop the bag in the trash can and head into her room. She's crying uncontrollably, sitting up in her crib. I find a pacifier and put it in her mouth, soothing her back down since she's not yet ready to get up. Leaving the room, I shut the door and try to wrap my brain around how to tell Rome.

I have a sinking feeling that this will be the thing that drives him away.

THIRTY-ONE

Rome

Harley hasn't been herself for an entire week. She hasn't been receptive to any of my sexual gestures. She seems to have a new reason to hate me every day, and I have no idea how to make her happy anymore.

"I'm going over to Savannah's tonight," she says from the bedroom.

"Why? It's my night off."

I put garlic in the oiled pan. I had plans to make us dinner and put our daughter to bed early, then make love for the first time in two weeks. Other than a little oral, we've done nothing.

"She's having the girls over for some wine."

I nod. "When will you be home?"

She comes out, putting her earrings in. Her hair is down and curled, and she's wearing a sundress with strappy sandals. She's gorgeous when she first wakes up, but tonight she looks like she's going on a date. It turns out I'm jealous of my own sister.

"I'm sure it won't be too late," she says, putting some stuff in her purse.

"What's going on with you? You've been avoiding me."

She ignores my question and stares around the apartment. "This place is a mess. Her toys are out of control."

She picks up Calista's toys. Calista stares at her while she eats some puffs from a bowl on the coffee table and watches television.

"Rome!" Harley takes the bowl from Calista. "You can't give these to her. She'll never eat her dinner." She throws them into the sink.

Okay, time for a talk.

"First of all, I can. I'm her father. She's starving and I'm making dinner, but it's gonna be awhile. I was going to make *us* dinner, but now you're going out."

She stares at me as though she's double-checking that I had the audacity to talk to her like that. She's not having it. "But you can go out and get drunk with Denver and Liam?"

"I don't care if you go out, but I thought—"

"I sit around most of the day with her. By myself. Which I love, but I want one night alone and you're giving me attitude about it?"

"No, I'm not." I clench my teeth, trying not to lose my temper. Something is definitely going on with her.

"You are. You come and go and do whatever you want. I haven't even taken my exam yet."

I hold up my hands before taking the pan off the stove because this looks as though it might be a long conversation. "I never said you couldn't. We have a calendar for a reason." I point at the big one she put on our wall. "We're a team, but I'm not a mind reader."

"Mama? Dada?" Calista asks, crawling off the couch and coming over to Harley. She tugs on her dress and Harley picks her up.

"It's okay," she soothes our daughter since we've never once raised our voices like this.

Is this the start of our demise?

"Just go." I hold my arms out, and Calista comes to me. "We're having daddy and daughter date night then."

Harley stands there for a second as though she wants to tell me something, but our eyes test one another, waiting for the other to apologize. She grabs her purse. "Don't let her stay up late so she's a nightmare for me tomorrow."

She's out the door before I can respond, which is probably a good thing since Calista is present.

"We need to figure out what's up with Mommy," I say to Calista.

* * *

Calista and I go to the diner to let someone else cook for us. After my argument with Harley, I'm not in the mood. Calista gets a scoop of ice cream and Karen asks to feed it to her. I'm not complaining.

Afterward, once I've had time to cool off a bit, I figure Harley has a point. Terra and Mare has been taking up all my time and I've barely been home. So after I read Calista a book and get her to sleep, I put away all her toys, then clean the dishes and the fridge. Hell, I even dust the television and the lampshades. I haven't been pulling my weight around here and I'm going to fix that.

I'm cleaning in the bathroom and grab the trash, then put a new bag in the trash can and head into the kitchen.

"Almost finished, then it's relaxation time on the couch.

Hopefully Harley's super happy when she gets home and wants to repay me with some sex," I say to myself.

I pull the kitchen bag out of the garbage and grab the baby monitor, heading down to the bin in the alley to throw away the garbage.

"Li!" I say as I approach, seeing him throwing away his garbage.

He crosses the alley. "What's up, man? How's Terra and Mare going?"

"Good."

We shoot the shit for a while and discuss him maybe having a signature night at our place, a special dish he's been thinking of that wouldn't work at Wok For U.

He eyes me with garbage and the monitor. "Never thought I'd see you so domesticated."

I look down at myself and join in his laughter. "Yeah, but why didn't you tell me what I was missing all this time?"

Li married his high school sweetheart and they have three kids. He was always the settling down type. In our yearbook, it should've said "Most likely to be the all-American Dad" under his name.

He glances at the garbage bag again. "Looks like you're not that far behind me, huh?" He leans forward. "Don't worry, your secret is safe with me."

I tilt my head, trying to figure out what he's talking about.

He eyes the bag again. I look at the garbage in my hands and see a pregnancy test box pressed against the outside of the white trash bag.

"Well..." I'm stunned. I can't even form words.

He smacks my back. "Like I said, your secret is safe with me. I better get going. Sunday nights are crazy."

"See you."

I turn my back to him and rip open the trash bag until the test box is in my hand. Sure as shit, it's a pregnancy test and the stick falls onto the black pavement. It's upside down, so I can't see what it says.

Harley would've told me. This is something we would do together. She'd tell me she was late, we'd pee—well, she'd pee—on a million sticks and we'd sit on the bathroom floor for three minutes, both silent and contemplating what we were going to do. Together. I missed this with Calista and I definitely don't want to miss it with my next one.

I throw the bag in the dumpster, pick up the stick, and slowly turn it over.

My heart drops to the pit of my stomach.

It's positive.

It's fucking positive.

Another baby is on the way.

Calista's gonna be an older sister.

No. Harley would've told me. I know she would have. Maybe it's Brooklyn's or Holly's. Definitely not Sav's. Maybe it's Juno's, though I'm not sure who the father would be. Maybe Colton? But I'd know if it was Harley's. Right?

As much as I try to convince myself, the doubt is still there. I tamp down my excitement of being a father again until I know for sure which woman peed on this stick.

Pulling out my phone on the way into the apartment, I conclude there's an easy way to figure this one out.

Me: *How's the wine?*

Harley: *Good. Sweet.*

Me: *Red or white?*

Harley: *?? Why are you so concerned?*

Me: *I'm bored.*

Harley: *White right now.*
Harley: *You're acting weird.*
Me: *When are you going to be home?*
Harley: *I never texted you once while you were with
Denver and Liam, so maybe grant me the same courtesy?*

I sit on the couch, staring at the phone, wondering how
to respond.

Screw this. I'm not the type to sit around and wait.
We're going to figure this shit out right now.

Then I stare at the monitor. Fuck. What do I do about
Calista?

Ten minutes later, Denver walks into my apartment.
He's dressed in athletic pants and a T-shirt and falls onto
the couch. "You owe me big. I had a survival trip last night."

I toss him a blanket. "If she wakes up, just soothe her
back to sleep. Sometimes she can't find her pacifier, so look
for that first."

"Sure thing. What's so damn important anyway, and
where the hell is Harley?" He glances around before grabbing a throw pillow and putting it under his ear.

"Nothing, and Harley's with our sisters. Girls' night."

He cringes. "Sucks for you. They're probably all
bitching about you."

"Whatever. Call me if anything horrible happens."

He nods, his eyes already closing. I turn on the monitor
to maximum volume even if Calista is literally twenty steps
away.

I hop in my truck with the pregnancy stick in my
pocket.

Who's going to be a mommy and daddy this time
around?

THIRTY-TWO

Harley

"Are you sure you don't want some?" Savannah asks, holding the wine bottle toward the only empty glass at the table—mine.

"My stomach hasn't been great today and I have to study for the exam." I hate lying, but the guilt of not telling Rome yet is eating away at me. No way I can tell his sisters, though I'm dying to talk to someone. But it feels wrong to talk to anyone about the pregnancy before I talk to Rome.

I have no idea how he'll handle the news. I mean, another baby? I don't understand. Our life has been a bit chaotic, but I've taken that pill every damn day. Isn't it supposed to be more effective than condoms? Am I the only woman on this planet who can get pregnant while using contraception?

"He did it again. Wyatt threw out all the stuffed

animals because he said what Gizmo's doing to them is freaking him out."

"What will you do when you have kids?" Juno asks, one leg propped up on the edge of the chair as she sips her third glass of wine.

"We'll have to keep the stuffed animals up high, I guess."

"Good luck," I say, and Brooklyn laughs.

"I love this new fridge." Holly's hands run down Savannah's newest purchase—a top-of-the-line stainless steel fridge—as if it's a model with abs of steel. "I keep telling Austin we need to update, but..."

The girls' eyes all turn down toward the table.

Savannah's the first one to speak. "You should. I know Austin's probably hesitant since it still looks like my parents live there, but you guys need to make it your own."

Holly comes over to the table and sits next to me. We're the only two here not related by blood. She shoots me a look, and I understand what she's conveying. We didn't experience the loss. The Bailey siblings share something no one outside of them can ever completely understand.

"I don't know. Austin says maybe we should build our own home." She shrugs and twirls her wine glass.

"That's ridiculous. It's paid in full," Brooklyn says.

"Exactly. We could sell it and you'd each get a share," Holly counters.

Juno and Brooklyn glance at Savannah.

"No, Holly." Savannah places her hand on top of Holly's. "We'd much rather have you remodel it and keep it in the family."

Holly's smile is tight. "I'll talk to Austin."

The conversation turns to lighter topics. Juno razzes

Savannah about Liam and Savannah rolls her eyes. Brooklyn asks Juno about Colton and Juno rolls her eyes. We talk about wedding plans that have yet to be made for Holly and Austin, Brooklyn's essential oil business, and the farmer's market this weekend.

It isn't until the doorbell rings that I remember Rome texted, asking what time I'd be home. How could he even bother me about that? I gave him his space. Still, my eyes find the clock.

"I'll grab it." Juno stands since she's the closest to the door. "Is this Liam, your late night booty call?"

Savannah flips her off. "I'm not sure if you noticed or not, but we hate each other."

Juno laughs, her auburn hair swinging as she walks to the front door. She opens it and says, "Oh no, you don't. Girls' night." I can't see the front door from where I'm sitting at the table, nor can I hear the guy's voice well enough to know who it is, but Juno's voice gets louder. "No, you can't see her. She'll be home later."

The door shuts and Juno comes in laughing.

"Who was it?" Savannah asks.

Juno points her finger, doing eeny, meeny, miny, moe between the three of us with a significant other until she lands on me. By that time, the door is already swinging back open and Rome is storming down the hallway.

Rome has this way about him when he walks into a room. Usually I feel comfortable, like he's a friend from childhood. But tonight, he looks as if he's on the warpath. His eyes are laser sharp and ready to shoot. They scour the table until they zero in on my empty wine glass and his shoulders falter. Without a word, he swivels on his heels and walks out of the room.

"What the hell is his problem?" Savannah asks, but she saw it too. His reaction was quick but deliberate and Savannah is too damn smart not to have caught it.

"I'll be right back." I stand from the table.

"He can be such a jerk." Brooklyn carries on, her voice drowning out as I open the door to find Rome heading toward his truck.

"Rome!" I call.

He places his hand in the air. "Just go have your fun. I got the answer I needed."

"What are you talking about?"

He opens the passenger door. A second later, the pregnancy stick I peed on last week is in his hand. My knees almost fall out from under me, but I manage to stay standing.

I threw that out. Put it in a plastic bag, knotted the bag, and threw it out. How on Earth... I suppose it doesn't matter now.

I come over to the side of the truck. "I can explain."

"Explain why you didn't trust me enough to tell me? Why I have to find a box in the trash can?"

I back step into the darkness and close my eyes. "It's not about trust, it's just..."

"What?" He's so eerily calm, I'm not sure where to go from here. Screaming I can deal with.

"I don't know. I should've told you, but I needed time to absorb the information."

He slams his door and walks over to me under the light of Savannah's driveway. "We're supposed to be a team. This is never gonna work unless you trust me."

I blow out a breath. "I get that, okay? I was just... you've been so stressed out with the restaurant. We barely see one another." I throw my hands in the air.

"So what? You figured you were going hide it from me until when, Harley? You had a bowling ball for a stomach?"

"No! I wouldn't do that."

His fist slams on the truck's hood and I jolt back. "Why? I don't understand."

"I... I..." There's no excuse other than my own fear, so I remain silent, staring at my entwined fingers.

"You know what? Forget it." He rounds the front of his truck.

"Where are you going?" I step forward.

"To think." He slams his door.

All I see is his pissed off expression before he turns the ignition and the interior lights dim into darkness. I watch him pull out of the driveway, and his tires squeal before he speeds down the road.

I cover up my sob and realize how wrong I played this fork in our road. The first time, we were both to blame, but this time? This time it's on me.

"Harley?" Savannah says, sliding out of the front door. "Did Rome leave?"

I nod.

"What's going on?" She approaches me as I stand like a statue in the driveway as if he's going to return.

"I'm pregnant." My hand falls to my stomach as though I have to non-verbally show her as well.

"What?" Her voice is low, a note of disbelief and judgment in there.

"Before you question how we could let this happen, I was on the pill. And we used a condom with Calista, so I guess your brother has some kind of magic sperm that swims at the speed of light."

"Ew, let's not talk about my brother's sperm, but congratulations." She opens her arms. "No matter what, it's something to celebrate. Believe me, babies aren't always planned, but that doesn't mean they aren't little miracles."

I stare at her as though she's someone else.

She shifts under my gaze. "Not for me, but for other people. I've raised enough siblings already." She leads me to the front stoop and sits down beside me. "Do you want to talk about it? Why is he mad?"

"I didn't tell him. He found the test. I'm still trying to figure out how that happened."

She nods. "Why didn't you tell him?"

I shrug. Savannah's been on our side through most of this. I mean, she let me move in with her, but I'm not sure I'm comfortable telling her that I worried he'd feel trapped. That in a few months' time, he went from a bachelor to a dad of one with one on the way. How much can a guy take before he decides to bolt?

"I can just see the stupid Buzz Wheel now." My head falls to my knees and my arms hang at my sides.

"Don't worry about that thing. It takes two, Harley, remember that. Not to sound like a health teacher, but only abstinence is a guarantee you won't become pregnant. Rome knew the risks."

Did he though? I'm not sure her argument holds much weight.

"I think I'm going to go."

"Are you sure? The girls will understand if you want to talk to them about it."

I shake my head. "Nah, I'm going to cut out early and if we could—"

"I won't say a word until you two tell me."

"Thanks." I stand and head into the house to say goodbye.

After I leave Savannah's, I find myself driving around Lake Starlight instead of going straight home. Rome being unwilling to talk to me upsets me more than if he screamed in my face. For the first time since we started down this path, I wonder if we've reached the end of the line.

THIRTY-THREE

Rome

Harley got in late. I can only assume she's told my sisters about her being pregnant, which means my entire family should be calling me first thing in the morning.

Her sliding into bed and turning on her side as I pretended to be asleep isn't as bad as me sliding out of bed this morning and heading to the restaurant as if I'm expecting a morning delivery.

It isn't until later in the afternoon, when Harley comes in to work her shift, that it gets more awkward. Where I usually get a big kiss hello and recap about this morning with Calista, I get a low good afternoon and she disappears to the bar.

Colin's side-glance says I'm not the only one who notices.

Instead of addressing the situation, I drown myself in

work. Screw dealing with my feelings. It's overrated anyway.

Rachel, one of my waitresses, comes in a half hour later. "Table nine wants to talk to you."

This isn't unusual. I guess the patrons of Lake Starlight don't understand that you don't ask to talk to the chef unless you want to compliment or complain. You don't seek him or her out just to chat about the last time you saw them. But this is a small town.

The minute I enter the dining room, my eyes find Harley. It's an instinct, like breathing. I always want to check on her as though I'm her bodyguard.

Our eyes meet briefly. Her hair is pulled back, and her eyes have deep bags under them that her makeup can't cover. But what wrenches my heart from my chest is the fact that her gaze swiftly leaves mine as though I disgust her.

I blow out a breath and head over to table nine, where friends of my parents sit. Val and Cory Martle say how proud they are of me and how wonderful the food was. They ask about Calista, so I pull out my phone to show them a picture. Val coos, her gaze going to Harley.

My jaw clenches, but I turn around. "Har."

She stops mid-pour and plasters on a fake smile.

"Come over, I want to introduce you to some people," I say, my arm outstretched as though we're not in the middle of a cold war right now.

She stops pouring, puts the drinks on Rachel's tray, and wipes her hands before weaving through the tables.

"Mr. and Mrs. Martle, this is Harley, my girlfriend." I place my hand around her waist, but she doesn't lean into my hold as she normally does. Her hip never touches mine as she leans forward and shakes their hands.

"Pleasure to meet you," she says.

"Your daughter is the cutest thing. I miss that age." Val looks at Cory and he laughs.

"Oh, you'll have your own grandchild one day," he says before sipping his wine.

"Thank you. She's becoming a handful. Just this morning she tried to jump off the couch."

"She did?" I ask.

Harley nods, barely looking at me. "Yep. Takes after her father from what I hear."

It amazes me how well Harley can pretend things are okay. It's actually kind of scary.

"Oh yes. I could tell you about Rome. I don't think he owned a pair of pants he'd actually keep on until he was six." Val smiles at me fondly.

"He was always testing his parents," Cory fills in.

"Sounds like Calista as of late." Her hand falls over her stomach for a second and I wonder what she's thinking. Probably secretly hoping the next one isn't like me. She looks behind her to see another waiter at the bar. "I better get back to work. It was very nice meeting you both."

She shakes their hands again, smiles at me, and walks away. The smile was forced, and I wonder if Val and Cory noticed how distant we seem.

"She's delightful. Your mother would be happy." Val hugs me.

"Thanks. I better get back into the kitchen." I hug them both again and leave the table, deliberately not looking at Harley.

The afternoon drags on. Usually the days Harley works are my fun days. The ones where I take small breaks and head to the dining room to shoot the shit about a movie or a band we disagree about. Let's face it, there's still so much we don't know about one another. Usually I prepare her lunch and she gives me advice on seasoning as though she's a chef. But today, I don't go out there and she doesn't come into the kitchen at all.

At five o'clock, right before all the reservations are due to arrive for our dinner service, my phone rings.

"What's up, Sav?"

"Hey, it's Liam actually."

I stop cutting peppers and wipe my hands.

"There's been an accident and we're on our way to Memorial."

My breath lodges in my throat and I unbutton my chef's jacket. "Who?"

"Calista, man. She fell and cut her forehead. We've tried to get it to stop bleeding, but we're going to take her in."

"I'll be right there. Just wait there." Then I think better of it. "No, go, but please, Liam..."

"No worries, I got this. She'll be fine. Don't worry." He hangs up.

I know I can trust him, but damn. I feel like I'm going to be sick.

I throw my chef jacket on the counter. "Colin, you need to handle service tonight. I'm leaving and I'm taking Harley. Sorry, man, you gotta earn your paycheck today."

He laughs before he sees my face. The spoon drops from his hand and panic laces his features when he realizes I really am leaving and he'll be on his own.

I ignore him and run out to the dining room. Harley's laughing with a coworker, but her back grows rigid the closer I get.

"Rachel, I need you to cover the bar tonight or say it's closed. Harley, we're leaving." I grab her hand, but she slides it out of my grasp. *This is no time to show your stubbornness, woman.*

"Okay," Rachel says, her eyebrows crinkling.

"We'll talk later," Harley whispers to me.

"We're not going to talk. It's Calista."

Her eyes widen. "What?"

"She fell and Liam and Savannah are en route to Memorial."

She unties her apron and tosses it behind the bar, running into the kitchen to grab her purse. I follow her out the back door and hop into my truck. That's when I realize that Harley's not in the passenger seat. She's about to climb in the Cadillac.

"Get in the car," I say, opening my door.

"I'll drive myself."

"No. Get in the truck!"

"You don't want to talk to me, so I'd rather be by myself."

Fucking hell. I climb out of my truck, go around the Cadillac before she can climb in, and pick her up, carrying her to my truck. Once she's securely in, I climb in and drive out of downtown Lake Starlight as though it's the Daytona 500 track.

"Don't touch me like that again," she says, her knee bouncing. "Did they apply pressure to the cut?"

"I'm sure they did."

"And they couldn't stop the bleeding?"

"I'm guessing not."

"Why is Liam calling? I left her with Savannah."

"I know as much as I told you. We just need to get there." I take a sharp right turn, hoping I can cut off some time by going the back way.

She crosses her arms. "Don't get all angry at me. I'm just asking."

"Are you okay? Isn't stress bad?" My eyes zero in on her stomach.

She follows my line of vision. "I'm fine. Not like you care."

"What the hell are you talking about?" My grip tightens on the steering wheel.

"You're ignoring me. Thanks for the cold shoulder, because that's making this all much easier to deal with." She looks out the window.

"I wasn't ignoring you, but how about we talk about you not trusting me? What did you think I would do? Run away? Thanks for the vote of confidence." I turn the wheel at the last minute, almost missing the emergency entrance to Memorial.

"I didn't know how you would react."

I slam on the brakes in the first parking spot I can find. She pushes open the door and runs to the entrance without waiting for me.

I guess our conversation is over.

I catch up to her at the nurses' station, but notice Savannah in a chair, her entire body shaking as she sobs.

"Where is she?" I ask my sister.

Harley looks back and runs over to Savannah, sitting down in the seat beside her. "How is she? What did they say?"

"I'm so sorry. I turned around for a second to grab her a juice, and next thing I knew, she was coming over to me with blood pouring down her face. I ruined my niece."

A nurse looks at Harley. "Are you the mother?"

Harley heads back to the nurses' station, leaving me with Savannah.

"I'm sure she's fine." I don't have time to console her though. I need to see my daughter.

"Come on back." The nurse presses a button.

Harley sprints to the door. I follow. The two of us walk fast then have to slow down to keep pace with the nurse. Can't she give us the room number and we'll go ourselves?

She opens the door to the room, and there's Liam doing animal sounds with some toys, but he's making the wrong sounds. He picks up a plastic cow and says baa. Calista cracks up. My heart relaxes and returns to a steady beat.

Harley runs over and touches the bandage on Calista's forehead.

"Mama!" She smiles at her then pushes Harley away, wanting Liam to continue their game.

He takes the hint and picks up a dog, saying meow. Her laugh is the best sound in the world right now.

"The doctor said they'll keep monitoring her," Liam says. "Said maybe we rushed it by bringing her here, but that it's always better to be cautious with a child with Von Willebrand." He gets up from his chair so I can sit down.

"Thanks so much," I say. "I should make sure Savannah's okay. She's so shaken up out there."

"Nah, I got it. She called me when it happened, and thankfully I was at Smokin' Guns, so it didn't take me long to get there. You stay here. I'll make sure she gets home and is in better shape."

Harley throws herself into Liam's arms. "Thank you so much. I owe you."

Liam looks at me over her mess of blond hair. "You owe me nothing. I'm glad she's good."

I share a thank you look with him, but Calista picks up the cat and says *woof woof* then laughs at herself.

Harley kisses Calista's face and looks over her body.

"What are you looking for?" I ask.

"Bruises. I want to double-check she's okay."

I help her investigate our daughter, who appears to be great.

A half hour later, a nurse and doctor come in and tell us they're going to keep her a little longer to make sure the protein in her blood works and that she develops a clot. I act as though I understand but realize quickly I need to do my own research on this disease.

Harley nods, understanding exactly what they're saying. Of course she does. And now we have another baby growing inside her that could suffer from this same disease.

THIRTY-FOUR

Rome

Calista falls asleep. The nurse comes in to change the bandage, Harley hovering over her shoulder the entire time. The nurse tells us it will only be a little while longer, that the cut looks as though it's clotting.

"I've never been so scared in my entire life," I murmur, holding Calista's hand. "What if it had been worse?"

Harley says nothing for a minute, holding our daughter's other hand. "The first time she got a bloody nose and it wouldn't stop, I lost all sense. I feel bad for Savannah, because I was as petrified as she is. I grew more used to it each time, but she hasn't had an episode in so long, I think I forgot how scary it is."

"I'm sorry, I have no idea how you did all that alone." I look at her, truly look at the woman I love. She doesn't know it, and I'm not even sure she'd believe me if I told her.

She shrugs as though she just loaded the dishwasher or

charged my cell phone for me. She raised this amazing little girl for eighteen months all on her own. That's huge, and it's about time we have a heart-to-heart about our next addition.

"Harley—" I approach the subject like a hesitant dog taking a treat from a mean owner.

"I'm sorry," she blurts. "I didn't mean to keep it from you, it's just... I mean, I'm pregnant."

I laugh because that pretty much sums it up. With the words "I'm pregnant," everything else in our lives bears down on us. Here I am just opening a restaurant, already running on empty with my schedule. To add another child into the mix is ridiculous and crazy, and people are going to look at us as if we're aliens with three heads and two bodies.

"It's not funny. I mean, how can this be happening?" Her head falls to the bed, her blond hair a veil over her face.

I look at Calista sleeping peacefully. My heart and mind are at peace now that I know she's okay. We'll get through every other moment like this, but we need to do it together. God, we're so much better together than apart. I'm the man I never thought I'd be because of Harley and Calista. Harley makes me into the man I want to be. A man like my father was.

"Hey." I reach across and brush her hair from her face. "It's just an unplanned pregnancy. Think of it this way—at least you know where to find the father this time." I chuckle, but she picks up her head with a glare that could strike me dead. "I'm kidding."

She groans. "People in this town are going to think I can't keep my legs closed."

"Who cares?"

She blows out a breath and looks at Calista. "But I can't help but love the fact that we'll get another one of her." She runs her hand down our rosy-cheeked daughter.

"Do you think I'm a bad dad?" I voice the fear that's been nagging at me, wondering if that's why she didn't tell me.

Her hand falls and she looks at me. "No. Why would you think that?"

I shrug. "Why didn't you tell me when you thought you might be pregnant? Why didn't you trust me to handle it?"

Her lips thin and she looks at her hand around Calista's. "I already feel like a noose around your neck. Adding another baby is only going to tighten that noose. Don't you ever think about where you'd be if I never showed up here?"

I slide out my chair and pat my leg, but she shakes her head. "Come on," I say. There's no way we can continue having this conversation while so far apart. "Please?"

She reluctantly walks over, and I pull her onto my lap.

"I'm not sure what I have to do to convince you that you showing up is the best thing to happen in my life." I press my hand to her stomach. "Calista is my world, and this little one will be too. But none of that is possible without you. You're not a noose. Yeah, our life will be crazy for a while, but I think we're able to handle that. I mean, we're the comeback kids, right?"

She laughs and places her hand on my cheek. "I'm sorry I didn't tell you right away."

I place my hand over hers. "That's okay, but next time you tell me, and we'll wait out the three minutes together, got it?"

She raises her eyebrows. "Next time?"

"Two is easy. If we're really gonna be the comeback kids, we need at least three. Unless..." I run my hand over her stomach, and she looks at the action. "You're carrying twins."

Her eyes widen and I laugh.

"Hey." I bring our conversation back to a serious level and stare into her eyes. "I love you. I don't throw those three words around loosely, so put them in safe keeping. From the moment you walked into Terra and Mare, my life hasn't been the same, and I never want to go back to the way it was. I always did play well with a team."

She kisses me and pulls back, resting her forehead against mine. "I love you, Rome Bailey."

"It means nothing unless you seal it with a kiss," I say, tapping my lips.

As our lips are about to meet, a screeching voice sounds in the room.

"*Oh. My. God!* My great-granddaughter!" G'Ma D sits in the chair Harley was in moments ago and presses her lips to Calista's cheek, leaving a red lipstick mark.

Calista stirs and looks at us, smiles, then turns to see G'Ma D. "Doodoo," she says in her sleepy voice.

I exchange a look with Harley.

"Oh, you can call me whatever you want." She hugs Calista tightly as she leans over the bed.

"Doodoo!" Calista wiggles because heaven forbid anyone show her affection when she doesn't want it these days.

G'Ma D sits back down in the seat. "Thank goodness for Liam, huh? Savannah told me all about it. She's a mess in the waiting room." She thumbs toward the door.

"I'm sure she would've been fine in Savannah's hands." Harley stands. "I'm going to go see if I can catch her."

Once Harley's out of the room, G'Ma D sets her eyes on me. "You!" She points. "Good thing Calista got hurt."

My head rears back. "What?"

"Otherwise you would've continued being an ass to

Harley. What were you thinking? This is your chance to right a wrong."

"I don't even want to know what you're talking about." I arrange the farm animals back up on the bed for Calista.

"This new baby. You get to experience everything from day one and you act like a spoiled brat because she didn't take the test when she was with you? Good thing I've been a great mentor to your sister. She knew exactly what to do."

A second later, Savannah and Liam walk in with Harley.

"See, she's great," Harley says, pointing at Calista. "Kids are resilient."

Calista spots the animals again and holds up a cow. "Nayyy."

"Oh shit. She's mixed up all her animals." I act panicked and pick up a dog. "What's a dog say, baby girl?"

"Meow," Calista says with a laugh, her head falling back on the pillow.

"Shit, babe, how hard did she hit her head?" I act worried, and Harley rolls her eyes at me.

Savannah runs forward to the edge of the bed. "Not hard at all." She picks up a chicken. "What does a chicken say?"

Calista grabs it. "Moo."

"Oh my God, look what I did!" Savannah sounds half ready to sob.

I laugh. Savannah looks at me, confused for a moment, before looking at Harley, who gives her an apologetic smile. I kind of like Harley apologizing for me. It's sweet.

Savannah hits me on the head. "You asshole."

"Azz hhhoole," Calista says.

Everyone laughs. Savannah's shoulders slump and her chin falls to her chest as if she can't win.

"Way to teach my daughter a bad word," I joke.

"It's fine. She said it last week when Rome was on the phone with his alcohol rep." Harley raises her eyebrows at me. I kind of like us together—a lot. "Now go home and relax."

Harley nudges Savannah toward Liam, who puts his arm around her. I narrow my eyes at them, but Harley shakes her head, telling me to shut up.

"I gotta go too. I just needed to see that she was okay. Bye, sweetie." G'Ma D waves at Calista. "It's poker night, and I've been watching those Texas Hold 'Em games. Ethel is gonna wish she picked some other game." She kisses Calista on the forehead. "Did you really hit your head?"

"Doodoo." Calista smiles. "Bye-bye."

The three of them say their goodbyes.

As they leave the room, G'Ma D's loud voice can be heard saying, "Good thinking on the hurt kid thing. That really got them together."

I glare at Calista's forehead, seeing no sign of blood on the bandage. Surely they didn't set up this whole thing.

The nurse comes in. "Okay, doctor's cleared her. I just need these papers signed."

Harley signs the papers as I inspect my daughter.

"She *has* a cut, right?" I ask the nurse.

She glances at me like "why would you ask that question?" Harley looks over her shoulder with a similar expression. Once they're done, the nurse stacks the papers on the table.

"You're going home." She touches Calista's toes, and she giggles.

"Home," Harley says and picks up Calista.

I meet her across the room, taking them both in mine. "Have I told you how much I love you?" I say to Harley.

Calista's hand runs down my five o'clock shadow.

"I'm pretty sure it'll never get old."

I bend down and kiss her. "Let's go home."

One of Calista's hands lands on each of our faces, pulling us apart. "No, Mama. No, Dada."

We break apart and laugh at our daughter.

"I see a lot of quickies in our future," I say then wink.

"Maybe we need to take that trip to the spa."

I look at Calista in her arms. Yeah, I'm not quite over this situation yet. "Do you think we should move her crib into our room for tonight?"

Harley shakes her head and laughs. Then we leave the hospital as we were meant to—as a family.

Rome

"Night, Daddy," Calista says as I kiss her forehead.

"Night, baby girl," I say.

"I'm not a baby."

I ruffle her hair. "Sorry, big girl."

She grabs her blanket and gets comfortable in bed. After flipping on the nightlight, I shut the door and head down the hall.

We're still above Terra and Mare because the baby won't need much room at first, but we'll have to figure something out and soon.

Harley's on the couch, her legs stretched out in front of her on the table, a pillow underneath them. The swelling has been horrible for her.

"I'm kind of depressed she's already over the dada name," I admit, falling into the couch next to her, my hand landing on her stomach.

"It was like the flip of a switch," she says, knitting something.

I take the long needles from her hands and put them in her yarn box. She's picked up the habit as a hobby. They all have. All my sisters, minus the twins.

She eyes me with suspicion. "What are you doing?"

"The doctor said we could try to induce labor. Doctor's orders are doctor's orders." My hand falls between her legs.

"I'm about as comfortable as an elephant in a Volkswagen Beetle." She shifts, but I fall to the floor, situating myself between her legs. "Rome," she sighs.

She sits up a little straighter when she realizes I'm not trying to get her pants off.

"What are you doing?" She notices the ring in my hand and shakes her head. "Now? You're doing it now?"

I laugh at her slight whine. "I know you told me to wait until after the baby, but I can't. I wanted to surprise you."

"You choose a Saturday night when I'm as big as a house, in yoga pants and a T-shirt with no makeup on?"

"You're always beautiful."

She blushes and I know I have her. I thought long and hard about this, and I don't want our baby coming into this world without us having a bigger commitment than live-in boyfriend and girlfriend.

"This wise woman once told me not to propose to a woman unless I loved her because love is the sticky stuff that keeps a marriage together."

She shakes her head as though she's annoyed, but I know she loves that I remember her words. "Sounds like a pretty intelligent woman."

"The smartest I've ever met. Except for her decision to let me father her children."

Her hand slides forward and she caresses my cheek. "I bet you're a great father."

I wink. "I love you, and if that's the sticky stuff we need, then I feel confident we got this marriage thing in the bag."

"Really?" she asks, a smile tipping up the corners of her lips.

"Yep. Because I love you so damn much, our sticky stuff is overflowing."

She laughs. "Good thing I love you the same amount."

"Then we have the sticky stuff in droves."

Another laugh spills from her mouth. "I guess so."

"So what do you say? Will you marry me? I could promise you the moon, the sun, and the stars, but all I'm going to promise is to prove to you every day how much you're the love of my life. Sure, we're on our way to being parents of two, but we got this." I wink again.

"How could a woman turn down a proposal like that?" She nods. "Yes, I'll marry you."

Joy filters through my blood, leaving me with a full-body buzz. I pick up the ring that I put on a necklace. I knew with her swelling, there was a chance the ring might not fit.

She looks at it after I clasp it around her neck. "It's so beautiful, but—"

I know what she's going to say—what about the cost? We should save that money for a place, but she's yet to realize that she's number one in this family. It's going to take a long time before she believes it, so I'll just put more ointment on all those wounds she got from growing up in foster care. Sooner or later, she'll be fully healed.

After all, she took a man who wanted to be a forever bachelor and birthed him into a baby daddy. Only an amazing woman could manage that.

I rise up on my knees to kiss her, but she clutches her stomach.

"Um," she says, looking down.

"What?" I ask.

Water from between her legs soaks the couch.

"Don't freak out, but it's time."

I go into our bedroom to grab the suitcase we packed last night. My phone vibrates inside my pocket, and I pull it out on the way back down the hall.

It's a message from Harley in the family group text.

Harley: *My water just broke. Juno can you come over whenever you get time and watch Calista since she's sleeping? Everyone else we'll let you know as soon as we have news at the hospital.*

"You're playing with fire," I say, dropping her suitcase by the door and moving to help her up.

"We told them we'd let them know, and if we only message Juno, it'll upset everyone else. It's easier this way."

I take her in my arms. "How do you know my family better than me?"

She shrugs then paces for ten minutes before Juno knocks on the door.

"About time, what the hell?" I ask.

"Sorry, I ran over here." She heaves a breath. Thankfully she lives close by, which is why she was chosen as the Bailey babysitter for Calista. "You guys picked quite a night to have this one born."

I'm halfway out the door, but Harley stops. "Why? What happened?"

"Savannah's house flooded." She cringes. "A pipe or

something burst while she was out of town, and since no one was over there..."

"Oh no. What's going to happen?" Harley asks.

"Yeah, we'll figure that out after we get you to the hospital. You know, with doctors who can deliver our baby." I tug on her arm, but her feet stay firm.

"Not sure. She'll probably have to go live with Holly and Austin for a little while, I guess."

"Okay, great," I say, tugging on the sleeve of Harley's jacket.

Her lips tip down. "I feel horrible for her."

"Yeah, I know." Juno sits on the arm of the chair.

"Okay, let's go." This time I actually put my arm around her shoulders and lead her out.

"Bye guys, good luck!" Juno says.

I shut the door behind us.

"You can relax, you know. I was in labor with Calista for a long time."

I'm still pissed I missed that one, but I've let it go. Well, I'm getting there.

"Hold up." I open our door again. "First of all, lock the damn door, my daughter is sleeping down the hall. Second, be a good little sister and get that stain out."

She glances at the couch and rears back. "No way."

She walks over, slams the door in my face, and I hear the lock click.

At least she did one thing I asked.

I guide Harley down the stairs and into my truck, then I speed to Memorial just like when we got the call about Calista all those months ago.

Twelve hours later, baby Bailey makes his appearance. Meaning Calista got to wait in the waiting room and will be the first to see her brother.

I head out to the waiting room, and Calista runs to me with two balloons on strings. They read, "It's a Boy" and "Congratulations." She's in her "Today, I became a big sister" T-shirt.

"Baby," she says.

"Yes, you have a brother."

She grins. "Let me see!"

All my family stands, but I put up my hand. "I'll be right back. We want to share this moment with Calista if you don't mind."

My siblings and Liam shake their heads, smile, and sit back down.

Calista walks with her hand in mine, staring into each room we pass. "Mommy?"

"Not yet."

When we arrive at the right room, Harley's on the bed, nursing Dion.

We wanted to stick with the Greek mythology names and, after consulting Selene, decided on Dion after Dionysius, the god of wine, festivals, and parties. Seemed fitting given that he is my child.

Harley looks at the two of us and smiles. "Hey, sweetie, want to see your brother?"

Calista stares at her with disgust. "What is he doing?"

"He's eating."

"Your boobie?"

I pick Calista up to bring her closer to the bed. This isn't the Hallmark moment we thought we were going to have with her. I set her on the bed, and she crawls down to the end.

"He gets milk from me."

"Like cows?"

"Yeah, like cows," Harley says, sneaking peeks at me with a "what the fuck" look.

"How does he get milk?" She gets up on her knees and stares down but still keeps her distance.

"My body makes it," Harley says.

"How come I have fridge milk?" Calista asks.

Harley laughs and looks at me. Yeah, moment over.

"Because you're a big girl." I ruffle her hair. "Don't you want to say hi to the baby?"

"He's little," she says with no enthusiasm. "Can I go play with Uncle Denver?"

Harley's lips dip and I shake my head.

"Guess I'll get our family," I say with a sigh.

"Yeah, I think he's done nursing." Harley hands me the baby and covers herself.

He's so small, but at the same time, I feel as though I'm holding the weight of the world in my hands. I hold him out toward Calista. "See, look at him."

She nods, slips off the bed, and walks out of the room.

"Hold up, sweetie."

I place Dion in the bassinet, and three minutes later, our circus of a family stomps down the hall. They're loud and boisterous and make a scene everywhere they go. They file into our room, taking up every nook and cranny, and while they take turns with the baby, I situate myself on the bed with Harley, watching my annoying family love on our son. She squeezes my hand as we watch Denver teach Calista thumb wars.

"We heard the news, Sav. We're so sorry," Harley says.

Savannah sits in the chair next to the bed. "The place is going to take months to redo."

"What are you gonna do?" I ask. "Stay at Austin and Holly's?"

I catch the two look at one another behind her. They'll do it because she's family, but I know with their wedding approaching, they probably want the privacy.

"No. I would never intrude."

"She's going to stay with Liam." G'Ma D appears out of the circle of family members. "You don't mind, right, Liam?"

He glances at Savannah with narrowed eyes and stuffs his hands in his pockets. "No."

But if I had to guess, he does.

"I am *not* moving in with Liam," Savannah says, not bothering to look around.

"What's the big deal? Denver lives there. You guys can be like *Three's Company*," Kingston says.

"Reverse *Three's Company*," Denver adds. "Come on, Sav. It'll be fun, and there's nowhere half decent to rent in town right now. What are your options?"

I look at Liam, whose face is growing redder the longer the conversation continues. His eyes dart to Savannah every time she should be answering the question. She looks over her shoulder, and their eyes meet. Harley squeezes my hand one more time in case I'm not witnessing it. *Oh, I'm right here, babe. Something's off.*

"Would it be a problem?" Savannah asks him.

"No," he croaks.

"Perfect. I don't know why you people can't think of these things yourself." G'Ma D holds out her hands. "Now give me the baby."

I kiss Harley's temple, wondering how I was able to get the first girl to keep my feet grounded to love me. She looks at me, and we don't need to say any words; it's all in our eyes. That sticky stuff between us multiplies every day.

The End

So??? Let us start by saying, secrets aren't our thing and we didn't really know how hard this was going to be. We had to be careful with our teasers not to name a dad, any excerpts we shared couldn't have Rome's name. Or Rayne's famous slip of the tongue. She might be the worst secret keeper in the universe! How we were able to keep this secret for so long is surprising to both of us.

While writing Birth of a Baby Daddy, Rayne felt as though she was missing Rome's voice, but she realized that just like our famous Lennon from Mad About the Banker, when a comical secondary character gets their own book, you're seeing a very different side of them. The way Rome was able to weave in and out of the first two Bailey books usually bringing laughs with his dialogue is a whole lot different than the man who finds out he's now a father.

Rayne begged for this secret baby trope to be in The Baileys repertoire. Not that Piper was opposed or even fought not to include it. But it's a trope Rayne had been wanting to get into a Piper Rayne book for a long time so she was so happy when Piper coined the title Birth of a Baby Daddy.

As with Jilted though, navigating Rome and Harley's story was hard because these two strangers had to get to know one another as well as tread through all the issues involved in co-parenting. We desperately wanted their relationship to develop naturally and not be a case of instalove. They obviously had the heat in the bedroom, what with Calista's conception two years prior, but Harley had trust issues and Rome was a happy bachelor when his baby mama landed in Lake Starlight. It was important to see them coming together as a true couple in order to believe in their happily ever after.

Many thanks to everyone below. Without them we'd be lost!

Danielle Sanchez and the entire Wildfire Marketing Solutions!

Ellie from My Brother's Editor for line edits.

Shawna from Behind the Writer for proofreading.

Sarah from Okay Creations for the cover and branding for the entire series.

Sara from Sara Eirew Photography for the loving picture of Brooklyn and Wyatt.

Bloggers who consistently carve out time to read, review and/or promote us.

Piper Rayne Unicorns who shout from the rooftops about our new releases and love our characters like we do.

Readers who took a chance on our book with so many choices out there.

I think you know who is coming next—our lovable Savannah Bailey (haha) and the man who loves to press her buttons, Liam. Unfortunately, we can't get a preorder up on

Amazon yet due to a three month out rule, so please sign up for our google sheet. We'll only contact you once the preorder and book goes live!

That's right we're taking a quick dive into Manhattan to hang out with the Mancini brothers in the White Collar Brothers series. The first book. Sexy Filthy Boss, is up for preorder now and releases in June. But don't worry, we'll be back in Lake Starlight with the Baileys in the fall!

Hugs to everyone!

Xo

Piper & Rayne

ABOUT PIPER & RAYNE

Piper Rayne is a USA Today Bestselling Author duo who write "heartwarming humor with a side of sizzle" about families, whether that be blood or found. They both have e-readers full of one-clickable books, they're married to husbands who drive them to drink, and they're both chauffeurs to their kids. Most of all, they love hot heroes and quirky heroines who make them laugh, and they hope you do, too!

ALSO BY PIPER RAYNE

The Baileys

Lessons from a One-Night Stand

Advice from a Jilted Bride

Birth of a Baby Daddy

Operation Bailey Wedding (Novella)

Falling for My Brother's Best Friend

Demise of a Self-Centered Playboy

Confessions of a Naughty Nanny

Operation Bailey Babies (Novella)

Secrets of the World's Worst Matchmaker

Winning My Best Friend's Girl

Rules for Dating your Ex

Operation Bailey Birthday (Novella)

The Greenes

My Twist of Fortune (FREE)

My Beautiful Neighbor

My Almost Ex

My Vegas Groom

The Greene Family Summer Bash

My Sister's Flirty Friend

My Unexpected Surprise

My Famous Frenemy

The Greene Family Vacation

My Scorned Best Friend

My Fake Fiancé

My Brother's Forbidden Friend

The Modern Love World

Charmed by the Bartender

Hooked by the Boxer

Mad about the Banker

Complete Set (all 3 books)

The Single Dad's Club

Real Deal

Dirty Talker

Sexy Beast

Complete Set (all 3 books)

Hollywood Hearts

Mister Mom

Animal Attraction

Domestic Bliss

Bedroom Games

Cold as Ice

On Thin Ice

Break the Ice

Complete Set (all 3 books +)

Charity Case

Manic Monday

Afternoon Delight

Happy Hour

Complete Set (all 3 books)

Blue Collar Brothers

Flirting with Fire

Crushing on the Cop

Engaged to the EMT

Complete Set (All 3 books)

White Collar Brothers

Sexy Filthy Boss

Dirty Flirty Enemy

Wild Steamy Hook-up

The Rooftop Crew

My Bestie's Ex

A Royal Mistake

The Rival Roomies

Our Star-Crossed Kiss

The Do-Over

A Co-Workers Crush

Hockey Hotties

Countdown to a Kiss (Free Novella)

My Lucky #13

The Trouble with #9

Faking it with #41

Sneaking around with #34

Second Shot with #76

Offside with #55

www.ingramcontent.com/pod-product-compliance
Lightning Source LLC
Chambersburg PA
CBHW061224310726

48971CB00007B/1936